TWO TO TANGO

BRITS IN MANHATTAN BOOK TWO

LAURA CARTER

Boldwood

First published in 2018. This edition first published in Great Britain in 2023 by Boldwood Books Ltd.

Cover Design by Rachel Lawston

A CIP catalogue record for this book is available from the British Library.

Paperback ISBN 978-1-78513-539-2

Large Print ISBN 978-1-78513-540-8

Hardback ISBN 978-1-78513-538-5

Ebook ISBN 978-1-78513-541-5

Kindle ISBN 978-1-78513-542-2

Audio CD ISBN 978-1-78513-533-0

MP3 CD ISBN 978-1-78513-534-7

Digital audio download ISBN 978-1-78513-536-1

Boldwood Books Ltd
23 Bowerdean Street
London SW6 3TN
www.boldwoodbooks.com

1

BROOKS

'Harder! Faster! That's it. Just like that. Hit me!' As I fire the words, sweat beads form on my temples.

'Fuck, Brooks. You're riding me like a bitch!' Kit is barely comprehensible through his panting breaths.

'Yeah, well, if you hadn't waited all your goddamn life to start coming to my gym, it wouldn't feel like you're dying right now.'

'Christ, you sound like Madge.'

I laugh. Kit's wife and I have been telling him he's been piling on the pounds for months. Correction: years.

Our good buddy, Drew, is leaning on the ropes of the boxing ring, watching me put Kit through his paces in the center. I hear his deep chuckle from across my shoulder. 'Just pretend Brooks is six feet four inches of pizza, Kit. Tear into him like you would a meat supreme.'

'Shut the fuck up, Drew. You know, I'd probably exercise more if I wasn't still scarred from last time.'

Drew holds up his hands. 'Hey, it wasn't me who shot a puck in your nose, buddy. Blame the man you're sparring with.'

Kit turns back to me, sweat pouring down his face and arms,

his black hair stuck to his forehead, his training top saturated. His eyes narrow.

'You want to hate me over that game of hockey, that's fine,' I tell him. 'Put it behind your punch.' I raise the training pads that are strapped to my hands. 'Come at me. Give me three more. Left, right, left.'

When he's done, Kit accepts a bottle of water from Drew and slips out of the ring. I switch the training pads for boxing gloves and stand in the center, waiting for Drew to come and give me a real workout.

'You did good, Kit,' I say, as I fasten Velcro around my wrists. 'A few sessions with me in the ring, and a couple sessions in the gym each week, and we'll have you shifting pounds and fitter than ever.'

I've been a fitness trainer and gym owner long enough to know that some people need praise. Others need to be pushed harder. Kit is definitely the kind of guy who needs a little ego massage.

'I could murder a pizza,' he says, after downing a bottle of water. 'That's your fault, Drew. All I can think about now is an extra-large meat supreme.'

I shake my head and bounce on the spot, warming up for Drew.

'I don't remember seeing pizza in your nutrition plan. I should know. I wrote it.'

He growls. 'You and Madge are going to have me wasting away. I'll look like the skinny assholes on the front cover of *Men's Health and Fitness* or whatever those magazines are that you all read.'

'Let's not get ahead of ourselves, huh, buddy?'

With that, Kit storms out of the boxing room and into the main fitness suite, leaving Drew and me smirking at his back.

'I think I'm going to enjoy training Kit,' I tell Drew. 'All right, loosen up those shoulders.'

Drew follows me, rolling his shoulders up and back, limbering up his arms, rotating his torso to stretch out his lower back. The dark, tired eyes I too often see on my best bud aren't showing tonight.

'You look relaxed, man. Being promoted to named partner at the firm obviously suits you.'

One side of his mouth quirks up. It's a facial expression that makes me smile inside. We were always told to smile properly for cameras when we were kids. We both had this half-smile thing going on at school. I vaguely remember we thought it was cool back then. I guess old habits die hard.

'It's not just the promotion, Brooks,' he says. 'I feel like I've got everything I always wanted. I got my name on the door at the firm and I've got the best girl I never knew I needed. Everything feels too good to be true.'

I tap a gloved fist against his shoulder. 'I'm happy for you, man. If anyone deserves it...'

'Yeah, I should say the same to you. I'd like nothing more than to see you happy.'

Happiness. There's a concept. One that died for me a long time ago, and one I'm definitely not in the mood to talk about. Contentment, though. That's a goal I might achieve, one day. That's something to strive for.

'All right, fists up. Show me what you've got. I've been waiting for this workout all day.'

* * *

I'm standing in front of a mirror in the gym changing rooms, running a small amount of product through my towel-dried hair.

Kit approaches from behind, his reflection appearing next to mine.

'I'll catch you tomorrow, Brooks. I've got to get back to Madge and the kids. I say the kids; hopefully, the horrors are in bed.'

Turning, I knock my fist against the one he holds out. 'You don't mean that.'

He shrugs. 'God knows I must have sinned in a past life. But you're right; I wouldn't be without them. I might be thankful when they're self-sufficient, though.'

'Ha. Be careful what you wish for,' I tell him. 'When they're teenagers, they just find different reasons to make you want to tear your hair out.'

'Can't wait. Catch you tomorrow, same time? Thanks for tonight.'

'Anytime, buddy.'

I move to the large locker I keep permanently stocked with clothes and take out a T-shirt. When my head pops through the neck, I see Drew sitting on a bench in front of me, pulling on a pair of shoes.

'Is Cady acting out?' he asks.

Bending to straighten my dark jeans over my boots, I say, 'Imagine a female version of us at eighteen years old.'

'Fuck.'

'My sentiments exactly. I'm thirty-five, and my daughter has a better love life than I do.'

'Jesus. As long as she doesn't have the same type of love life you have.'

I get his point. My type of love life is one-night stands a couple times a month. That's definitely not what I want for Cady. I shudder at the thought.

'I don't even want to think about that.'

'Probably for the best. Okay, I'm ready. I'll meet you in the bistro.'

'I won't be long; I just need to speak to a couple of the staff about closing up. Order whatever you want from the kitchen – it's on the house – then we can go grab a beer.'

After checking my list of clients for personal training sessions tomorrow and making sure the class schedule has no last-minute changes, I speak to my night team and head into the bistro.

The café bistro is a large, open space with modern, glass tables. We have a small menu offering proteins, veggies, and healthy carbs. We also have a salad and smoothie bar. I eat here often. It's one of the perks of owning the gym.

The bistro is a relatively new addition to the site. Drew helped me out with it by having his firm deal with the legals around the construction work.

As I walk past the busy tables – some people eating meals, some having smoothies, some just drinking coffee and chatting – I can't help but think it's a far cry from where I started out.

The first gym I ever worked out in was an old warehouse on the edge of New York Bay: the Staten Island side, where I grew up. I was seventeen. I've always been a tall, broad guy, but back then, I was just a kid who liked to play the guitar in my high school band. The difference between me and the rest of the guys in high school was that I had knocked up my childhood sweetheart, Alice. And I was ready to marry her.

The kicker was, Alice loved me but her parents didn't. They thought I was a waster. Well, I knocked up their daughter when she was sixteen – of course they thought I was a waster. By comparison to Alice's private education and her family's weekend home in the Hamptons, I had nothing. I came from nothing. My mother worked in a bar and my father was a *jack-of-all-trades, master of none*, as the saying goes.

But I'd have been damned if I didn't try to prove everyone wrong. I was willing to do everything and anything I could to convince Alice's parents to let me marry her. She was the mother of my child, and the girl I was crazy in love with.

So, while I finished high school, I started working as a mechanic to earn some cash, and I joined the gym. I wanted to work like a man. Prove that I could provide for my family like a man. And I wanted to build muscle, to start *looking* like a man.

That first gym I went to was owned by a guy we all knew as Crazy Joe. I'll never forget him. He really was crazy. He served in Vietnam and, by his own admission, smoked too many joints and took too much LSD in the seventies. He was covered in tats. Ready to beat men to a pulp 'for exercise.' He was drunk on whisky most of the time. But he's where it all started for me.

His sanity aside, Crazy Joe was all right. He'd have these moments of tenderness and enlightenment. Who knows, maybe that was just the LSD talking, but he sort of took me under his wing. He got me into boxing every day. I ran with him on the streets, and we lifted weights together. Hell, Crazy Joe gave me my first tattoo. Though my arms and chest are covered in ink now, I still have that first tat on my bicep.

What I didn't realize then was that I would never be good enough for Alice's parents. No matter how much gym time I put in. Whether or not I still went to school while working as a mechanic. Despite the fact I went to their house every night to see Alice and Cady, not out of a sense of obligation but because I was desperate to see my girls. None of it mattered to them.

They still saw me as nothing but a weight on their daughter, pulling her down. Of course I didn't want to be a weight, but I did want to be an anchor. For her. For our family.

My fight to prove myself and to win Alice started when I was seventeen. It has never ended.

'How's the steak?' I ask, taking a seat on a stool next to Drew.

'It was great. I swear it gets better every time,' he says, winking at Angie, my best chef and an old family friend.

'Such a charmer,' she says, shaking her head and waving a hand.

'Has everything been okay tonight, Angie?' I ask.

'Busy, but you know me, I like to keep busy. I bumped into your Cady this morning. She was heading to the library. She's a looker these days, isn't she?'

'God, tell me about it. I'm thinking about locking her in her bedroom and putting a chastity belt on her until she's forty.'

Angie throws her head back as she laughs, her blonde-gray ponytail swaying. 'Well, her ma was a looker at that age. Not that I have to tell you as much.'

My mind drifts to Alice; her soft smile, her gentle touch, the sweet scent of strawberries that always seems to surround her.

'No, you don't have to tell me that,' I say, fighting to keep my lips straight, rather than scowling. The woman knows how to kick a man. But she's always been a good friend to my mother and there have been times when she's helped keep me on the straight and narrow. Hell, sometimes her brutal honesty can be endearing. 'On that note... Drew? Beer?'

He wipes the corner of his mouth with a napkin and slides his plate across the counter. 'Thanks, Angie. Don't tell my mother but you've always made the best food of all the moms.'

'Get out of here.' She beams, more with pride than embarrassment, I think.

The summer night air is warm as we head a few blocks west, toward Central Park. We take up two stools at an intentionally rustic bar. I guess you could call it a haunt of ours, although we come here less now than we used to. I'm busy, with the gym being at full capacity these days. Drew has been working crazy hours for as long as I can remember, and now he has Becky too. But it's Friday and we're going to have a couple of beers before Drew picks up Becky from the swanky restaurant where she works as a patisserie chef.

Damn, after the news I received today, a few beers will be more than welcome.

A young waitress makes eye contact. 'What can I get you, gents?' From the length of the minidress she's wearing, together with her slim hips and flat stomach, I'd guess she's in her early to mid-twenties. Her hair is perfectly styled. The gloss finish shines beneath the bar lights, showing the multiple colors that have been woven through it. It tells me she can afford a decent stylist. But the small hoop that pierces the inside of her ear tells me she's kind of edgy. I'm going to guess she's a student. An art student, maybe. Working a bar for some extra cash.

She plants her hands on the wood-top counter. Despite the crowd, she takes time to bend forward toward us, intentionally displaying two pert breasts beneath the low neckline of her dress. She's obvious but she is attractive.

Drew pays her only a cursory glance, and she focuses her attention on me as a result. 'Two Johnnie Walker Blue Label, on the rocks,' I tell her.

She draws one side of her mouth up until a dimple shows. 'Hard liquor,' she says, emphasizing *hard*.

It's forward, too forward, but I'd be lying if I said my member didn't twitch. She could be someone to take me out of my head later, when I know I'll otherwise be lying in bed dwelling on what will never be with Alice.

I watch her set about making our drinks. When she places them in front of us, she says, 'I've never seen you in here.' As she does, she slips me a napkin on which is the name 'Jennie' and a cell number written in lipstick.

'Try opening your eyes,' I tell her with a grin, taking the napkin. Her eyes do, in fact, shoot wide.

When she walks away, Drew lifts his drink to his mouth. 'You're going to take her home, aren't you?'

'She's like an eight and she's gagging for it.'

We both watch as Jennie glances back across her shoulder and suddenly laughs. She's cute.

'And you tell her to open her eyes? Risky tactic,' Drew says.

'Not when you've got nothing to lose. If you start with nothing, you can only gain, right?'

Drew's brows furrow. 'You okay, bud?'

'Fine. Just busy.' I swig from my glass and enjoy the burn of whisky in my chest.

'That's what you've said the last three times I've asked you recently.'

'So stop asking.'

He raises his glass as if accepting my point, and sips. I shouldn't have snapped, but goddamn Angie brought my mind back to Alice. I just haven't shaken it off yet.

'Speaking of busy,' Drew begins. 'I thought we were going to find some time to talk about your franchising the gym?'

I have thought about franchising the gym. Years ago, all I wanted was to be a successful businessman. To make something of myself. To make money for my family, enough to win back Alice. Now...

'What's the point? One gym keeps me busy enough. And I have enough money saved to put Cady through college.'

'You've got the best gym in the city, Brooks, and a hell of a reputation to go with it. You've wanted to expand for as long as I can remember. I think now is a great time. I can e-mail you some documents, some things to think about.'

I drag my hands roughly across my face. 'Yeah, send them

across. I'll take a look.' I drain the liquor in my glass and plant the empty down, too hard.

'All right, buddy, what's going on?'

I sigh as I look at Drew, the man who knows me better than anyone, and I cave. 'Alice is pregnant.'

Drew offers no response other than to hold up two fingers to Jennie, who carries a bottle over to refill our glasses.

'I don't know,' I continue. 'On some level, I guess I've always thought we would end up together. She's had two failed marriages. She's older now. It's not like her parents control her the way they used to. But a kid? I mean, that's... she's not going to leave this one.'

I raise my chin to Jennie, who flashes me a coy smile. Then I take a gulp from my freshly topped-off glass.

'I know how long it's been. I know we were kids when we had Cady. It's just still...'

Drew pats my shoulder as he finishes my sentence. 'A punch in the gut. I can finally understand it, buddy. I thought I'd lost Becky once and it wrecked me. I just hope you don't stop yourself from ever finding someone. Don't hold on to it so long you let it ruin your life.'

I laugh. A short, harsh sound.

'Like another eighteen years?'

* * *

At 1.30 a.m. and five or six whiskies later, I'm standing outside the bar with my back propped against a yellow cab. A mild liquor fog has settled in my mind. Enough to blunt the turmoil of my own thoughts about Alice and her baby. Not enough to stop them completely. I stayed for another drink, or two, after Drew left, and then I flagged the cab when I noticed Jennie packing up for the night.

She finally appears through the double doors to the bar, stepping onto the sidewalk with a short leather jacket covering her little black dress.

She's laughing with two others who were working behind the bar tonight. Before she sees me, I hit send on the text I've already typed.

I watch a pouty smile appear on her lips as she takes out her cell phone and reads my words:

Your place or mine?

She lifts her head and looks left, then right, where our eyes connect. I open the cab door and she whispers something to the girl she's with before coming to me.

'Well, my eyes are open now, and it looks like you want a cheap fling.'

I raise my hand to her neck and move my face within an inch of hers. 'First, I don't think you're cheap. I think you're hot and looking for a good time tonight. Second, yes, I do want a fling. One night to show you how a man should treat a woman. Nothing more.'

Her eyes seem to grow heavier; then she bites her lip and slips into the back of the cab.

Third, tonight, I could really use a distraction.

2

BROOKS

It's a little after five in the morning when Jennie leaves. I close the door behind her with no intention of seeing her again. It was fun, hot, a distraction. Nothing more.

I slump down on the sofa, naked but for my shorts. My abs are decorated with scratch marks from Jennie's nails. I lie back and stretch my arms above my head. I'll try to catch a few hours' sleep before I get ready to pick up Cady for breakfast.

When she was a kid, I would see Cady every weekend, without fail, and as often as she wanted to see me any other time. As she got older – and found boys – she came to stay over less and less. Now, we tend to meet for lunch or coffee, or she'll come by the gym if she's in the city. Does it get me down sometimes that I don't see her as often as I'd like? Yes. Do I fully understand having raging hormones and feeling like the world is on your shoulders as an eighteen-year-old? Yes. In fact, it's remembering so well that scares me so goddamn much.

I tossed and turned but I must have dozed off at some point because I wake with a start, though in my mind I'm still sixteen and lying in a bed with Alice, listening to music.

The clock tells me the time is 8.20 a.m. I'm not meeting Cady until ten.

After mixing up a chocolate K-Z protein shake – courtesy of one of my sponsors – I move back into the lounge. I live in a fairly modest place, given how much money the gym turns these days, but it is a city apartment with a basement garage for my truck and it's within running distance of the gym. True, my view is of the red bricks of another high-rise, but I'm not around a lot to see the view in any event. It's a two-bedroom place and I really don't need more space than that. The living room/dining room/kitchen area is airy. The walls are white throughout. Some are decorated with bright, abstract art, mostly picked by Cady. In the living room, I have a large, flat-screen TV and an L-shaped sofa. Some might say it's a man's apartment. They would probably be right.

I grab a guitar from the three set in stands along the living room wall, choosing my six-string acoustic over electric or bass. To be honest, I don't play electric or bass much these days, even though they were my preferred option when Drew and I had our band in high school.

Planting my protein shake in its plastic bottle on the coffee table, I sink into the corner of the sofa with my guitar and start to strum. Soon, I find myself slipping into the rhythm of the Goo Goo Dolls' 'Iris' and start to sing along. It doesn't stop my mind from wandering.

Alice is having another baby.

I know there's no chance for us. Yet, for some reason, each time she marries, gets a boyfriend, or becomes pregnant, it's like someone taking a fucking axe to my chest.

I don't want to feel this way. I want to be over her. But how the hell do you get over a first love, the mother of your child, and the woman you have spent your life trying to impress?

Everything I have done since I was sixteen years old has been about her. For her.

What is the point? What is the point to any of what I've done?

The lingering thought that I should expand and franchise the gym comes to me now. Drew is right; it would be a sound business move. A natural progression, even. But who would I be doing it for if not Alice?

* * *

The suburb where Alice now lives is like a real-life version of Wisteria Lane. Not that I watch *Desperate Housewives*, obviously. Cady has the show saved on my DVR, that's all.

Despite not being too far out of the city, the houses are large – real family homes – and painted white, blue, yellow. A life I couldn't have even dreamed of giving Alice, not back then.

This subdivision could be idyllic, except Cady gives me the lowdown on the residents. The Georges and the 'big affair.' The Hamiltons and their illegitimate child. The fight between the Smithsons last week that led to Mrs Smithson throwing Mr Smithson's clothes out of the upstairs window.

Despite all this, if I'm honest with myself, I'm envious of Alice and her pretentious home in her pretentious neighborhood. I'm jealous that she's living the life I always wanted to have with her. A family. A family home. Our daughter.

I can't bring myself to drive up to their house to collect Cady. When Cady was a toddler, I would be forced to carry her to Alice's door, usually after she had fallen asleep in my car. As she grew up, my ability to withstand my own emotions weakened and my reasons for taking Cady to her front door lessened. For years now, in this suburb and the last, I've parked at the end of the street and waited for Cady to come to me.

It's 9.58 a.m. I'm two minutes early and Cady will be five minutes late, at least, so I turn off the engine and wait, my elbow hanging over the window, the sun warming my skin beneath my T-shirt.

I know it sounds ridiculous – a broad, muscly man like me, waiting out on the street as if he's running scared. But see, I am afraid. Having to pick my own daughter up for coffee, instead of being there to tuck her in at night, to help with homework, to tell her things will be all right when she's having a bad day, that's hard enough. I don't need to see Alice and really tear my wounds open.

I flick radio channels as I wait, settling on Blake Shelton's latest Billboard hit. Cady eventually comes toward the car at six past ten – not too bad for her these days. Gone are the times when she would run along the street toward me. Now, she struts in her black skater skirt, her black ankle boots, and a black leather jacket. All despite the fact it's seventy-seven degrees out.

She doesn't meet my eye as she moves around the truck and slips into the passenger side. She pulls her bag – black – from over her shoulder in silence and dumps it in the footwell. Then she sits back, clicks in her belt, and sighs as she straightens her thick bangs and usually blonde bob.

I brace my hand on the steering wheel and look at her.

'Morning, Dad,' I say, mimicking her voice. 'Oh, hey, morning, Cady. Yeah, I'm great, thanks for asking. And you?'

I watch as her lips fight to keep their belligerent expression, then break into a smile. Eventually, she flashes me those huge, blue eyes that are so like her mother's.

'Hi, Dad.'

'You have pink hair.' I point out the obvious.

She shrugs as she smirks. 'It's just a wash. Mom hates it.'

'I guess that means you'll continue to do it?'

'Maybe.'

I shake my head. 'Well, I kind of like it. It suits you. So, you want to get breakfast in the city?'

'Yeah, I'm going to see Zach when we're done.'

'Zach?'

She shrugs again and I wonder if it's legitimate for me to strap those shrugging shoulders to the seat.

'My boyfriend. He goes to NYU.'

I feel my eyes attempt to pop right out of my head.

'A new boyfriend? He's in college? What was wrong with the other kid, from your class? Where is Zach from? He's too old for you.'

'Dad, he's like two years older than me. Chill out. You're gonna give yourself a coronary.'

'A coron... This discussion isn't over.'

Like a petulant child, I purse my lips, knock the truck into drive, and pull out of the perfect freakin' suburb toward the city... and, incidentally, toward Zach, my daughter's college boyfriend.

I park in the basement garage of my building and we walk to the Butterfly Café, a new place that Cady tells me is 'shabby chic.'

'What exactly is shabby chic?' I ask, tucking my white wicker chair under the white table. I nudge the floral planter from the middle of the table to one side so I can see my daughter.

She chuckles. Damn, I love that sound. Always have.

'It's this stuff,' she says. 'The whitewash, the paisley prints, flowers. Kind of vintage but modern. Pretty.'

'Right. And that pink hair, is that shabby chic?'

Her brows scrunch and her button nose wrinkles. The sight is like someone holding a hot-water bottle to my chest.

I fight against my laughter. 'Why do you have that look? It's a wash, it's pink, and it's a little bit like that Frenchie character from *Grease*, so it's vintage. Am I wrong?'

'Oh my God, Dad. On so many levels, just, oh my God. First,

the only part of shabby chic that relates to my hair is chic. And, seriously, you know the characters from *Grease*?'

I do laugh now. 'It's a classic. Plus, your mom used to force it on me.'

Just like that, my laugh cuts off and I'm staring at the laminated breakfast menu in front of me, trying not to remember times spent watching *Grease* through one eye as I was in a lip-lock with Alice.

Cady orders quinoa porridge – her latest fad – and I order an omelet, as she fills me in on her summer break so far. As our breakfast plates are set in front of us with peppermint tea for her and an Americano for me, she gets to the story of her first meeting with Zach.

'He plays in a band and a bunch of us went to the gig, in Brooklyn.'

'Brooklyn? You're only eighteen.'

She rolls her eyes. 'It was on campus. Plus, we stayed over. Amber knows one of the other guys in the band.'

I almost choke on my eggs. 'You stayed over? With who? With this Zach?'

'Well, there were a bunch of us. It wasn't like it was just the two of us. Anyway, like you said, I am eighteen.'

Jesus. I feel my head starting to heat. Any second now, my gray T-shirt will be showing my stressed-out-dad perspiration under the arms.

I eye her over my coffee cup as I take a mouthful and try to think of how best to handle the situation. 'Does Alice know you stayed over?'

Yep, I'll start by hoping Alice has already dealt with it.

Cady shrugs. 'She knows I stayed out, yes.'

'Cady, quit the attitude and quit shrugging your damn shoulders at me. And quit using lines on me that I used on your grandparents. You say she knows you stayed out, which is code for you stayed with Zach and she doesn't know.'

She clears her throat and sits straighter.

I suddenly feel like my fifth-grade teacher, Mr Perkins, the way he would raise one brow and tut as he chastised me before sending me to the principal.

'Look, he's twenty and in college. You're about to go to college. I'm not going to pretend you two won't... you know.'

Her cheeks burn red as she looks around the café, probably hoping for the fire alarm to sound or for a cab to drive through the front window. I'd be grateful for one of those things myself.

'Dad, seriously. I know about the birds and the bees. We aren't having this conversation.'

I lean back in my chair and tell her with a look that we absolutely are having this conversation. 'Listen, Cady, I'm not going to be a hypocrite. I just want to know that you're being sensible. Make sure you know the guy and like him. Make sure he's decent. Don't disrespect yourself by letting just anyone—'

She pushes herself out of her chair and stands in a ridiculously melodramatic fashion. 'Christ, Dad, I do know him. And I know he really likes me, and I like him. And we're not sixteen.'

As calmly as I can when an eighteen-year-old is shouting at me in a public place, I tell her, 'Sit down, Cady, right the hell now.'

I guess I pitched it right because she does sit. 'You sound just like her.'

'By "her", I assume you mean your mother. Look, I get that you think you know everything right now, and hell, you probably know a lot more than Alice and I knew at sixteen. But we're both just trying to stop you from making the mistakes we made.'

She drops her wrist to the tabletop, rocking the teaspoon against her cup and saucer, drawing looks from other customers.

'So now I'm a mistake?'

I roll my jaw, counting in my head to control my temper. 'No, but you are proving that you're a goddamn child.' I drag my hand through my hair on an exasperated sigh. 'You are anything but a mistake, Cady. You're the only thing I've ever done right. But if I could have had you a few years later when your mom and I... There are some things I would have, should have, done differently. I'm just pointing out that you could learn from me. Have fun but be sensible.'

We stare at each other long enough that I wonder if we're in an indefinite standoff, or whether I got through to the girl who is just as stubborn as her old man. Finally, her lips break into an almost smile.

'Are you going to take me for my birth control appointment?' she asks.

'Do you want me to?' I ask, reciprocating her teasing. 'Are we going to talk about why you wanted to see me today?'

She shrugs, and I swear I have to bite down on my tongue. 'You're my dad, aren't you?'

'Actually, I'm aware of that. Every time I see a new strand of gray hair in the mirror, I'm reminded I'm your father. And I love to see you but I saw you last weekend so I wasn't expecting to see you for, like, I don't know, a decade.'

She laughs as I finish the sentence in a mock-teenager tone, the kind you might hear in the movie *Mean Girls*. Again, I've watched it with Cady and the fact she has the same name as the lead character is purely coincidence. No judging.

'I wanted to see you, that's all.'

I watch her, silently, waiting for her to fill the gap. I've learned over the years, if I want my daughter to talk, this is how. Kids – sorry, young adults – don't like silence.

She breathes out heavily. 'It's just, I'm fed up with hearing about the baby's room, and the baby scan, and the nursery conversion, and what a wonderful family Mom and Richard and the baby will be. I mean, I know I'm moving to the college dorm and all, but...'

'You won't be pushed out, Cady. Your mom wouldn't do that. I know it's hard.' God, do I. 'But I know Alice, and Richard, want you to be a part of their family. You *are* a part of their family.' I reach out and lift her fallen chin until her eyes meet mine. 'And you can talk to me anytime, kiddo. All right? You can stay anytime. Plus, when you're at NYU, we'll be able to see a lot more of each other.'

Her smile creeps onto her lips. 'Can I get a free gym membership?'

'You already have it.'

'For my friends?'

'One friend.'

'And food in the bistro?'

I chuckle. 'And food in the bistro.' I cover her hand with mine. 'I love you, kiddo.'

She rolls her eyes. 'Love you too.'

'Good, you can buy breakfast.'

'I don't love you that much. Anyway, I have places to be.' With that, she stands, plants a kiss on my brow, and quickly navigates the tables to slip out of the restaurant. I watch her walk by the glass window. She stops on the sidewalk and looks right at me. Then she shrugs.

Ah, Christ, she definitely got my attitude.

3

IZZY

'Izzy, I'm off to work.' My sister's voice is a garble that reaches me from her bathroom, which backs onto my bedroom wall. When I hear her spit, followed by the running tap, it confirms my suspicion – she was talking through a mouthful of toothpaste.

When my bedroom door opens, I raise my head from the suitcase I am packing. Anna – or Annabella if we want to use her Sunday name – looks as classy as ever in navy chinos and a polka-dot blouse. She looks far more sophisticated than her job as a journalist at one of the trashiest online newspapers in the world might suggest. Of course, that's because Dad's credit card pays for her couture wardrobe. Still, she's using her English degree, as Mum likes to remind me. And I secretly love living with my own personal A-list news gossiper. I don't even have to trouble myself with buying magazines.

'Have a great time in NYC. I know you'll be fabulous.' She finishes with her trademark killer smile.

'I wish I had a dose of that confidence.'

'Nonsense.' She checks her Rolex. 'Right, must dash. I will see you in a couple of weeks. Text me when you land in the Big Apple.

And don't be afraid to bring me back something divine. For the record, I adore this season's Mulberry frame bag.' Before my door closes behind her, she calls, 'Powder blue.'

I lean over to my music dock and press play. Cher's version of 'The Shoop Shoop Song' comes through the speakers and I sing along as I finish packing. I've packed for all eventualities. There's no way this suitcase is going to be under twenty-three kilos. I'm used to wearing yoga pants and sports bras every day but my book tour is going to mean promotional interviews and reader signings. I'm going to need dresses and smart clothes. Things I don't wear often these days at all. I'll even have to wear makeup.

Since I got my book deal twelve months ago, and for the two years before that when I was desperately trying to build a brand of fitness training and nutritional advice, I've concentrated on my career and not much else. My boyfriend dumped me – brutally and by phone – although, he was a pretentious arsehole, so I should probably count my lucky stars. Friends stopped inviting me places because I (apparently) made them feel fat by ordering the egg white omelet, butterless vegetables, and fruit instead of chocolate pudding. It's not often I allow myself to drink alcohol, and I hold evening fitness classes six days a week in any event, so my previous existence as one of London's notorious Chelsea socialites – well, it died a slow but very definite death.

Sighing, I sit back on my haunches and assess the mountain of clothes, shoes, and accessories that made the first cut. Time to get tough. I tie my mass of blonde locks into a ponytail and start taking anything that is not an absolute must from the piles, throwing the discarded items across my king bed to the other side of the room.

I've given up two belts, one pair of ankle boots and a jacket by the time the landline phone rings. Damn it.

My sister and I live in a two-floor apartment in the Chelsea and Kensington Borough of London. It is two floors of a large, white, terrace house. You know the type, quite typical of London seen in movies. Old house, high ceilings, inordinately expensive rent that Mum and Dad still currently supplement for Anna and me. I'm hoping I'll be able to change that soon.

I hop over my case and the clothes strewn around the cream-colored carpet, and bound downstairs for the phone.

'Hello?'

'Isabella, darling, it's Mummy.' She says it in a way that's almost comical. As if she's been asked to perform her best impression of the Queen, but for a theatre audience, so she has to shout it in a sing-song kind of way. I swear, when I was a child, she was well spoken, but she was Mum, not Mummy; grass was pronounced grass, not graaas. As my father's cracker business – as in cream crackers and cheese, not Christmas crackers – skyrocketed, Mum became 'Mummy' and Dad became 'Daddy.' We had always mixed with the middle classes but my parents started to mingle in higher society. Anna and I were moved to a 'posher' posh school. Mum slowly began to exaggerate her spoken vowels and always used our full names, Annabella and Isabella.

'Hi, Mum, what's up?'

'Oh, darling, I do wish you would speak properly.'

Rolling my eyes for no one's benefit except my own, I tell her, as politely as possible, 'I'm packing, Mum. I have to leave for New York in a few hours.'

'Ah, yes, I forgot about your little trip.' I grip the phone so tightly, it feels like my knuckles might pierce my skin. 'I wanted to invite you to the Savoy for tea next week for Granny's birthday.'

'I won't be back from the book tour then. I'll take her somewhere when I'm in London again.'

'Well, how long is this book tour?'

'I've told you all about it. Two weeks. I have some signings lined up and a couple of interviews.'

'Hmm. Right. Well, at least then it will be over and you can start concentrating on more important things. Like—'

'How many times do I have to tell you before you'll accept it? This is what I do, Mum. I'm a fitness instructor. I teach nutrition.'

'That's wonderful, darling, until the latest exercise fad has been and gone. There is no ladder to be climbed in the profession of fitness. You have the highest class of degrees from a highly respectable university. You could be anything you want to be, Isabella. The world is your—'

'Oyster. Right. Except, this is what I want to do, Mum. I have to go. Enjoy tea with Granny. Tell her I said happy birthday.'

Hanging up the phone, I feel like pulling my hair out. Actually. But I really don't have time for that. I must pack for New York.

* * *

'Izzy! Over here!'

I see a paper sign marked in – is that lipstick? – with my name. Then I see Kerry's head popping around the side, where her perfectly painted pink nails are gripping the paper.

That's my publicist. Flawless and fabulous Kerry. I have no doubt her leather pencil skirt and pink blouse – which matches her nails exactly – and those excruciatingly high black heels are all designer. But the fact is, with her figure and looks, it wouldn't matter if the clothes had been dredged from a gutter. She would still look 100 per cent a-mazing. Of course, the look is all part of her job. 'You have to know how to promote yourself if you want to be able to promote others,' she always tells me. I'm pretty sure that's a play on the saying about loving oneself before you can love another – you know the one, Anyway, she's a fearless beast when it comes to flaunting her clients and that's what matters to me.

'Kerry, hi!' I let her fold me a little too zealously into her arms and we perform the perfunctory air-kiss routine.

She sets off walking and talking, so that I am left trudging after her with my suitcases, dragging one in each hand. I managed to sleep for a few hours on my night flight but I'm still yawning as I walk.

'You have a magazine interview tomorrow,' she announces. 'Your book signing on Thursday has been shuffled to five thirty at Barnes & Noble. We'll get you there at five. It will be set up ready for you, of course. Oh, I've booked you a radio interview for next week. We have various things lined up next Tuesday for publication day, although most of the promo is online.' She stops and turns quickly, making me crash into her swinging shoulder. As if the bump didn't take place, she continues. 'What are your thoughts on holding one of your *Salsa Yourself Slim* classes in the city?'

'Ah, yeah, that sounds great.'

'Good. Because I've started to put some feelers out with production companies. I was thinking we could film the session.'

'Well, I already have classes on YouTube.'

She laughs at me in a way that makes me feel like a small child. 'No, not just YouTube videos, Izzy. I'm talking real production, for a DVD or an online course. Interactive exercise.' She takes a high-gloss brochure from her bag and hands it to me. 'Here, take a look at this. I'd love to get you into this gym. A guy called Brooks Adams owns it. You might guess that from the name, ha. Who names a gym after himself? Anyway, he's the man everyone in New York wants to be trained by right now. Let me know what you think.'

She spins on her devil shoes and heads out of the Arrivals exit.

I follow her to a parked black Cadillac and finally turn over my suitcases to a suited driver.

Kerry continues to talk but when she tells me she will handle everything and that she'll ping me a full schedule by e-mail, I allow myself to zone out.

I have been to New York a number of times: with my parents, with my girlfriends, once with a boyfriend. Regardless, the view of the city never gets old. I smile at the sight of the Brooklyn Bridge, set against the morning's sky. When we get closer to the city, the high-rises force me to take a breath so deep, my chest rises. The Chrysler Building. The Empire State Building. The general buzz and hum of the busy streets. Even the endless streams of yellow cabs.

It's all busier, brighter, bigger than London. I love it. I love it so much, I think maybe I was a New Yorker in a past life. Then again, maybe I was a squirrel or a hippopotamus or something, and now I just happen to love this city.

4

BROOKS

I'm sitting in my office sampling new products – currently eating a gluten-free, high-protein bar, and reading the related marketing paperwork from the supplier – when there's a tap on the door.

'It's open,' I call.

The door opens onto the mezzanine balcony of the gym and my friend Sarah, in her sweaty gym wear, is leaning on the door frame. Even with a red face and her dark hair tied into a knot on the top of her head, she looks good. Don't read into that. I am 100 per cent friends with Sarah and no more. That's why I can tell her, 'You look in good shape,' even when she's wearing tight-fitting Lycra.

'I ought to. I spend ten hours of my life in this place each week. I avoid carbs like they'll give me the plague, and I can't remember the last time I gorged on a tub of my favorite thing... BJs.' That's her code name for her best guys, Ben and Jerry. She plants a hand on her hip in an oh-so-Sarah way. 'I've actually just been to the Zumba class. I've gotten into the idea of dancing to stay slim since that new fitness girl came on the scene. You know, the British one. She does some dance-yourself-skinny kind of thing. Anyway, I've seen one or two of her YouTube videos and thought I'd give Zumba a try.'

I lean back in my desk chair and swivel. 'Did you rate it?'

'It was cool. A nice change from being in the gym. That woman you have instructing is kind of crazy, though. Said she's been divorced something like ten thousand times and, hell, for a middle-aged woman, she rocks the twerk.'

'Nice critique. I'll be sure to rate her high in the box that says "twerking" in her performance review.'

She laughs, something I love to hear from her. Despite her tough bravado, behind closed doors, Sarah can be really down. I mean, who can blame her when she was widowed so young? But I get a kick out of seeing her happy.

When I realize I've paused to reflect on her smile, I break our silence. 'Hey, I'm almost done here for the night. Don't suppose you'd indulge in some Monday night wings?'

I would usually use the guise of Monday night football to cover my obsession with wings but it's out of season.

'Wings?' She gestures to herself, pointing from her head to her toes. 'And ruin this? Actually, I might have to go back to the office. Drew is pulling an all-nighter. Another time.'

She drops a kiss to my cheek, comments on how bad she must smell, and leaves. It's funny to remember that Sarah and I actually met because Sarah is Drew's legal secretary. Drew introduced us more years ago than I care to remember. Now, Sarah's a pretty close second to Drew in my best friend rankings. Although, she did just lose points for refusing wings.

With Drew at work, I call a few of my other friends. Kit refuses on grounds that his wife, Madge, won't let him out. Madge is pretty awesome, for the record, but Kit is like a big kid and since they have two young children now – the real kind, not the thirty-odd-year-old, hairy kind – sometimes, she has to enforce a few rules with him.

I call Edmond. Also known as Super-chef and the owner of the swanky restaurant Becky works in. It's a long shot because I know, if he is free, he's probably spending his rare night off with his wife and kids. Sure enough, he answers the call and tells me that because the restaurant is closed on Mondays, he's having a quiet one with his family.

I try Marty, the other half of Statham Harrington law firm, alongside Drew. He's taking some clients to a boozy dinner – code for schmoozing.

On the 'good friends' front, I'm all out. I can't really be assed to make small talk with the guys from the gym. Even when we're out for drinks, I always get the sense they see me as their boss and don't fully relax.

The proverbial lightbulb suddenly shines bright in my mind. Jake.

I mentioned I went to school with Drew. Grew up with him, really. Our families both lived on Staten Island when we were kids. His mom all but adopted me when my folks decided to get a divorce and were gunning for each other's blood every night. Well, Jake is Drew's kid brother. He's a twenty-five-year-old man now, but to me he'll always be Drew's kid brother – who we tortured for fun but always loved. He's doing well for himself these days, working for a hedge fund in London. He flew over here so we could all celebrate Drew making named partner at Statham Harrington. As far as I know, he's still in the city.

I hit his number in my phone. 'Brooks, my man. How you doing?'

'Jakey. You still in New York, buddy?'

'Not for long but I am right now. I'm currently watching some awful game show with my folks, going out of my mind.'

'Is your mom in earshot?'

'She sure is. That's why she just tossed a sofa cushion off my head. Hang on.' I hear him in the background: 'I'm going into the other room, relax. You wouldn't have answered that question right anyway. Ouch! Stop throwing cushions!'

I'm shaking my head but can't help smirking when I hear a door close and he comes back on the line. 'Sorry 'bout that.'

'No worries, man. You want to escape for beer and wings? We can't do Monday Night Live but we can catch some football reruns. I doubt you've seen them in London. You can stay at my place.'

'I'm on the next ferry to the city.'

* * *

'All right, guys, I got one Texas smoked burger with sweet potato fries, and one extra-large stack of firecracker wings.'

Jake has his head tipped back to drain the dregs from his bottle of Samuel Adams, so I tell the waitress, 'The burger is his. Wings for me. Thanks.'

She puts the plates on top of the sticky bar we're perched at. There's something about a sticky wood bar in a sports joint that just works. And Mitch's Sports Bar happens to have the best wings in the city.

'You want another two beers, Brooks?'

That's Mitch. Second-generation Mitch, who now runs the bar since his old man died a few years back.

I've wasted no time in getting my first wing to my mouth, so I nod with a mouthful of hot sauce.

Jake is chomping through his first bite of burger as if he hasn't been fed for a decade.

'I'm telling you, they don't make burgers like this in England.

In London, it's all about presentation and good British beef. Screw that! I want good, hearty, mess-on-a-plate pulled pork. I don't give a crap where the meat came from, I just want the thing to be smoked properly with a solid barbecue sauce. This is a burger. I ought to take a picture of this and tweet it to the Royal Family.'

I wash down my first wing with a swig of beer and subtly swallow the belch that threatens to pop up. 'I don't think the Royal Family will engage with a burger war on Twitter, man.'

He takes another bite that has me in awe of the man. Showing me the half-chewed contents of his mouth, he says, 'Yeah, maybe I should just eat it. Should you really be eating this stuff, Mr My Body Is a Temple?'

'Are you kidding? I work out so that I *can* eat this stuff. You can't starve yourself and build muscle. Wings are good protein.'

Jake gives me a disbelieving look from behind his beer bottle. 'I'm sure that's not what goes in those nutrition plans you've got every New Yorker raving about.'

I ignore his comment and work through another wing. I know my fitness brand has taken off. Damn, I have a wait list of hundreds for PT sessions and nutrition advice, but I feel weird when the guys blow smoke up my ass. They just know me as Brooks. Not Brooks 'Trainer to the Stars,' as one magazine put it recently.

When the Jets score a touchdown, I drop my bare chicken bone on my plate and jump from my stool. 'Yes! That's what I'm talking about! Pay up, Jakey-boy! I told you there was a touchdown left in this quarter.'

'It's a fucking rerun. You've already seen it.'

'I told you when we made the bet I hadn't seen it. Pay up.'

'Ah, fuck. Here, have your five bucks. I can't spend it in London anyway.'

I tuck his money into my back pocket and sit. 'Ahh, are you

sore, Jakey? Good luck to your hedge fund clients. With the bets you place...'

He thumps me in the arm but does it with a smile on his face. When the quarter ends, the television switches to commercials and I take a chance to really focus on working down my mammoth plate of meat.

'See, Brooks, this is exactly what I'm talking about.' I follow the direction of Jake's pointed beer bottle to the large screen behind the bar. 'This woman is selling fitness and not eating barbecue wings.'

I watch as a skinny blonde on the TV dances in front of a class. The words *Salsa Yourself Slim* flash up on the screen. The shot moves to an image of the same woman wearing purple yoga pants and a neon sports bra on the cover of a book. The voice-over says, 'Look and feel great with Izzy Coulthard's new book, *Be Green. Be Clean*. Learn her top tips to salsa yourself slim, and try delicious, detoxifying recipes.'

I suck the firecracker sauce from my fingers. 'No way. Clean eating, all that raw carrot shit, will get you skinny. No doubt about it. But if you want to really be healthy from exercise and a good diet, you've got to eat. You can't eat like a rabbit and put in a good workout. You need protein to repair your muscles and give you the strength to put in a solid session for your heart and lungs. I concede, maybe I don't encourage sugar- and salt-laced barbecue sauce in my nutrition plans, but I do push eating meat.'

Jake holds up two hands as if in surrender. 'Hey, I'm on your side. But I've got to tell you, if it's a choice, I'd prefer to wake up to her body than yours.'

'Jesus. Can we get back to talking football instead of you thinking about being naked in bed with me?'

He doesn't talk football. He starts talking baseball. With one ear focused on him, my eyes find the blonde dancer on the large screen again. Yeah, I'd take her body over mine too.

Three beers, a win for the Jets, and a bout of meat sweats later, I let us into my apartment. I flick on the standing lamp in the living room and draw the curtains closed across the floor-to-ceiling windows.

I gesture to the sports bag slung across Jake's shoulder. 'You can take Cady's room.'

'How is the little mite these days?'

I fill two glasses of water from the refrigerator filter and hand one to him. 'Imagine yourself at eighteen, then give it female parts and a pretty face.'

'Oof.'

'Exactly. Listen, I'm going to hit the sack. I've got a full day at the gym tomorrow. There isn't a TV in Cady's room but make yourself comfortable out here as long as you like.'

* * *

I know I'm dreaming. I know that I'm not actually working out on the shoulder press in my gym, that I'm actually lying in my bed, sleeping. But it feels real enough for me to keep going. As I'm finishing up my final set of reps, the heavy fire doors to the main floor of the gym blow open, as if they weigh nothing. I raise a hand to shield my eyes as a bright light beams through the doorway, like rays refracted through a shard of glass. Through the intense light walks a blonde woman. Her hair is tied back. She wears tight purple yoga pants and a blue sports bra, displaying every fine inch of her body. I recognize her from TV.

I get off the machine. The gym is full but the blonde is focused solely on me. She glides toward me, her feet barely touching the ground. Damn, she's pretty.

I'm about to speak, to introduce myself, maybe tell her I've seen the commercials for her new book, when she reaches me and places her finger across my lips.

What is happening?

I don't care. I know I could wake up at any moment and I'll be damned if I'm going to waste this moment. She's so hot for me.

I open my mouth quickly and take her finger between my teeth. Her eyes go wide and in her irises, I see flames. A hot, orange blaze.

She leaps up and I catch her long, toned legs around my waist. I crash my mouth against hers and we ravish each other, tongues lapping, each swallowing the other's groans in the middle of the packed gym.

I carry her to the wall behind the hip-abductor machine and press her back to it, taking her weight with my body as she bites my bottom lip. I pull back from her to draw the zipper down the front of her bra. *Nice.*

'Brooks,' she moans.

Only, it isn't her voice. I recognize that voice. I look up at her face. It's no longer the woman from the commercial looking back at me. It's...

'Alice. God, I've wanted this for so long.' I close my eyes as I press my lips to hers, gently this time.

'Me too, Brooks.'

I pull back quickly as the voice shifts to a masculine one. I drop her onto the floor, noticing that the lover who was a woman is now Jake.

Holy crap!

'I told you I preferred your body,' Dream Jake says.

Wake up! Right the hell now!

* * *

I sit up in bed, my face screwed tight with disgust.

'What on earth?' My whispered words are lost in the empty bedroom. The alarm on my bedside table tells me it is 3.57 a.m. 'Christ.'

I flop back against my pillows and rub my face. There's no way in this freakin' millennium I am going back to sleep and risking being in a lip-lock with Jake.

I reach under my bed and pull out my Mac. Maybe I'll look over the franchise stuff Drew sent to me.

After twelve minutes of reading his high-level review points, I realize I don't have the energy for it.

Instead, I write an e-mail to the guys, asking them if they want to get an ice hockey game going soon.

5

BROOKS

'That's twenty. Nice job.' As I take the weight of the bar my client is using for bench presses and lift it onto the rack, Rick brings himself upright and wipes his forehead. I note for my record the increase in his weights this session. 'How are you feeling?'

He drinks from his sports bottle. 'I've never felt in better shape in my life.'

I drop a hand to his shoulder. 'Let's move on to dead lifts in that case.'

We're on the mezzanine floor of the gym, looking down over the cardio machines, as I set up Rick's weights and get him started on his reps, always keeping one eye on his form.

'Brooks, you got a second?'

I turn to see Charlie, my floor manager, coming toward me in chinos and a blazer. It's her day for dealing with corporate membership renewals so she isn't in her usual sports gear.

I tell Rick to keep going, then say to Charlie, 'Sure, what's up?'

She leans closer and lowers her voice to little more than a whisper.

'I've got a crazy-ass publicist and a mini-celeb in reception.

They're kicking up a stink because I've said they can't come into the gym without a membership. They demanded to see you. Said they tried calling before they turned up. I wouldn't bother you with it, but they're causing a scene in front of the bistro and it's full down there.'

I can't help my sigh. It's always the wannabe celebs who think they have some kind of God-given right to work out here.

'You've told them we don't do special treatment?'

'Only ten times. I could shoot for the eleventh.'

'Tell them to take a seat and calm the hell down. I'm not cutting my session short but we'll be done here in five. I'll come down then.'

'Thanks, Brooks.'

As she walks away, I tell my client to rest between sets. Then I call back to Charlie. 'Who is this person, anyway?'

She stops and glances down at the clipboard in her hand. 'Izzy Coulthard. That *Salsa Yourself Slim* woman from the TV commercials.'

* * *

Despite the liveliness of the bistro, as soon as I walk through the double doors to the reception area, my attention is drawn to two women wearing stubborn pouts and sitting on the leather sofas next to the front desk.

Charlie tells them, 'Here's my boss now,' and they stand to face me. The brunette, whom I take to be the mouthy publicist, is standing on too-high heels, hands on her hips, her nails coated in bright-pink polish. She's striking, yet my eyes flick over her and land on the blonde I recognize from TV. Izzy Coulthard. And good God, she's even hotter in person. The TV did nothing to show that her slim figure, toned as it is, has all the right curves in all the right places. Her purple yoga leggings from the cover of her book have been replaced by jazzy blue print leggings, which she wears with a hot-pink running top. Her hair is tied into an immaculate ponytail, not one wisp out of place. And, oddly, given she is asking to work out, her face is full of makeup. A serious instructor would not work out in a full face of makeup.

I cross to the desk. 'Ladies, how can I help you?'

An awkward silence ensues while I stand in front of them, my arms folded across my chest. I look from Izzy to the publicist. Waiting. The publicist opens and closes her mouth without speaking, then slowly, as her gaze runs from my head across my folded arms, she reaches out a hand for me to shake. Is she ogling me?

I take her hand in a short shake. As if the move snaps her out of a trance, she speaks loudly and quickly. 'Finally, someone with some authority around here.'

'Excuse me?'

She flicks her bobbed hair from her eyes and flashes me a flirty smile. 'Well, I was explaining to this woman, your receptionist, that this is Izzy Coulthard. I'm sure I don't need to explain to you that Izzy is here on a promotional tour for her new, highly anticipated fitness book.'

I stare at her blankly, as if I've never seen the stunning blonde by my side on TV.

She continues to speak. 'I'm her publicist, Kerry. Izzy wanted to check out the gym to see if we could...'

I tune her out as my attention shifts back to Izzy. The woman from my hot-as-hell dream. The woman who morphed from herself to Alice and finally to Jake.

Christ. My body shudders as I remember that nightmare.

From the parting of her lips and the widening of her eyes, I'd say Izzy just picked up on my not-so-subtle revulsion, and she is

100 per cent affronted. I could fix that easily. I could explain that I'm not shaking off the thought of banging her in my dream but the thought of getting jiggy with Jake.

Of course, that won't put an end to the incessant ranting of the ignorant publicist who is still talking at me.

'...I tried to explain to your receptionist that it would be good marketing for the gym if Izzy were to be seen working out here, and—'

I dart my focus back to Kerry and hold up a hand. 'I'm sorry to disappoint you, Kerry, but we don't have the capacity for walk-ins. I have a full members list.'

She tuts. Actually *tuts* at me. 'This is Izzy Coulthard.'

'Sweetheart, she could be Angelina Jolie. I don't bow to status or threats from publicists. And, for the record, Charlie is my floor manager, not a receptionist. And if there were any chance of me letting Izzy work out in my gym today, insulting my staff is the last thing you should be doing.'

I resume my folded arm position and glare at Kerry until she looks away.

'Look, we didn't mean to cause an upset.' Izzy speaks with a British accent. A cute British accent. She glances around the space and the people in the bistro who have gone quiet and are watching our show. When I look at her this time, I notice a small dimple in the center of her chin, and the amazing brightness of her blue eyes. 'I just want to work out.'

Don't be lured in by it, Brooks. She's just another jumped-up wannabe, whether you've fantasized about tapping her or not.

'Do you run?' I ask, before images of her legs wrapped around my waist can penetrate my thoughts. At least I tried to stop them from doing that.

'Ah, yes, I run.'

'Well, since you're dressed for it, I'll do you a favor.' I incline my head toward the neon-blue sports bag on the floor by the sofa and exhale sharply through my nose as I realize it is a high-end designer label and probably cost my month's rent. 'You can leave your gym bag in a locker here and go for a run. When you leave the gym, run eight blocks to the left. You'll be in Central Park.'

For the second time, her lips part. This time, her mouth opens wider.

'Are you joking?' Kerry chides.

I shrug. 'The offer's there. Take it or leave it.'

Kerry puts a hand on my arm, a move I think is intended to be aggressive, or powerful, who knows? 'But I called and told y—'

'I picked up your voice messages before I came down here. All three of them. The first asked if you could come here today. The second gave me an hour to respond. The third said you were on your way.' I take her hand from my arm. 'I don't take kindly to people telling me what to do with my gym, Kerry. Try advance notice and a polite request next time.' I turn to Izzy, who still looks a little astonished. 'If you want to borrow a locker, Charlie will fix you up.'

With that, I turn my back on them. Before I reach the double doors, I glance back at Izzy.

'Hey, none of my business, but if you want that book to sell, you might want to reconsider your choice of publicist.'

I let the doors close behind me and smirk all the way up the stairs. Who the hell does she think she is?

* * *

Back in my office, my smirk disappears and it's easier to tell my hackles are standing up. That attitude. Rude to my staff. Rude to me. Rude about my gym. And all in front of customers.

Without realizing, I've started pacing the floor, my usual calm shot. I thought Brits were supposed to be all pleases and thank-yous and queues. Not hoity-toity divas.

I rub a hand roughly across my short beard and crack my neck. *Shake it off, Brooksie. Shake it off.*

Taking a bottle of sparkling water from my minifridge, I sink into my desk chair and lean back into the padding as I drain the bottle, enjoying the cool, calming effect of the liquid. I fire the empty into the trash can in the corner of the room and stare at my desktop screen saver. A picture of Cady is swirling around the otherwise black monitor.

I don't know why I do it – morbid fascination, maybe. I wiggle the mouse, type in my password, and open the internet browser. I only type 'Izzy C' before Google offers me her full name.

Hitting return brings up multiple images of Izzy Coulthard, aka Brit with a stinking attitude. I click on images and the screen fills with pictures of her. Mostly, she's dressed in sports gear. Tight fitting and brightly colored. Her hair is always tied in a high pony-tail, as slick as it was today. Her arms are toned, even though her skin is pale in every image. Her face is flawless, yet not made up. She looks better without all the makeup she was wearing today. More natural. Like a real fitness instructor. I wonder why she was wearing makeup today; it surely wasn't to mask a lack of confidence.

In all the shots, she's working out or looking at the camera, straight faced.

Figures. I've spent minutes in her company and can't imagine her smiling.

As I scroll down, the images keep loading. Finally, one picture makes me pause. I click it to zoom and take her in. Her head is thrown back, her mouth is open, her perfect teeth are on display. She's laughing, hard. It lights up her eyes – the brightest, bluest eyes I've seen. Her dainty hands are placed across her waist.

I rest back in my chair and take in the image. Everything about her. I'm still staring when my cell phone rings, stealing my attention.

The name on the screen causes me to do a double take. It's surprising it hasn't gone to voice mail by the time I slide my thumb across the screen and put the phone to my ear.

'Alice. Hi.'

She clears her throat. Good, this is awkward for us both, then. 'Hi, Brooks. How are you?'

I shrug, not that she can see me. 'I'm fine. You?'

'Mm-hm, good.' Cue uncomfortable pause. Hey, I didn't make the call – it's not on me. 'Well, I mean, I'm good generally. You, ah, I guess Cady told you I'm pregnant?'

'Right, yeah, she mentioned it. Congratulations... by the way.'

Did she just snort? 'Thanks. So, that's not actually... I'm calling about Cady.'

'Of course, right.'

'Brooks, I don't know what to do with her. I'm going out of my mind. She's got this older boyfriend, a college guy. She didn't come home on Saturday night. She called and said she was staying with a friend but I saw her friend's mom yesterday and she said they didn't stay there. Cady stank like a brewery when she finally did come home.'

I take a breath. Part of me thinks Cady's just being an eighteen-year-old kid. The other half of me wants to wrap her up in cotton, so I get where Alice is coming from. 'I'll talk with her. I spoke to her on Saturday but I'll try again.'

Alice sighs. 'Brooks... I... How would you feel about her coming to stay with you full-time? Just for a while. I can't. I mean, I'm pregnant and...'

I feel my brow scrunch. She wants to kick out my daughter? 'Are you kidding me?'

'I just think she'd be better off—'

I scoff, feeling my blood boil in my veins. 'She's a kid, Alice. She might give it the tough eighteen-year-old routine but she's just a kid.'

'She's your kid too, Brooks,' she yells down the line.

'Hey, calm down. You know I'd have her with me twenty-four/seven if I thought it was the best thing for her, so drop the attitude. Maybe ask yourself why she's acting out now, of all times. She feels pushed out. You're pregnant. She needs to know she's still your girl, Alice.'

The line goes silent and I know she'll have her fingertips pressed to her soft lips, her eyes closed.

'I just don't want her to...'

'Make the same mistakes as you did. I know.'

What she doesn't know is that those words hit me like bullets to my chest, blazing through me, breaking bones, burning a hole in my heart, piercing my lungs, and making it hard to breathe.

She blows out slowly but heavily, as if through pursed lips. 'You always could read people, couldn't you?'

Nostalgia Lane? Really? That's not my address.

Suddenly uncomfortable in my seat, I stand and move to the window, looking out over the city. 'I'll talk to her. Just try to include her. Maybe set up a girls' day. I'm sure she could use a woman to talk to. You set something up and I'll pay for Cady. Don't push her out, okay? Don't make her feel like she isn't welcome in your home.'

'You know she is. Of course she is.'

'I know that. Just make sure *she* knows it.'

'Okay. Thanks, Brooks. It's good to talk to you about her. You know, when I try to talk to Richard, he—'

Richard. We're going to talk about the latest husband?

'I've got to go, Alice. If you need me for anything to do with Cady, you know how to find me. Anything at all.'

'Oh, yeah, course.'

'Bye, Alice.'

'Goodbye, Brooks.'

I end the call and lean into the sides of my fists, pressing them against the cool glass of the window. I fill my lungs with one steady, calming breath, reminding myself that she's not *my* Alice. She's not the Alice I was in love with eighteen years ago. And I will never have her again.

My melancholy is replaced when I see the bright Lycra of the British diva, heading back toward the gym. So, she did go for a run. Her hair swishes as she runs. Her arms move parallel to each other, drawing perfectly straight rotations. Her style is good, efficient. Her thighs look strong. Her stride is set at a solid pace. She moves effortlessly, but I know she's working her body hard.

When she stops outside the gym, she presses the phone holder that's strapped around her bicep, presumably to turn off or change her music, then she starts to stretch. Her top rides up as she takes her arms above her head and leans to one side, stretching the sides of her torso from the hip. Her stomach is perfectly flat. Her skin inviting.

It is such a shame she's an obnoxious—

'Brooks, I'm done for the day. I'll see you tomorrow.'

I spin quickly and feel as guilty as I must look. I feel as if I've been caught red-handed with contraband.

'Thanks, Charlie. Have a good one.'

When I turn back to the window, Miss Attitude has vanished from the sidewalk.

I check my watch and get a little buzz when I see it is second lunchtime. See, I train folks who work office jobs over actual lunchtime, so I eat two smaller helpings before and after then.

Meh, small for me. I guess you could call it a little Brooks quirk – I'm always hungry.

The bistro is still busy. Adding the café to the premises was one of the best business decisions I've made. People fill the seats all day, whether it's breakfast, brunch, snacks, coffee, smoothies, dinner. There's a cheerful vibe about the place – people high on endorphins putting the world to right.

Dipping my head to the familiar faces around the bistro, I move toward the smoothie bar. Before I get to the counter, my ears find the English girl, then my focus lands on, well, her ass, then the rest of her. She's leaning on the counter with both palms, standing on her tiptoes for no apparent reason, as if she's walking on eggshells.

'Oh, no, those combinations don't really do much for me. Let's make it easy. I'll take the green roots smoothie but leave out the shot of that Xcell protein. I don't rate that stuff at all. Could you also switch out the cucumber and add kale? Do you have asparagus? That would be great in there. You know, I could leave you one of these...'

I watch, one brow raised, my teeth digging hard into my cheek, as she takes one of her books – the one from the TV commercial – from her sports bag and holds it out to Angie.

'This is my new book. It has great recipes. I think they would do really well here.'

I try to keep my cool, since that's what people expect from me – hell, it's what I expect from me – but my words are sharp. 'What do you think you're doing?'

Izzy jumps and spins quickly, leaning back when she realizes how close my face is to hers. 'I was just—'

'You were just shitting all over the recipes I put together. You were just bad-mouthing one of my sponsors, when I'll bet you've never even tried their products.'

'I—'

'You were just pimping your book in my gym, uninvited.'

I fold my arms across my chest and glare at her as she takes a step back. When she looks down at the ground, guilt strikes me. I went in too hard. I don't know why. It's not like me.

An apology of some sort is on the tip of my tongue when she whips her head back up and there's bloody murder in those blue eyes. They no longer shine; they're cold as an ice queen's.

'You know something – I'd heard about this gym, and about you, Mr Brooks Adams, Trainer to the Stars.' She puts on a mocking tone that makes her sound petty. 'Kerry wanted me to come here because she said the gym, and you, are the best in the city.' She throws her head back on a fake and damn annoying laugh. 'Well, at least I understand why now.' She gestures with her free hand from my head to my toes. 'It's obvious, isn't it? When a personal trainer looks and talks like you, there are no distractions. Your clients can focus 100 per cent on working out because there's no risk of them falling for their trainer.'

Now it's my turn to laugh. 'Really? You're throwing out cheap shots about my looks because you're having a tantrum? For a moment there, I almost forgot that you're a wannabe with a hell of a lot of attitude. Thanks for the reminder.' I turn to Angie, who is watching the show with an empty blender cup held midair. 'Give her what she wants just this once, Angie. It will be the first and last time.'

Shaking my head, I abandon the lunch idea and turn to leave the bistro. But it seems Izzy Coulthard just doesn't know when enough is enough.

'You really are precious over a piece of bloody cucumber!' she shouts after me.

'At least cucumber tastes of something. I mean, kale? Really? Be original.'

Her jaw drops before a childish scowl takes over her face. 'Yeah, well, kale tastes better than those shitty protein shots.'

'That's BS. And, for the record, you don't need to salsa yourself slim if you eat like a goddamn rabbit in any case.'

I leave the bistro as she shouts something about the diet of a gorilla.

Did that really just happen? In front of customers? Did I just argue with a woman over cucumber and kale?

By the time I reach the mezzanine level, I'm laughing. For some ungodly reason, I'm in kinks. I really did argue with a woman I don't know over cucumber.

I have a flashback to her childish pout. Like Kirsten Dunst in that cheerleader movie that Cady watches. What was that, *Bring It On*? That's it. I swear Izzy's pout was worse than teenage Kirsten Dunst. I laugh harder. Damn, it feels good.

It could be her pout. It could be the realization that, while I was having an argument with a hot woman over vegetables, I didn't think about Cady going off the rails, or the fact the only woman I've ever loved is having another man's baby.

Either way, give the most obnoxious woman in the world her due, I never laugh after I've heard from Alice. Never.

6

BROOKS

I see Drew and Kit walk into the gym. I watch their reflections hover while they wait for me to finish my last reps of bicep curls. Although I spar with people and do a piecemeal workout during the day, when the gym is quiet, I like to fit in a full body workout whenever I can. Sometimes that's at 9.00 a.m., sometimes right after lunch, or like tonight, it can be around 9.00 p.m.

I grunt through the final curl and lean close to the mirror to put the weights down on the rack. As I wipe sweat from my neck and arms, Drew and Kit come closer, both wearing jeans and button-downs. Both with wet hair from showering.

'Do you want us to wait for you?' Drew asks.

'No, don't worry. I'm about done. I'll clean up and see you at Black Velvet.'

It's not like I'm out every night of the week. I was out over the weekend. And Monday night with Jake. Now, it's Wednesday and I'm going out again, so I guess I can see why some might think I'm a drunk. I'm not. Generally, I drink a couple of times a week. I don't get wasted. But Jake is heading back to London tomorrow, so the gang is getting together for a send-off. The good thing about the city is, whether it's Wednesday, Friday, or Sunday, there's always life in the bars.

After stretching, I head into the men's changing rooms. I take my shower, then pull on my jeans and boots with a long-sleeved T-shirt that doesn't hide the tips of the ink from my shoulders and chest that sneak above the neckline.

A quick check of my watch tells me it's been twenty-five minutes since the guys left. I need to get moving.

In my office, I dump my dirty clothes into my laundry basket and lock up. As I'm heading out, my cell starts ringing.

Taking the stairs two at a time, I slide my thumb to answer without looking at the screen. 'Yo! I'm on my way. Get me a beer and whatever Jake wants.'

'Who would have thought the most miserable man alive has friends?'

I pause at the bottom of the stairs. 'Who is this?'

'Kerry. Izzy Coulthard's publicist. We met today? You were extremely rude?'

'Aha. What do you want?'

'While it pains me, Izzy likes your gym. She moaned about the owner being a jerk and the smoothie recipes being in need of improvement but—'

'Listen, Kerry, I have somewhere to be. What's this about?'

She makes a noise, like a grunt or growl that sounds as if it came through gritted teeth. 'We need a space for Izzy to shoot a DVD of her *Salsa Yourself Slim* classes, and you, unfortunately, have the best space in the city. So, I'd like to book into one of your studios.'

She can't see me, but I'm shaking my head in sheer disbelief. The audacity of these women. I hear her flicking pages down the line.

'Ideally, we would do tomorrow. We really need to get moving on this and I have a film crew ready to go. At the latest, we could do Friday. What works for you?'

I scratch my head. Like they do in comic sketches to get the point across to viewers that they're confused. 'Are you shitting me right now? You behave like you did this morning. And by that, I mean both of you. Then you demand a favor from me. Command me to do something like I'm your puppet.'

'Don't be precious about this, Brooks. You don't have to like me, or Izzy. The fact is, the publicity would be good for your gym too.'

I scoff. 'You are some piece of work, Kerry. You know that? I've met two-year-olds with better manners than you.'

'Really? I hardly see you as the soft, caring, fatherlike figure. Ugh, I shudder to think what your spawn would be like.'

'This isn't helping your cause.'

'Goddamn it, what will?'

There's shuffling and crackling, then the muffled sound of whispered bickering. Then the British vegetable lover is on the line. 'Brooks, it's Izzy. Look, I know we didn't exactly get off to a flying start today but I'd be really grateful if you would let us use your studio tomorrow.'

'Ha! So you can pimp your book to my staff again?'

She sighs. A noise of pure exasperation. It's extremely satisfying to me. 'I'm sorry about that. I wasn't trying to... I can see how it must have looked and I apologize. But I'd be truly, truly grateful to you. Indebted to you, in fact, if we could book in.'

'Indebted. Would you let me have one of your books as a thank-you?'

'Of course I w—'

She stops when I snicker.

'Right. That was a joke. Good one. What can I do? What will it take?'

While these women drive me crazy, I can't help but enjoy the sound of her begging in that hot accent.

'Oh, I don't know. Maybe a six-letter word beginning with P?'

I hear her exhale. 'Please.'

'Say it like you mean it.'

'Brooks. Darling, Brooks. Pretty please, with buttercream icing and a cherry on top, will you let me use your studio tomorrow?'

I feel one side of my mouth curl. Damn, I enjoy hating this woman.

'I'd love to help you out here, Izzy. Really, I would. I think it was the way you bad-mouthed my gym, my sponsors, and my recipes that did it for me. But you see, I have a full schedule of classes tomorrow, so I don't have a free studio.'

'But—'

'I enjoyed listening to you beg, though, darling Izzy.'

She gasps and I have to fight to keep my amusement from spilling out. 'Fine. Bugger off, Brooks, you... you... meathead.'

'Meathead? Seriously?'

'Yes, meathead. And, for the record, your attempt at a British accent sucks egg. Extremely smelly, rotten egg.'

I'm still laughing when the line goes dead. For the second time, Izzy Coulthard has my ribs aching.

* * *

Black Velvet is the kind of bar that is always busy and never seems too crowded. You might call it classy. Not somewhere you would have found me ten years ago. In fact, five years ago, when I had my gym based in Brooklyn, you still would have been more likely to catch me in an old bar with sticky floors and a kind of grungy feel.

I spot the guys right away, in the same booth we seem to have adopted ever since the bar opened. Jerome – ex–football player turned club owner – is a client of Drew's and, like most of Drew's exorbitantly wealthy clients, they throw him perks. Judging from the bucket of Dom Pérignon in the center of the black table, shining under the light of a waterfall crystal chandelier, I'd say tonight's perk is a bucket of champagne.

Kit sits with his arm across Madge's shoulder. Sarah is looking at something on Jake's phone. Drew is laughing with Edmond, who must have snuck out of the restaurant early and brought Becky along with him. Edmond's wife, Amelie, is putting in a rare appearance too. When I say Amelie, think the Johnny Depp movie *Chocolat*. Edmond's wife looks just like Juliette Binoche: beautiful, sweet, high cheekbones, short, dark hair.

I deal with handshakes, fist bumps and cheek kisses, struggling to navigate around the booth, then slip onto the black velour seat next to Sarah. When I have a glass in my hand, Drew makes a toast. 'To my kid brother. Heading back to London's women and booze. It's been good to see you.'

'Good luck with that hard life there, Jakey,' I say, tongue in cheek, when I clip his glass with my own. I swallow the fizz, appreciating the bubbles but wishing I was drinking beer.

'Yeah, to the hard life,' Kit says. 'And by the way, if you ever need any help with that...'

Right on cue, Madge drives the palm of her hand into Kit's shoulder. 'Hey, jackass, I'm right here.'

Knowing this is how the two of them roll, we all enjoy the joke. Kit and Madge were Drew's college friends but they've morphed into being our friends. They're a solid couple and sometimes I think being able to joke with each other is what keeps them strong. Especially with two young kids. I know from the nights I looked after Cady alone in the early years that two young kids can't be easy. And Cady was a good baby... so I was told. Truth be known, I envy Kit and Madge.

As I'm watching my friends, Sarah nudges her shoulder against mine. 'Say, Brooks, Kristie Flemming told me there was a little, ah, altercation, at the gym this morning.'

I know exactly the altercation she means. The one and only time I've been unprofessional in front of guests of the gym. So, I do something that Drew taught me to do many moons ago, when he was a junior attorney. I deflect. 'Kristie Flemming. I can't place her. Anyone need a top-off?'

I reach for a bottle of bubbles and seek out a glass that looks like it could do with a top-off, which happens to be Becky's. Drew eyes me, knowing I stole his tactic, but he doesn't call me on it. There's no need since Sarah gets in there first.

'Brooks Adams, that was a blatant attempt to divert attention.'

I slide Becky's full glass back to her and roll my eyes as Drew smirks, enjoying the situation. He knows I don't like all eyes on me.

'Sarah, seriously, is there anyone in Manhattan you don't know?'

She ponders, overacting the point, the tip of her finger resting against pursed lips. 'Mm, no. I make it my business to know what's going on in my city. Think of it like citizen's watch. A good deed. And my good deed for today is asking, on behalf of Kristie, who is the woman you had an altercation with this morning?'

'Why does Kristie need to know that? So she can gossip to her wine club friends?'

'Wow. Nerve. Hit. No, like many women who pay the extortionate membership at your gym, Kristie has a huge crush on you.'

'That's insane.' I sip from my glass – a manly sip. 'My memberships are not extortionate. They include the pool, sauna, steam room, all classes.'

Sarah looks at Drew and says, in her law firm telephone voice, 'Your honor, the defendant is deflecting.'

Drew sits up straight. 'Mr Adams, please answer the question.'

I growl at Sarah. 'It was just some fitness woman who is in New York to promote her new book. She and her publicist came into the gym like God owed them a freakin' favor. They upset my staff. I didn't like it. That's all.'

'Reeeeally. See, Kristie said there was a spark between you and this woman. She also said the woman was a hot blonde and that she could have cracked nuts on her ass.' Sarah throws a glance to Drew. 'Rear, your honor. Could have cracked nuts on her *rear*.'

Trying not to let my amusement show, I say, 'If by spark, you mean the kind you get from dropping a lit match on a diesel bonfire, I'd agree, there was a spark. And you'd hope to be able to crack nuts on her ass. She might be an arrogant jerk, but she's selling fitness. You have to practice what you preach and all.'

'Hold up!' Jake says. 'Which blonde are we talking about here? And, side point but relevant, did she also have a good rack?'

I pick a peanut from a ramekin on the table and throw it at Jake, hitting him flush between the eyes. 'It was that chick from the TV commercials on Monday night.'

'The one from London?' Jake asks. 'The *Salsa Yourself Slim* chick?'

'That's her.'

Almost in perfect harmony, Becky and Sarah chime, 'No way!'

'I adore her videos on YouTube,' Sarah says.

'I make cakes for a living and she's managing to keep the pounds off me,' Becky adds, in her British royals–type accent.

'What is that? British solidarity? Have a word, Drew.' At that, Becky throws a peanut at me but I open my mouth and catch it, giving her a smug grin.

'You two should find yourself someone nice to gush over. Or, better yet, let me hook you up with nutrition plans. I'm telling you, Izzy Coulthard may seem nice on TV and YouTube, but she's got a pole so high up her ass, it's—'

'Okay, enough,' Madge interjects. 'Why was she in your gym anyway?'

'To work out. And to ask if she can use a studio for her new DVD.'

Sarah does a goofy dance in her seat. 'Eek. Can Becky and I come watch?'

'I would let you if I had said yes, but I didn't. I don't want her in my gym.'

Madge turns to me and looks me in the eye. 'Brooks, I've got two young kids. I really couldn't give two hoots about working out when I run around after my Tasmanian devils all day, but this could be good for you,' she reasons. 'It would promote the gym in the process. I may not work as a full-time publicist any more but I still know a few things.'

The others jump on the bandwagon, giving me more reasons to say yes than I can count. Some based on breasts and ass. Some based on girly fitness instructor crushes. Drew's based on helping to build memberships in anticipation of adding another gym to my portfolio.

Against my instincts, I'm left wondering whether it might not be the worst idea in the world to let Izzy 'Flower Power' Coulthard film in my gym.

7

BROOKS

I see the same look on Charlie's face that I know is on my own – somewhere between wanting to pull her hair out and pity.

'Next time I have a brain fart like this, please do everything in your power to stop those three letters coming out of my mouth,' I tell her.

'By three letters I take it you mean Y-E-S?'

Rubbing a hand across my chin, I just shake my head because it's too late. There really isn't any way to stop the circus show that has overtaken my unsuspecting gym and made it the farce of the city.

'Would you pin these around the place?' I hand her twenty signs, all black caps typed on white, and all saying the same thing:

SORRY FOR THE INCONVENIENCE. FILMING IN PROGRESS. THE CAMERA WORK IS LIMITED TO STUDIO A. PLEASE CONTINUE TO USE THE FACILITIES AS USUAL.

I head out of the reception area in search of the solitude of my office. I take out my phone and text Drew:

I am never drinking Dom again. I've been overrun by salsa-loving terrorists.

'Look out, dude.'

I pin my back to the wall of the staircase as two cameramen come charging past, carrying poles and a large camera and those things that look like umbrellas but do something to change the lighting in a shot.

As I reach the landing of the second floor, I hear the same freakin' dance track that's been on loop for the last two hours. The sound is coming from Studio A, where Izzy Coulthard will be filming her DVD *Salsa Yourself Slim*.

Dragging a hand through my hair and glaring down the corridor to the open door of the studio, I say for my own pleasure, 'I swear to God, one more fucking time and I'm cutting the plug.'

'Oh, please.' I recognize her accent before Izzy moves to stand in front of me. She's in psychedelic yoga pants and a workout bra. But that is no ordinary workout bra. Her breasts are pushed up like perfectly formed, round, teasing... I drag my attention to her face, watching her drink from her sports bottle, hoping she didn't catch my wandering eyes. 'You're getting just as much out of this deal as I am, so stop whining.'

I don't have a chance to respond before I'm watching her firm ass cheeks move like silk – smooth, alluring, enticing – as she strides in the direction of the studio.

Argh, she's right. I just need to suck it the hell up.

I'm still watching her as I round the corner toward my office and walk bang into the wiggling hips of a dancer, who is decked out in brand-new sports gear. Here, on the mezzanine balcony, overlooking my gawking regulars, blocking the route to my office, ten fit-as-sin dancers are swirling and grinding svelte hips, perfecting their pre-choreographed moves to Izzy's salsa class.

It's hard to know which comes first: my dry throat, my wandering eyes, the loosening of my jaw, or the twitch at the crotch of my sweatpants. I'm thirteen years old again.

With my forearm leading the charge and semi-blocking the view in a bid to stop me from getting in an embarrassing state in my underwear, I make my way through the crowd of temptation and into the sanctity of my office.

I take a bottle of water from my minifridge and soothe my dry throat, contemplating whether I should pour the whole damn thing down my boxer briefs to put out the flames. Hey, at the end of the day, I'm a hot-blooded man.

Pulling up my schedule for the day, I sink into my desk chair. I'm not sure how it happens but next thing I know, there are images of Izzy Coulthard on my screen. My mouse cursor is hovering over a YouTube video when I hear her voice in the corridor.

'You're looking great, ladies. You can head into the studio now. We're about ready to film.'

Pushing back in my chair, I see her through my open office door. The smile she offers the others leaves as quickly as they do, and Izzy comes to lean on the balcony rail. Her shoulders drop an inch and she seems to be focused on nothing, lost in thought. Wow, she is insanely attractive. Even more so now, with her hair tied back, her lips relaxed and not forced into a pout. I realize for the first time just how slim she is. I want to go to her, wrap my arms around her, and take care of her.

What the actual?!

'Izzy, now is as good a time as any to have a chat about presales.' Kerry, in her high heels and skinny jeans – completely out of place in the gym – comes into view. Izzy stands, turning to her. 'We need to do more ahead of Tuesday. The TV ads have definitely helped but we aren't seeing the numbers we'd hoped for. At least not yet.'

I watch Izzy's back constrict and then relax with a deep breath. 'What can I do?'

'The book signings start this afternoon, but I really think we need to give people a reason to want to know more. A reason to visit your page. I think you need to do what we talked about with your blog. The blog is doing okay. I think you have to drive more interest there and try to convert some of those readers to sales.'

'Kerry, I'm not comfortable with it. I don't see why I have to insult others to sell books.'

Those are not words I ever thought I'd hear Izzy say. Of course, the soft tone of her voice and the defeatist fall of her shoulders aren't things I've seen yet either.

Kerry waves a hand flippantly. 'Stop thinking of it as bad-mouthing. Think of it as playful. Joking around. Showing a new dimension to your personality that attracts people.'

'Surely, if what I'm doing is mean, people wouldn't like me. How would that help sales?'

'Look.' Kerry's tone shifts to annoyance. For some unknown reason, I have an urge to walk out there, give her what for, and take Izzy away from the situation. 'Any traffic is good traffic. This isn't a joke. People have put money behind this book. And I thought you told me this was your chance to prove something, huh? That you can be who you want to be and make a success of it?'

The physical shift in Izzy is visible. The change in the air is palpable. Whoever Izzy has to prove something to, the person is worth trying something she doesn't really want to do. She nods. 'You're right. Fine. I'll do what it takes.'

Yep, that's more like the Izzy I've seen.

I try to work but the constant stop, restart, boom boom

freakin' boom, is driving me crazy. An amped microphone projects Izzy's shouted instructions along the corridor. And, yeah, maybe curiosity gets the better of me.

My next PT client is coming in three minutes. So, I find myself moving along the corridor to Studio A. No wonder the music is so loud; they're filming with the doors open. Huge amps, the size my band used to gig with in high school, are lined along one wall of the open space.

'All right, ladies. Let's take it from the top.'

Restart and boom, boom, boom. My head is going to explode in time to this mind-battering track. Out in the empty corridor, I stubbornly fold my arms across my chest. I watch as Izzy begins to salsa. She moves one foot forward then back, her hip rolling under her tight leggings.

'Let's get some sexy arms, ladies. Show me how hot you are.'

With smiles on their faces, Izzy's fake clients move their hands over their bodies as they follow her moves. But there's only one person in that room I cannot take my eyes off. I imagine dancing with her. Rolling my pelvis against hers. Running my hands up her sides.

And then I'm doing it. I'm salsa dancing in the corridor. I'm moving my feet Latin-style. Holding out my arm as if I were gripping her waist and moving with her pressed against me.

'Brooks?'

I spin quickly and come face-to-face with Daryl: six four, built like the Rock, my goddamn client.

I stop dead, my arm still around Izzy's invisible waist. I look at my arm, as if this really cannot be happening. As if I didn't just get caught salsa dancing by my most butch client. I clear my throat. In the most masculine voice I can muster – somewhere between Johnny Cash and Barry White – I tell Daryl, 'Let's get to it, man.'

* * *

By lunch, Studio A has been cleared and the gym is in the process of being restored to normality. I have undoubtedly lost man points with one of my clients today but the gym may have gained more followers. Which really raises the still lingering question: do I want to franchise the gym?

My cell rings as I'm unstrapping my hands after fitting in half an hour on the punch bags. I use the strap to wipe sweat from my forehead and swipe my thumb across Cady's picture.

'Hey baby.'

'Hey, Dad. I'm on Fifth Avenue. I was supposed to be meeting a friend but her mom had some kind of drama and she has to babysit her kid brother. Anyway, she's going to be at least another hour and a half. Do you want to meet?'

I check the large clock on the boxing room wall. It's almost four and my next client is booked at six thirty. 'Ah, yeah, sure. Let me grab a quick shower. Where should I meet you?'

'Mm, outside the Lindt store?'

'Okay. I'll be there in twenty.'

'Cool. Oh, and Dad, don't wear your sweatpants, okay?'

My next breath comes short and hard through my nose. 'You know, five years ago, you thought I was cool.'

* * *

Fifth Avenue is as packed as ever, with people carrying shopping bags, women strutting in ludicrously priced heels, men in suits walking with cell phones and paying no attention to the people they're bumping into. Tourists stop to unfold and read a map, completely failing to grasp the grid system.

I spot Cady walking out of Lindt. Her hair is still pink. Her skater dress is teamed with black lace-up boots today and her leather jacket is tied around her waist. I dodge the traffic and run across the road to meet her, coming up behind her as she's about to put a dark chocolate Lindt ball into her mouth.

'You shouldn't eat too much of that stuff. It's just a ball of saturated fat and refined sugar.'

She turns to face me and rolls her eyes exaggeratedly as she puts the whole ball into her mouth with a satisfied groan.

'That's disgusting,' I tell her. She chuckles and covers her mouth as she bites down on the ball.

We set off walking without a plan. When her mouth is empty, she tells me, 'I'll give up chocolate if you give up beer.'

I narrow my eyes and pretend to mull that over. Then I grab her shoulder and turn her back toward Lindt. 'Let's get you another bag of those.'

She giggles and I swear, my life may not have panned out the way I would have liked, but if there's one thing I am proud of, it's this girl.

We window shop with take-out drinks. I get the lowdown on what's hot and what's not when you're eighteen these days. I'm lucky enough to get to sit on a chair in Abercrombie & Fitch and wait for Cady to try things on. Two young men with pecs and tans give me peculiar looks. A couple of girls, younger than Cady, bat their eyelids at me.

'Cady, are you done? I need to get out of here before I'm arrested.'

She comes swinging out from behind a red curtain, carrying two check shirts across her arm.

'Do you want those?' I ask.

'Yes, but I have money.'

Those five words thrill me. She knows the value of money.

That's something I want her to know and I'm not sure many kids do these days. I take the shirts from her.

'Since you didn't ask, I'll get these.'

When we're paid up, we head back out onto the street, Cady swinging her bag as she walks. She seems to have become happier since we were last together and I decide not to bring up the older boyfriend or underage drinking again. Not this time. Something tells me my girl could just use some love today.

'Ooh, could we pop into Barnes & Noble? Then I'm going to have to love and leave you because Meghan is on her way.'

'Sure, kiddo. What are you doing with Meghan anyway?' I hold open the door to Barnes & Noble for her to walk in ahead of me.

'Just going to grab some food, and maybe a movie.'

I can live with that. Cady takes off ahead of me and I'm left alone, doing a double take when I catch a face I recognize pinned to a sign by the cashier's desk.

Izzy Coulthard
Author of *Be Green. Be Clean.*
Signing, today, 5.30 p.m.

I check my watch as an irrational sense of panic makes my insides judder. She must be here now. Thumping my chest in a King Kong-esque way to kill the erratic beat beneath, I head in search of Cady.

Not seeing her on the ground floor, I move upstairs.

At the far end of the store, next to the café, I spot Izzy. She's alone, sitting behind a table, with her phone in her hand and a stack of her books at her side. Her head is down and she seems to sigh as her fingers move across her cell screen.

My stomach becomes weightless. She's an ass, I know. A beautiful ass but still a self-important ass. But her conversation with Kerry today, the way she stood, defeated, and now, seeing her alone at the table, I don't know, maybe it melts my iron heart or something.

I don't know how long I stand there watching her, hoping someone will take a book to her and ask her to sign it. I contemplate going myself, but she's more likely to think I'm gloating than genuinely asking her to sign a book I'll never read.

As if she senses me gawking, she raises her head. I panic, shuffling right, then dart left behind a shelf of books. I pin my back to the shelf, panting, as if I've just run a record time in the New York Marathon.

'Dad, what are you doing?'

I roll my head to the right and see Cady. My eyes quickly follow hers to the label on the shelf in front of her.

'Erotic romance!' I exclaim.

'Dad, shut up. Jesus!'

I'm at her side in a flash and see the *Fifty Shades* trilogy in her hands. She needn't know I've actually read the thing. No one needs to know that. But in light of the fact I have read it...

'No way!' I take the books from her hands and plant them back on the shelf.

'I'm not five, Dad. I do know what sex is.'

Christ. 'And if some boy sees you reading that stuff, he's going to think it's an open invitation to take a flogger to your ass. Let's go.'

'Oh my God. How do you even know what a flogger is?'

Am I allowed to laugh in this situation?

'Out. Now.' I turn her by the shoulders and fight my smirk behind her back as I guide her down the staircase and out to the street.

'Oh, Meghan's there. See you, Dad.'

Just like that, I'm abandoned on Fifth Avenue, my face uncharacteristically burning red for more than one reason.

I take out my cell phone and dial Sarah.

'Hey, you!' she answers. 'What's up?'

'Hey, Sarah. Could you do me a favor?'

'Name it.'

'Could you maybe round up a few friends and head to Barnes & Noble on Fifth Avenue? The, ah, salsa guru you like has a signing there. I... I don't even know why I'm asking but could you go get a book signed? I'll buy it. Get one for Becky and Madge too. Or, better, take them if they can get here like, yesterday.'

'Uh, I'm going to ask you more about this later but sure, I can do that.'

8

IZZY

This is mortifying. Maybe my parents were right. God, if they could see me now. That song pops into my head, 'If My Friends Could See Me Now,' from the musical *Sweet Charity*. Except, if my friends could see me now, I'm not eating fancy chips and drinking fancy wine. No, I'm sitting at a table in Barnes & Noble on Fifth Avenue, feeling utterly embarrassed. One book. From the stack of twenty on the table and the box full of additional copies hidden by my feet, I've sold and signed *one* copy of my book.

'It's one signing, Izzy. And it's your first one. We'll work on more promo,' Kerry tells me, returning from wherever she disappeared to ten minutes ago.

It doesn't matter what she says because I know this is bad. Presales aren't going well. It's my first book, so I knew it wouldn't hit the best-seller lists or anything – although there was a small part of me that hoped – but so far, it has sold a couple thousand copies, that's it.

How can I go home and look my parents in the face and tell them I made the right decision to follow my heart, then immediately ask them to write me a check to help with my rent?

Maybe Mum is right. I should give up on my need to perform and be something more ordinary. Perhaps I should do something stable. Something with a steady income that could pay my rent.

A lump forms in my throat and pressure builds behind my eyes. I take out my phone and check Facebook. Not because I want to especially, but because I can't let Kerry know that I feel... defeated. Well and truly, buried six feet under defeated.

'I'm going to take off,' Kerry says, checking her watch. By that, I suspect she means, she needs to deal with clients who make her money. 'The store will take care of any leftover copies. My suggestion is to sign them and we'll have them put on the shelves on release day. I'll chat with the manager on the way out. I need to go review your blog post.'

'My blog post, right.'

'Oh, don't be like that. It's just a little spice to your usual dry health and fitness stuff. Trust me, this will be worth it.'

I hug her goodbye and flop back down on my seat. Will it be worth it? The blog I wrote was not nice. I demeaned Brooks' gym, his techniques, and worse, him as a person. I mean, sure, he behaved like a knob and the man has such a shitty, abrupt, mean... I picture his biceps bulging under his white T-shirts. The tattoos decorating his arms and poking out through the top of his T-shirt. I bet his toned pecs and abs are covered in ink. I wonder if his back is—

Stop, Izzy.

I shuffle on my seat, clenching my thighs together. Okay, so his looks have got me a little... wired. But he is an absolute tool. I mean, I only wanted a green smoothie, for Christ's sake. And it wasn't my fault Kerry had a crappy attitude with him.

But the blog – is that really me? Is that what I've become? It feels dirty.

But there's no way I can face going back to Chelsea and telling people, telling friends and family, that I failed at this.

And I have failed. Just look at today. I lift my head from my iPhone to the empty space in front of me and feel like crying again.

I have no choice but to try to drive more readers to my blog and socials. I have got to do something.

As my vision starts to cloud, I see three women tottering on heels toward me. I glance across my shoulder, knowing there's nothing but a wall behind me but really not believing that these women might be coming to see me.

'Hey! Izzy? Oh my gosh, we love your salsa videos. I'm Sarah,' the tall, immaculate brunette says and then gestures to the shorter, blonde woman next to her. 'This is Becky.'

'I'm Kristie,' the third says and thrusts her hand at me to shake. Though she smiles through brightly painted, pink lips, the look on her face is more inquisitive than friendly, her green eyes scrutinizing me.

'Hi, it's a pleasure to meet you.' I stand up and the one named Sarah leans in to hug me. 'Would you like me to sign a book for you?'

'Absolutely,' Becky says. I recognize her accent immediately.

'Hey, you're British,' I say, stating the obvious. 'It's nice to meet another one of us across the pond.'

'I am. And I'll take three copies, please. I'm always looking for new food ideas. I'm a chef.'

'Oh, gosh, that makes me nervous,' I tell her, genuinely.

I take three copies of *Be Green. Be Clean* from the pile I never thought would go down and open each to the first page. My hand trembles as I take a Sharpie to the page and sign the books. When I'm finished, Sarah asks for four copies, and Kristie, who seems slightly chirpier now, asks for one.

'Oh, hey, ladies, over here.' I look up as Sarah waves over another two women in suits. 'This is Izzy. If you haven't seen her salsa classes, you must.'

I chat with the women until there's only Sarah and Becky left. They're easy to talk to and seem genuinely interested in my book. Becky is flicking through and commenting on recipes she says she is going to try. Sarah asks about the video I was shooting this morning. It doesn't occur to me for a few minutes that news of the DVD hasn't broken yet. It is in my blog post – which also slags Brooks Adams – but that hasn't gone live yet.

'Hey, how did you know about the shoot? Do you go to the Brooks Adams gym?' I ask.

Sarah bites her bottom lip, as if she's been caught playing truant from class. 'Mm, I do. But I know about the shoot because we're actually friends of Brooks.'

'Oh.' Friends of the guy I've slammed on my blog. 'Oh. I see.'

Sarah laughs. 'We know about your run-in, but it can't have been that bad since he told us you were here signing tonight. He said we should come down.'

I feel my brow furrow. 'He did? Why would he do that?'

My curiosity is quickly wiped out by the realization that Brooks sent people to see me. They aren't really here because they wanted to meet me and buy my book.

Sarah juts out a hand to my shoulder. 'That doesn't mean we don't love your work, though. I genuinely bounce around my apartment to your videos.'

Becky closes the hardback in her hands. 'And I really am going to steal some of these recipes.'

I force a smile, knowing it comes on only one side of my mouth. 'Thanks. I appreciate it.'

'Hey, if you're in the city for a while, we should all do coffee or brunch,' Sarah says.

Becky nods. 'I'd love that.'

Sarah scribbles her number on a receipt she pulls from her purse. 'Drop me a line if you find some spare time.'

When I'm alone, I start to sign the remaining books from the tabletop and the box beneath. I carry them to the cashier's desk and head out to Fifth Avenue. Despite the warm air, I wrap my jacket tight around me and walk with my arms across my stomach. I could really use a hug.

I walk. And walk. Weaving between streets and people. I keep walking until my kitten heels are hurting the balls of my feet.

Tonight was not a success. I sold books but basically all thanks to Brooks Adams, who doesn't even like me.

I stop dead in my tracks. If he doesn't like me, why did he send those women to my signing? It makes no sense. And he was so sharp with me. He seemed like such a dick. Admittedly, one hot, hot, hot dick but a dick nonetheless.

How did he even know I was in Barnes & Noble? Oh my God, did he see me? Did he spot me sitting alone, not signing any books, looking like a complete failure? Did he send those women out of pity?

Perhaps he reads my blog. Would he read my blog?

Oh sugar! My blog.

I pull my iPhone from my handbag and dial Kerry.

'I've changed my mind,' I say when she answers. 'I don't want to put out the blog. If that's what it takes to sell books, I don't want—'

'Too late, *chica*. It went live nineteen minutes ago.'

9

BROOKS

It just keeps going. The verbal diarrhea.

> The best gym in the city, I was told. Everyone wants to be trained by Brooks Adams, I heard. Well, while I can vouch for the perfectly adequate facilities of his gym, the man himself leaves a lot to be desired. I'd heard he was like diamonds to women: irresistible. In this woman's opinion, once you look beyond the allure of bulging biceps, there's nothing but an ill-mannered, arrogant ape.
>
> Putting the beast's personality aside for one second, I must say, I find it hard to believe that he looks the way he does (read: extremely buff) if he follows his own advice. The man was annoyed at me for requesting a green smoothie from his new bistro. Even though I offered one of my new recipes to the server (see links below to my new book *Be Green. Be Clean* – preorder quick, hard copies are selling out fast), Brooks Adams saw red (not green, at all). I won't go on about the quarrel we had over the matter, which was not only embarrassing to me but also other clients in the bistro. My point is this, Brooks

Adams doesn't believe in good nutrition, so what is he really
doing to get that body? I'll let you draw your own conclusions.
All I'm saying is, I'm guessing he doesn't practice what he
preaches.

Why not try a fitness and nutrition regime that works?
winks

'Is she for fucking real?' It's a rhetorical question but Charlie
answers, her tone as wary as her stance as she hovers at the
doorway of my office.

'I'm sorry, Brooks. I thought you would want to know.'

I finally take my eyes off the smug face of Izzy Coulthard on
my screen. 'I do, Charlie. Thanks.'

She leaves me shaking my head. I don't know if I'm shaking
my head in disbelief – how can anyone, especially in the same
professional circle as me, be such a jackass? – or because I
thought I recognized something in her today, something that said
there was a good side to her, and I'm surprised at my own enormous misjudgment.

I push back in my desk chair too harshly, sending it crashing
into the wall.

And I actually felt sorry for the woman. While I was arranging
for Sarah to go to Barnes & Noble, Izzy was probably posting this
blog from her cell.

What a fool. When will I learn that women, even the prettiest
ones, with the most beautiful accents, can be... poison?

My hands are balled into fists as I stare at the blog post, still
certain this cannot be real. It would be one thing if she didn't like
something changeable. If she thinks there are better health and
nutrition methods than mine, that's okay. But to trash my
methods and my gym. Then to attack my character. All in freakin'
public!

I don't bother reading the III comments already amassed in the hour this thing has been published.

'Goddamn it!'

I throw out an arm and knock a pen pot from my desk, scattering stationery across the floor. That only pisses me off more because now I have to pick the damn things up.

As I crouch to refill the pot, it occurs to me I'm not even maddest about other people reading the post. My clients are loyal. I'm more annoyed that I feel like a fool over a woman. I've spent eighteen years being crazy over a woman. But this one... she's something else.

I replace the pen pot, switch my jeans for shorts and then head down to the boxing room. I dip my head to two guys sparring in the ring and mutter acknowledgments to others around the room.

I find one free hanging bag, strap my hands, and put every drop of anger I feel into my fists. When my anger doesn't subside, I thrust a roundhouse kick at the bag, sending it swinging. The taste of salt pushes through my lips and onto my tongue. Sweat drips into my eyes. I can feel the focus of the faces in the room trained on me. I realize I must look insane, going hell for leather over nothing. But this is what I profess – take your shit and put it into your workout. She wants to know why I look the way I do? Because I have a lot of fucking anger and hurt. Because I'm fed up with always trying and failing to be something for one person. One person who will never take me back.

And for some goddamn reason, Izzy Coulthard has managed to bring my shit to the surface more fiercely than I've felt it for a long time.

'Brooks. Brooks!'

I grab hold of the punch bag and look at Charlie, not prepared to see the person standing beside her.

'I'm sorry,' Charlie says. 'She was adamant about coming to see you.'

Izzy eyes me cautiously. If she can see on my face the burning rage I feel at the sight of her, I don't blame her for being wary.

'Brooks, I'm so—'

I hold up a strapped palm and break the glare I'm giving her, trying to cool my temper. I won't do this again. I won't prove her and her pretentious, childish blog to be right. With professional resolve, I all but growl, 'Go to my office. We'll talk there.'

She nods and turns on her feet. I watch her walk away, noting the black filth on the bare skin of her heels and the shoes she's holding in her hand.

I have no idea what I'm going to say to her. All I know is that my anger usually simmers, quietly. But with this woman, for some reason, I feel out of control with rage.

The AC in the stairwell chills my saturated shirt and my body as I walk. I pull my shirt over my head and flick it across my shoulder, leaving me topless and sweaty, then start to unwrap my hands. I see Izzy pacing the floor of my office.

Taking a calming breath, trying to put myself in my usual mind-set, I move into the room and knock the door shut behind me. I don't meet her eye as I continue to unstrap my hands and drop my shirt onto the rim of my laundry basket.

'Brooks, I'm so sorry. Those words weren't all mine. I sent the post to Kerry and—'

'Did you write it?'

'Yes, but—'

I turn to her now, trying not to focus on how beautiful she looks in her green dress, which is patterned with vines of exotic flowers and butterflies – sweet and expensive looking. Ironic, given this woman is anything but sweet. I push the image of her sitting alone in Barnes & Noble from my mind. The moment in which I thought she might be something other than a loud-mouthed fame chaser.

'Is that really how you want to get book sales? By trashing my gym and my advice?'

'No, I—'

'Why? All over a kale smoothie? I let you into the gym to film. I noticed you didn't mention in your little blog post that the reason I didn't just let you walk right into my gym to work out is because I respect my clientele too much. Because I don't think that you should take the space of someone who has waited on a list for months, just because you have a book deal. Just because you're...' I gesture to her with my hand and stop short of calling her stunning or saying that she has the most mesmerizing smile I've ever seen, that her body is exactly what I would savor in a woman: svelte and feminine, while being strong and lean.

Her jaw drops and her eyes narrow. 'You know something, I ran here. Yes, ran, barefoot, from Fifth Avenue. I wrote the beginnings of that blog post but that was before...'

She shakes her head and seems to find another line of attack. She steps close to me, her finger pointing in my face. 'You! You. You...'

I inhale and instantly find out what a mistake that was as her darkly sensual perfume assaults my senses and ignites my libido, blurring my thoughts.

She drops her finger and steps closer to me still, so she's right under my nose, looking up through her lashes. Her eyes widen now, with surprise or perhaps knowing, and her chest rises and falls quickly. I feel her breath against my bare skin. And I want to rip that criminal dress from her with my teeth.

'Would you please put on a shirt?'

I force my eyes shut, killing the link, murdering the moment. Murderous. Yes, murderous, that was how I was feeling before her perfume. I put a hand on her shoulder and take a step back from her.

I grab a clean shirt and pull it over my head, telling her, 'You're better than this. You must be. Look what you've managed to do already. Your name is out there. You have a book deal. Don't let yourself fall into the trap of having to put others down to succeed.'

Her tongue slides along her bottom lip. Thankfully, she drops her head so I can't see any more. All the same, I can feel blood rushing to my crotch.

Christ.

'Don't crave fame and fortune so much, you forget how to be a decent person.'

Her head snaps up and her hands come to her hips. 'I am not *craving* fame and fortune. I want to put my work out there. I want to help people get fit. Unlike you, I want people to do it in a healthy, sustainable way.'

I scoff. 'We're back to this. Right. You don't even know the people I train, how they feel, or the advice I tailor to them. You run around professing that kale and cucumber work for everyone. Let me tell you, if you advise people to eat like pigeons, they will lose weight. But they won't feel good, it isn't sustainable, and they won't tone up.'

'How dare you!'

'How dare I? At least I'm saying it to your face and not on some pathetic blog.'

'My blog is not pathetic.'

She's all but screaming at me. Her cheeks are flaming red. It starts to tickle me.

'Please, you don't even follow your own advice. There's no way you eat lettuce leaves and have an ass like that.'

She spins around on the spot like a dog chasing its tail. It's hilarious. I bite my lip and cover my mouth with my hand to keep in my amusement.

'What's wrong with my bum? And why have you been looking at it, anyway?'

I can't help the short chuckle that escapes me. 'You have a fine ass, Izzy Coulthard, but you didn't get that from eating kale. Admit it or not, you like protein. As for why I've been looking at your ass, ibid.'

'Huh!' She straightens her already straight dress then points her damn finger in my face again. I contemplate taking it between my teeth. 'You just wait, Brooks Adams. You thought the first post about you was bad. You just wait!'

She stomps her foot like Thumper, making my laughter bubble out of me.

Ah, Jesus. I can't decide whether this woman is the best or worst thing that's happened to me in a long time.

10

BROOKS

He had the audacity to say I couldn't possibly follow my own advice because he likes my arse. Yep, he has been ogling my bum. As a side point, I'm sure that's some kind of harassment. Ladies, you should be careful when in Brooks Adams's gym. Maybe the gents should be wary too, you never know!

Let me tell you something. I could whip that protein-loving ape into shape. Two weeks following my recipes and my classes and he would feel much healthier. He might stop saying vile things to women and, as a consequence, he might find a home for his pent-up rage (read: testosterone).

Harassment? Ape? Pent-up testosterone?

Drew and Kit are standing over my shoulder as we read Izzy's latest blog from my office desktop.

'You really pissed her off,' Drew says, stating the obvious.

'What the hell am I supposed to do? I can't have this shit out in public. Look at what people are saying.' I scroll down to the comments beneath the blog post – all two hundred plus of them.

Kit whistles through his teeth. 'Ouch! Samantha Garfield from

Boston says women are already insecure about going to the gym without their trainers gawking at their bodies.'

I push out from my desk and start pacing as Kit slips into my seat. 'Oh, here's one from Simon Etching. I think I know who this guy is. He says he's trained with you for years and your advice has been tailored and exceptional.'

I exhale heavily. 'It's good, in theory. But it means my clients are reading this garbage.'

'Good point,' Kit admits. 'Yikes, there's a woman here slamming Izzy for trying to use you to leverage her own interests.'

'Whoever she is, I like her!'

'Whoa, whoa, back up there.' I look over to see Drew taking control of the mouse and scrolling the screen. 'Anna Coulthard is saying you guys should train together. You and Izzy, she means. She's saying she challenges you to follow Izzy's advice and Izzy to follow yours.'

'Coulthard?' I move over to the screen and start reading. 'It's her sister. She wants to write about it in some British newspaper. No way. Not ever. Izzy Coulthard is not training in my gym.'

I stand upright and find two sets of eyes on me.

Drew speaks first. 'It might not be a terrible idea, Brooks. It would mean publicity for the gym. A chance to set the record straight.'

'Clearly you haven't been in the same room as Izzy and me. We'd kill each other. Throw a diet of greens and pent-up frustration into the mix and I really will be the Hulk.'

'Or Popeye,' Kit says, mimicking Popeye swallowing down cans of spinach.

'No. Not happening.'

'Jokes aside, you could speak to Madge and get her advice. She looks after the kids now but you know she was a publicist, right?'

I rub my chin. 'Yeah, yeah. I'll give her a call.'

* * *

Whatever you do, take the moral high ground. Be nice. Be the bigger person.

Madge's words play over and over in my mind as I sit on my sofa with my laptop on my knee, trying to watch baseball on my flat-screen and ignore the ever-growing number of comments on Izzy's blog post.

It's like they're taunting me, forcing me to read them. I set the laptop to one side and grab my guitar. I strum a Tim McGraw track in an attempt to distract myself. This is not what I need on a Saturday night.

It's no good. I pick the laptop back up and start reading the latest comments.

Green Pixie: You tell him, Izzy. We're proud of you, girl. We don't think you're fame hungry. Love, your London Salsa Ladies.

Alvin Dawson: Brooks is dead on. You can't build core strength and muscle if you eat like a bird.

Melissa Z: I love the idea of Izzy and Brooks trying out each other's advice. That would be hilarious.

FitnessFanatic: Melissa Z, it wouldn't just be entertainment, it would actually be useful. All these trainers say their method is the best. Now's the chance to put them to the test.

Diane16x: This post is disgusting. Izzy Coulthard is trying to tarnish Brooks' good name for her own benefit. I've been a client of Brooks for five years and I've never looked or felt better. He doesn't adopt a one-size-fits-all approach like this Izzy woman tries to do. I say you should go back to England, Ms Coulthard, and spout your poisonous BS there.

'Wow, you go, Diane!'

Be nice. Be nice. Be nice.

'Don't respond, Brooks, come on buddy. Don't respond,' I tell myself.

The devil on my shoulder wins. I click to open a new comment box and begin to type. At first, I follow Madge's advice.

Dear Izzy, I apologize if you feel threatened by my methods and put out because I didn't allow you to train in my gym. I did, of course, give you access to a studio to film your new DVD. As I have previously explained, I have a wait list of clients. Some names have been on that list for months. I do not operate on a system of preferential treatment, therefore, I could not allow you to take a slot in my gym, thereby favoring you over others. I hope you can understand this. I am sure your classes and fitness advice work for many people. I wish you success with your new book and the upcoming DVD.

As I hit submit and complete the CAPTCHA – God, those things are annoying – I'm more riled than I started out. Why should I be nice to her when she's nothing short of awful in return?

Before I can add another comment, she replies:

Dear Brooks, I only wanted to try out your gym as a fellow instructor for one hour. You were rude and obnoxious. Good luck to anyone who decides to go to your gym and train with you!

I can't help myself.

Please. You are so celebrity hungry you think you are better than others. You strutted into my gym, upset my staff and clients, and tried to instruct my kitchen staff as to what they should be doing. Who the hell do you think you are?

I know I shouldn't have sent it as soon as I hit submit.
She replies in seconds.

Who do I think I am? Mr My Way or the Highway!

Angry, I thump out my next response.

You have no idea how I advise clients. Everything is tailored to their needs. Unlike your methods!

Izzy: Ha. As I said in my post, Mr Adams, put your money where your big, rude, ogling mouth is. You didn't want me in your gym because you were worried your clients would see a better alternative to your methods.

My knuckles are showing white as I type.

I did not ogle you. Nor do I scrutinize my clients in any way other than professionally, when they invite my assessment. You are so up your own 'arse' that you think every woman wants to be you and every man wants to nail you.

I've completely lost my dignity. Madge will be sitting at home, screaming at me.

Izzy: You are so far off the mark, you can't even see the mark. If you think your training is more effective than mine, Brooks, prove it. Follow my plan and see how much better you feel. It might even curb some of those tantrums you keep having.

I start to write a reply and stop. I have no intention of following her plan. How would that even work? But she has boxed me into a corner.

Acknowledging that I have already stooped to her level and made myself look like a petulant child rather than a thirty-five-year-old businessman with an adult daughter, I slam the lid shut on my laptop.

* * *

With the windows down and the wind in my face as I cross the Brooklyn Bridge, I already feel better about this whole Izzy situation. I heard nothing more about it on Sunday and refused to look at any more comments. It was a blog post. One silly little blog. It's done. She'll go back to England and I'll forget she ever existed.

Out of nowhere, a yellow cab slams on its brakes in front of me. I hit my hazard lights as I come to an abrupt halt behind it. Next thing I know, a police vehicle comes tearing across the bridge with its lights flashing.

Looks like I'll be late for my meeting. Not sure what lies ahead or how long I'll be stuck here, I turn on the radio and shuffle in my seat to take my iPhone from the ass pocket of my jeans.

'Folks, that was Dobie Gray with "Drift Away." Now we're back with Izzy Coulthard.'

I'm about to connect my iTunes to the car when her familiar voice comes through the speakers.

'Hi.'

'Izzy, we've talked about your new book, *Be Green. Be Clean*, which releases tomorrow. We've discussed your presence online with your *Salsa Yourself Slim* classes.'

'Yes.'

'But there's another element of your online marketing that viewers have been texting in about. You have a blog.'

She clears her throat. I set my iPhone down on the passenger seat before turning up the radio.

'I do, Steve. I use the blog to give my followers new recipe ideas and fitness tips.'

'Except, in the last few days, you seem to have used the blog to... how should we put it? Criticize a fellow fitness instructor. For our listeners, we're talking about Brooks Adams, owner of the Brooks Adams gym. What's the story there, Izzy?'

'Well, Mr Adams and I don't exactly see eye to eye. Our fitness advice differs and our manners certainly do.'

'Meaning?'

She scoffs. 'Meaning I have them and he doesn't.'

Ha! Pot calling the kettle black there, Coulthard.

'Although some might say the tone of your blog lacked manners yesterday.'

Yes! You tell her, Steve Sitwell.

'Arguably, it was not my most professional moment. That said, I stand by my comments. Mr Adams has been very rude to me. He has also made derogatory statements about my methods.'

'Oh, interesting. I just received a tweet from a listener who wonders whether this is a love-hate relationship?'

What?

'Ha! Between Brooks and me? No way in hell. Sorry, am I allowed to say hell on air?'

'Sounds like you just did. So, you wouldn't want to see Brooks again?'

'I. Ah. No. I wouldn't. Where are you going with this, Steve?'

Something I'd like to know.

'It has been pointed out to me that in your last comment on your blog on Saturday night, you invited Brooks to try out your fitness regime. Now, I have a number of listeners saying they would love to see that.'

No. Screw them. Let her get on a plane and fly out of my life.

'I did write that but I did so knowing that Brooks is too chicken to take me up on the challenge.'

Chicken?

I reach over to the passenger side for my iPhone and search for the station's number. Before I put thought behind my actions, I'm calling Steve Sitwell.

Someone from the studio answers.

'This is Brooks Adams,' I tell him. 'Steve Sitwell is currently talking about—'

'Hold on, I'm going to put you through.'

'Through where?'

'Brooks Adams. The man himself. You're live on air, buddy.'

Fuuuuuuuuck!

'Do me a favor and turn your radio down in the background.' For some reason, I turn down the radio in my car, just as Steve Sitwell instructs.

'Do you have something you would like to say to Izzy Coulthard, Brooks?'

I really have no idea. 'Ah, I, ah...'

She laughs in the background. Hearing her is like a red rag to a bull.

'Yeah, I do. If you want to trade fitness plans, Izzy, let's do it. Come into my gym for two weeks and I'll show you a thing or two.'

'I don't need your advice, Brooks.'

'Ah, that's right. Now who's chicken?'

'I'm no chicken. I'll come to your gym and I'll do your stupid routines and eat your protein. And you can follow my plan. You can eat greens and see how good it feels to detox. And... you can salsa!'

'Hold up! There'll be no—'

'We follow each other's plans to the letter or we don't do it at all. Are you afraid you'll harm your precious reputation with a few hip sways, Brooksie?'

'Don't call me fu—'

The line goes dead. He cut me off to stop me swearing. I quickly turn up the radio.

'You heard it here first, folks, Izzy Coulthard and Brooks Adams are going head-to-head. Boy, I think this is going to be good. Will you let us stay up to date with your progress, Izzy?'

'I. I don't know. But. Ah. I guess.'

What in God's name have I done?

11

IZZY

'You have got to be kidding me!' My voice is shrill, painful even to my own ears.

The fact that I'm sitting next to Brooks in Kerry's office is bad enough. Now she's saying I have to live with him for two weeks to make this thing work. It will be good for PR and we need to keep an eye on each other, she argues. She's lost her mind. Live with that gorilla?

Argh, why didn't I just tell them I couldn't extend my trip? Or say my grandmother died? Or that my dog ate my gym kit?

Kerry turns her laptop on the conference room table so the screen faces Brooks, Madge – his PR manager – and me.

'See for yourself. Your blog hits skyrocketed. You had more comments on your blogging war than you've had in the previous year.'

Brooks sniggers and I swear my palm is twitching to slap his face. But Kerry is right. My presales were low. In the last couple of days, preorders, YouTube views, interactions on socials, and new visitors to the blog are all up. Today, my release seems to be going reasonably well. I'm climbing the Amazon charts, at least.

Madge leans in to speak to Brooks, but she's still loud enough that I catch her words. 'Your membership requests are up too, Brooks. If you are going to franchise, this could be good for you.'

He rubs a hand across his short beard. I've never found beards attractive but on Brooks, not only does it work, but it makes me want to test the theory about beards and sensations. Ahem, you know the one. I like his rugged look. Tats, beard, muscles. It's so far from the suited, pompous Londoners I'm used to, the type my parents want me to marry. I like the way one prominent vein shows in his biceps, whether he's flexing or not. I wonder whether he's so ripped, the veins of his pelvis will show me a trail down to his... I shudder involuntarily. This is Brooks Adams I'm focusing on here. Scum of the earth. Well, except that one thing in the bookstore. No! No buts.

I blink three times in quick succession, realizing Brooks is watching me stare at him. *Sugar*.

'Look, it sounds like this could be good for both of us,' he says, surprising me. 'I'll do it. But the defamatory blog posts have got to stop. It's childish and pitiful.'

I feel my jaw drop. Now I'm childish and pitiful?

'And to be clear, just in case there was any insinuation that staying with me means staying in my apartment, you are absolutely *not* staying at my place for two weeks.'

That does sound better. Kerry had made it sound like she wanted us to be living in the same accommodation but, frankly... 'I don't like you. Nor do I want to be staying anywhere near you!'

'Yeah, ditto baby.' He shifts his focus, to address Kerry. 'There's a place on the same floor in my block, two doors down the hall from my apartment. It's available for short-term rental. Maybe you can fix that.'

I hold up a finger as a sound of pure contempt leaves my

mouth. 'First, never call me baby. Secondly, I don't want to be even two—'

'Done,' Kerry says, cutting me off. 'I'll make it happen.'

Grrrrrrr. If I could make someone feel intense pain with my mind, both Brooks and Kerry would be feeling it right now. Though I have to admit, it is the lesser of two very evil evils. 'Fine. Thanks, Kerry.'

With my inner grizzly growling, I hold up three fingers to Brooks. 'Third, each of us has to follow these plans to the letter. No cheating in between. Part of my plan is detoxifying your body, so don't go putting any beer or trashy protein in there. And you have to do the exercises I give you. None of that grunting, meathead, weight-lifting crap.'

He stands up and shakes his head like a headmaster might at a pupil. 'The same goes for you, Coulthard. If I give you steak, you'll eat steak. If I tell you to lift weights, you'll lift weights. And you can't go fitting in dance sessions and messing up my plan.'

I stand and mirror his hostile posture. 'Fine.'

'Fine.'

As we stare at each other, I notice for the first time the flecks of gold around his green eyes. They're like a fine chain holding a bright emerald. I've never seen irises quite like them before. He holds my stare until his eyes slip down to my mouth. The move makes me suddenly need to wet my lips with my tongue.

I have to tell myself that gorgeous eyes, rugged and muscular or not, I am looking at Brooks 'Big Head' Adams.

'Are we all set, then?' Madge rises from her seat, breaking our standoff. She places a hand on Brooks' shoulder and they exchange an unspoken communication.

'We're all set,' Kerry says, narrowing her eyes at me, as if to ask why I was just lost in all things Brooks. I would also like to know the answer to that question.

* * *

I drag my Louis Vuitton suitcase up another flight of stairs, then stop on the landing before tackling the next. I remove the elastic tie from my hair and retie a higher ponytail, lifting my hair off my clammy neck.

'You're telling me that of all the days and times the elevator could break, it's now, when I am moving into your building?'

Brooks' mouth curves at one side in a sick and twisted kind of smile, then he continues up another floor, with ease, though he *is* carrying a significantly smaller case than the one I'm lugging.

'Looks that way now, doesn't it?'

'You planned this, didn't you? You had the concierge do something. I bet if I were to stand in that elevator shaft right now, the lift would be there and it would take me up to your floor.'

He pauses midflight and smirks down at me. 'You want to try it, be my guest. Don't expect me to pick you up when you plummet to the basement.'

'You're sick, Brooks Adams.'

'No sicker than you. Carting this much luggage around is a sadistic thing to do. How much stuff can you really need, anyway?'

'You'd be surprised,' I puff, recommencing the struggle upward.

He moves around another stair wall and out of view. 'At least those greens keep you nice and strong, huh?'

I have never wanted to harpoon someone through the head so much in my life.

We finally make it to the twelfth floor. I'm pleased I decided to wear gym kit for the move but I'm still sweating from all the ugly places. I can feel stickiness between my boobs. I try to subtly dip my fingers into my sports bra to wipe it away but Brooks turns right as my fingers are wedged in my cleavage.

He has stopped outside an apartment door and raises one brow. 'I know you said you wanted a ride but playing with your breasts in the communal areas is a little desperate, Izzy.'

'Would you just bugger off?'

'Sure thing. I'll leave your ridiculously oversized luggage here, shall I?'

'Look, this constant fighting has got to stop. We're working together now.'

He tilts his head to one side in such a bloody supercilious way, I want to slap his chiseled face. 'I'm sorry, Izzy, you're right, fighting in public places is a little uncouth. Not like arguing via a blog post available to the world, for example.'

Stomping my feet as I pull my case, I move to his side. 'You really need to get over that.' I eye the blue door and the gold numbers 124 nailed to the center. 'Is this my apartment?'

'No, this is *my* apartment. You're two doors that way. I just want to show you this door and let you know that you are not welcome here. If you run out of milk or sugar or you watch a scary movie and need a buff man to put an arm around you, there are around one hundred sixty other options in this building. Consider 124 off limits.'

Dick. Big, massive, huge, enormous dick.

He steps to one side and gestures down the hall. 'Shall we?'

'Yes. For the record, I don't take milk or sugar. And if I did want a ride, you're the last man on earth I would stroke my tits for.'

'Classy, Coulthard. Real classy.' He chuckles and I have to fight not to laugh with him. 'And, for the record, the elevator has been broken for weeks. Come on, Tits, lead the way.'

I try to open the door but the key seems to be sticking, and ramming my shoulder into the wood doesn't help.

'Don't do that, you'll hurt yourself. Here.'

Reluctantly, I move aside and hand the keys to him. He manipulates the lock and opens the door. As he's staring intently at the lock and wiggling things on the door, I take a look around.

The open-plan kitchen and living room are bright enough, despite both windows looking onto another apartment block. The furniture is smart, for a rental. It's cold and bachelor-like, all black, white and chrome, but I will take that over some seventies green velour and psychedelic wallpaper, I suppose. Small mercies.

I head along the hallway to the bedroom. A double bed, not made. Crap, I didn't think about that. A wardrobe. One small chest of drawers. More of the white walls and dark wood. I cross the hall into the bathroom. Everything is white and looks like someone did a run on IKEA's entire budget bathroom range, but it's clean. I turn the shower knob. It works. That's a plus.

Okay, it's not the Ritz but it will do.

When I walk back into the living room, there's a cardboard box resting on the kitchen counter. Brooks is now holding a can of oil and fiddling with all three locks on the door.

'What are you doing?' I ask.

'Fixing your lock.'

Duh.

I lift the lid on the cardboard box. 'What's this?'

He speaks without turning away from his task. 'I figured you would need a few things. Water, towels, bed linens. Sorry I didn't have any kale or arugula in my fridge.'

My mind wants to throw out some quick-fire remark but my heart stops me. It's kind of... touching, that he thought of me. So instead, I thank him and set about emptying the box.

When he is satisfied with the locks, he opens and closes the door a few times. Then he sets off wandering around the apartment, checking the balcony doors and the locks on the windows. I silently admit it's nice to have a man in my temporary home, wanting to keep me safe. Maybe Brooks has a decent side after all, no matter how miniscule it might be.

'Is this place like yours?' I ask when he comes back into the living room.

'I have a two bedroom but the layout is similar. Same view.'

I find glasses and pour us each a glass of water, sliding one along the kitchen worktop to him. 'I don't understand why they put the buildings so close together. I mean, who really wants to stare at someone else's apartment?'

He puts down his glass and exhales while shaking his head. 'Sorry it's not Buckingham Palace, princess.'

'Sorry, I didn't mean anything by it. Your gym does well; you could surely afford a view.'

'Wow. Just when I think you might be human, you prove to me that you're nothing but a spoiled brat. My place works for me. You have no idea what I have coming in or out of my bank.'

'The lift doesn't even work.'

He starts to leave and I put a hand on his arm to stop him. Wow, that's firm.

'Sorry. Sorry. I come out with things before I think.'

'Stop saying sorry. Just don't do things to apologize for.'

I nod. 'Sorry.'

'Christ.' He sounds angry but the tiny curve of his lip when I slap my hands across my mouth betrays his amusement.

'I apologize,' I tell him, smirking.

'I suppose you have the best view in London?'

'Not especially, though my folks rent my sister and me a place in a great location.'

'Your parents pay your rent? Are you kidding?'

'I... no. I intend to pay for it when I have a steady income.'

'That's incredible and yet doesn't shock me at all.'

I want to give him a sassy retort but I don't have one. Deep down, I know that letting my parents bankroll me at twenty-eight is a little pathetic but it really is the done thing in Chelsea. I open my mouth and close it again without making a sound.

'I'll leave you to it. You've got my number if you need me.'

'W-wait. We start this thing tomorrow. I need to, you know, ask you questions and stuff. We need to set some rules.' The words are true but sound frantic, like I'm desperate to keep him here. I change my tone. 'You must need to know things about me to tailor a plan to me?'

His reluctance is palpable. 'I guess. But I need to go and get something to eat. I'll come back after dinner.'

'You said you had a tuna steak before coming to collect me from my hotel.'

'I did. Now I'm hungry again.'

'You're a beast.'

'And you're a stick insect.'

'Whatever. Look, I could eat. Why don't we have dinner together and talk about tomorrow? I need to grab a shower. Maybe we could order in? There must be something healthy around here. I mean, we are in Manhattan.'

'Fine.'

Gosh, he's hard work. 'Fine. Do you mind if I take a shower and wash this grime off?'

'Make sure you wash the sweat from your tits.'

I turn to scowl but his head is already lowered as he scrolls through his phone.

I grab a towel – Brooks' towel – and my toiletries bag and head into the shower. I clean my teeth over the sink as steam begins to fill the room.

The door startles me when it pops open. I turn my head to look down the corridor but it's empty. I close the door again and keep cleaning my teeth. The door pops again. Argh! I close it again and put my toiletry bag on the floor as a doorstop.

I climb under the warm stream of the shower and start to think about some nice, healthy food. Maybe sashimi or a tofu broth. I realize I'm hungrier than I thought.

After a shorter time than I would usually take, I step out of the shower and wrap a towel around myself. I pick up my toiletry bag and find my moisturizer. With one leg up on the sink, I start to rub in the new brand of product I picked up in duty-free to try.

12

BROOKS

I can't wait to see her face when our extra-large meat supreme pizza is delivered to the door. If I'm going to be forced to spend time with this woman, I might as well entertain myself in the process.

I continue trying to sit on the kitchen stool without thinking about how much I need to take a leak but I've turned gray in the time the woman has been in the shower.

I can't take it any longer. Maybe she has an en suite, like in my place. If there's no second toilet, I'm going to have to go to my own bathroom. I head toward her bedroom. I don't hear the shower running but I do hear humming. A sweet, almost angelic sound that makes me think it can't possibly be coming from such a hostile woman as Izzy.

I'm stopped in my tracks by a sight that has me swallowing hard. The bathroom door is ajar, the mirror above the sink steamed. I follow the foot that is raised onto the side. I follow it up a long, smooth, damn fine leg. I take a deep breath to calm my racing pulse as I watch Izzy's hands move over her skin as she rubs in body lotion.

Down, boy! She's bad news.

I turn too quickly, wincing as the floor creaks beneath my feet. I walk straight for salvation, away from temptation. Before I close the apartment door behind me, I hear the bathroom door slam shut. Did she know? Did she want me to see that?

Was the hand down the bra thing for my benefit too?

One thing I am certain of: this stupid PR exercise is going to end in two weeks and that spoiled, hot-as-hell brat is going back to London. Then my life will resume some sort of order.

Back in my apartment, I unzip my pants and take my much-needed leak. Before fastening my jeans again, I give my man a little stroke. Just a small one. I'm sorry, buddy. Give me two weeks, that's all.

I grab two bottles of beer from my fridge before heading back to Izzy's apartment, feeling like Tantalus. I shall not be tempted. I shall not.

Izzy is sitting on the sofa, wearing lounge bottoms and a T-shirt. A thin one. A thin, white T-shirt. And she's braless. I think of her personality and it's enough to quash any sexual thoughts.

'Here.' I hand her a beer. 'A congratulatory beer for publication day.'

'That almost sounded genuine. Thanks, but I don't really drink.'

I lower myself into a lounge chair. 'Don't really?'

'I used to. Before I found fitness. But I don't like to put that stuff in my body. It has so many toxins.'

'Jesus, Izzy. People tell me to let my hair down. Compared to you, I feel like I have long, curly locks blowing in the wind on the back of a Harley.'

'Hmm. Nice imagery. I can see you with long hair.'

'Drink it or don't, but tonight, I need a beer.'

She nudges the bottle away from her on the coffee table and

I'm reminded of Cady as a four-year-old when I told her to eat her green beans.

Izzy hands me a pad of paper and a pen. 'Shall we get started?'

'Sure. What's your height?'

'Five six.'

'Weight?'

Her eyes narrow. 'One sixteen.'

'One hundred and sixteen pounds? What are you, a child?'

'That's within a healthy weight range. Do you treat all your clients like this?'

'Good point, well made. I'm just saying, you could do with adding a few pounds.'

She stares at me as she scoops up the beer bottle and drinks. 'And you have far too much bulky-bulkersome going on.'

'Bulky-bulkersome?'

'I'm just saying, you could do with *losing* a few pounds.'

'Was that supposed to be my voice? I don't sound like that and your American accent is way off.'

'Whatever.'

'Ah, back to grown-up Izzy.' Someone might need to check me into AA at the end of these two weeks. 'What's your BMI?'

We work down my usual questions and move on to hers. My stomach is growling fiercely by the time there's a knock on the door.

'Finally!' I offer Izzy my wallet as she gets up from the sofa.

'I've got this,' Izzy says.

I'm already laughing inside as she unlocks the door.

'Mr Adams. Extra-large meat supreme with extra chicken.'

My humor bursts from my gut when Izzy turns to me, white faced, her jaw dropped toward the floor.

She snatches the pizza and pays the delivery guy, all the while mumbling curse words, most of which I miss under the sound of my laughter.

She comes back to the sofa and thrusts the box at me. 'Here, I would rather starve than eat that rubbish.'

'Oh, come on, don't be such a baby. You're already drinking beer and we don't start this farce until tomorrow. Relax tonight. I imagine it's for the first time in your life, anyway. Try it and see how it feels.'

I open the box. The smell of tomatoes, cheese, and pepperoni hits my nose. I take a slice and sit back with the point of the triangle in my mouth.

'Oh my God, this is amazing.'

On a 'Humph,' Izzy unfolds her legs from beneath her and leans in to take a slice. 'I'll eat your bloody pizza but only because I'm hungry. You're a pig, by the way. Chew your bloody food before talking to me.'

I'm laughing again, almost delirious. I loathe this woman. I hate her so much, it's hilarious.

13

BROOKS

Day 1

Izzy arrives at the gym around nine. She's wearing large sunglasses, even though she's inside, and looking down from the mezzanine level to where I'm training a client.

'Don't tell me Tom Ford has started doing shades for artificial lighting,' I call up to her.

She lifts the glasses to the top of her head and scowls down at me as she sucks through the straw of a smoothie cup.

'Steve Sitwell from NYC FM is here. He wants to talk to us about our competition,' she says.

'Yeah, well, he'll have to wait. I'm busy. And, baby, there is no competition.'

'What have I told you about calling me baby?'

I get a cheap thrill out of watching her stomp huffily away.

I put my client through one more round of squats, then guide him through stretches. 'Nice workout, Jimmy,' I tell him.

'I'm feeling good, Brooks.'

'That's the aim. It's week twelve so we should revisit your goals and think about where you want to go from here. Let's finish stretching those hamstrings and go up to my office.'

Upstairs, the door to my office is closed, despite the fact I left it open. When I step inside, I'm assaulted by woman. A floral scent, not perfume, hits my nose. Izzy is sitting behind my desk with a pink laptop. A bright box of tissues has been placed on the edge of the desk. And the shelves that line the back wall are empty.

'What are you doing? Why are you sitting at my desk? Why does it smell like a beauty salon in here? And where the hell are the tubs of protein that were on my shelves?'

She holds up a finger. 'Just one sec.' She continues to type on her screen as my blood reaches boiling point. 'There. E-mail sent. What was your question? Oh, your protein crap. I removed temptation. You can thank me later.'

'Thank you?' I'm about to lose my cool when I remember my client standing behind me. 'I need my office so you and your pink laptop will have to vacate.'

'But where will I work?'

'I don't know, Izzy: the bistro, anywhere that isn't my office.'

She rolls her eyes and closes her laptop. 'Are you an only child? I bet you are.'

Pointing out to the hallway, I say, 'Out. Now.'

'Fine. Don't forget we need to speak with Steve Sitwell.'

Lord, give me strength.

'Come on in, Jimmy. Take a seat.'

As he and Izzy pass each other, she tells him, 'If you want a clean, refreshing nutrition plan, Jimmy, I'll be in my new bistro office.'

I know she only said that for my benefit by the smug look she casts across her shoulder before she leaves.

Jimmy takes a seat on the opposite side of my desk and chuckles when I pick up the pink tissues and throw them into my wastebasket.

'Did you get married and forget to tell me, Brooks?'

'Man, don't even joke about that shit.'

By the time Jimmy leaves, I'm ravenous. The almond milk, ginger, and carrot smoothie I was allowed for breakfast – which was as disgusting as it sounds – is just an unpleasant memory. In fact, it did nothing to curb my appetite this morning.

Silently cursing Izzy, I head down to the bistro. I spot her right away, talking to a man I assume is Steve Sitwell. Not ready to deal with another round of smart-ass quips on an empty stomach, I catch Angie's attention.

'Good morning, soldier. What can I get you?'

'Eggs, please, Angie. Could you rustle me up two poached on brown?'

'Um, well, you know I never refuse you, Brooks, but...' She glances to the table where Izzy is sitting.

'She told you not to serve me, didn't she? Well, she needs to remember whose name is above that door. I'll have the eggs please.'

'Okay, handsome. Whatever you say. Coffee?'

'Yeah, great, thanks.' I sit on a stool in the corner of the bistro while I wait, drawing as little attention to myself as possible.

As I'm waiting, a message comes through to my cell from Madge.

How is the first day going?

I fire a quick reply.

The woman is driving me crazy!

She replies with only five words.

Think of the greater good.

It had better be for the greater freakin' good. Two weeks of this is going to be painful.

'Here you go. One coffee. Two eggs on toast.'

'You're a star, Angie.' I'm licking my lips as I pick up a knife and fork. But when I look back down at my plate, it is snatched away.

'I absolutely do not think so.' Izzy holds my plate in one hand, her free hand on her hip. 'No dairy. No bread or pasta. And absolutely no caffeine.'

Have you ever been told you have tickets to see your favorite band? Like, the band you've been desperate to see live all your life. Then, right before you get to the arena, you're told the concert is canceled? Yeah, well, that's how I'm feeling about my eggs right now.

'Give me my eggs.'

'No.'

I stand up. 'Give me the eggs, right now.'

'No, Brooks. You agreed to follow my plan.'

'Izzy, I'm starving.'

A camera flash draws my attention from my little heaven on a plate. Steve Sitwell is taking photographs of our latest altercation. Great. Freakin' marvelous.

'You know what, Izzy? Fine. You're right. We agreed to follow each other's plan to the letter.'

'Yes, we did.'

'Great, well, you can eat the eggs. I want you to have more protein for your weight training, so go ahead. Devour my first real meal of the day. Oh, and don't worry about me, I'm sure I can find some sparkling water to fill me up.'

'I'm not hungry. I had breakfast three hours ago.'

'But we've established that hunger doesn't dictate whether we eat. So, let's take a seat and you can tuck in.'

Her eyes flicker toward Steve Sitwell and I know she'll agree.

'Fine. They look delicious.'

I follow Izzy, Steve, and my breakfast back to their table, and I'm forced to swallow my drool as I watch Izzy eat my perfectly poached eggs, while Steve interviews us about our plans for each other.

* * *

After lunch – if you can call a plate of cucumber and arugula lunch – my grizzly has been sufficiently tamed for me to tackle my first workout session with Izzy.

We're in Studio A, the dance studio where Izzy filmed her *Salsa Yourself Slim* DVD. It's a decent-sized space, with a wall of windows and three walls of mirrors, meaning it's bright and uplifting. In part due to the light, in part because there are so many Brookses reflected in this room. Izzy doesn't seem to find that entertaining when I say it aloud.

Izzy is standing at the head of the room, flicking through tracks on her iPhone. Satisfied, she sets it in the dock and Latin music fills the room.

I stand in the middle of the space in my shorts and T-shirt, wondering what on earth I am going to be doing.

'My plan is to show you some basic moves today; then, because I'm only allowed to follow your workout plan, you'll have to use my YouTube videos. I spoke to Charlie and she's getting a projector in here for you.'

You spoke to my staff? I bite my tongue, literally. 'Great. Let's get going, then.'

'Not so fast, bulldog. You need to stretch. Arms up.'

Following her lead, I stretch out my core, my arms raised above my head. But when she folds from her waist to touch her toes, my testosterone gets the better of me. I stare unashamedly at her Lycra-clad ass, thinking how much I would like to get my hands on those cheeks.

'Brooks, seriously, focus!'

Oh, she's hot and she knows it.

I bend to touch my toes. Once the stretching is done, Izzy comes to my side and shows me some basic salsa steps. I watch her first as she steps forward and back, her hips rolling with each move. I don't have to imagine how good she'd be in bed because she's showing me all her moves. My hands ache to take hold of her waist and pull her to me.

A cough at the doorway steals my attention and forces my lascivious thoughts back into their cage. Steve Sitwell is standing on the threshold with a lady I don't recognize.

'You don't mind if we sit in, do you? This is Elaine. She's from *Diet and Fitness Magazine*.'

Elaine looks short next to Steve, perhaps because he's so tall. She holds up a hand as a quick greeting.

'I'd like to get some shots of you training, make a few notes. Kerry sent me along. We would like to run an article in the magazine about your competition.'

It seems bizarre that there is interest in this. Perhaps they can already see that these fourteen days in Izzy's company are likely to end in murder, and definitely blue balls, but I'm hoping that's not so obvious.

The music gets going and Izzy tries to incorporate the few steps she has shown me into a routine. I feel like the biggest dick in the world – in a bad way. Seemingly, if it isn't running or team sports, I have two left feet. Try putting two left feet, rigid hips, and no clue what I'm supposed to be doing to a Latin beat. You've got the image. It's like King fucking Kong stopping in the middle of city destruction to do a badly coordinated Riverdance. At one point, I'm fairly certain Elaine snickers.

'This is ridiculous. How much longer do I have to do it? I haven't even worked up a sweat.'

Izzy clicks off the music. 'We'll go through it one more time. The reason you're not sweating is because you're overthinking. If you forget the steps, just keep moving. It's a great workout for your core and legs, as well as cardio. You just need to stop hating for long enough to actually work out.'

She misses the roll of my eyes as she turns back to the music dock.

'From the top.'

Grrrr!

* * *

Standing in front of the mirrors in the weights section of the gym, I don't have enough fingers to count the pairs of male eyes watching Izzy.

'Brooks, these are four-kilogram dumbbells. I can lift more than this. I'm not a five-year-old.'

'Could have fooled me,' I mumble.

'What was that?'

'Nothing. I'm starting you off light. I don't know how strong you are yet. But we aren't going to lift heavy weight. You don't want to bulk up; you want to be strong and toned but still feminine. To do that, you need to do more reps of lighter weight. So, quit moaning and get to it. You had me dancing around like a fool for an hour; you can listen to me now.'

'It's not dancing like a fool, it's—'

'Goddamn it, Izzy, just give me a break. You're exhausting.'

She scowls but starts her first set of bicep curls.

'Roll your shoulders down and back. That's it. Can you feel the difference?'

As well as rolling her shoulders, she rolls her eyes. 'I know how to do bicep curls.'

'If you knew how, you could have started correctly in the first place and saved me having to tell you.'

Something that sounds very much like 'bugger off' leaves her mouth. I'm beginning to think of it as a term of endearment.

Once we're done with weights, I set her off running sprint intervals on the treadmill. By the time I'm done, she's slumped on the end of the tread belt, her head between her legs.

'Are you all right? Izzy?'

'Yes. I'm good.'

'If I push you too hard, you have to tell me.'

'I said I'm fine,' she snaps.

I hold up my hands. 'Let's stretch, then. Do you need my help?'

She shakes her head and rises to her feet. I leave her to stretch but keep an eye on her. I know I pushed her hard but right until the last, she seemed to be able to take it.

When she's done, I leave her wiping down her face and topping off her water bottle, and I make my way up to my office. I'm starving and the worst part is that I have vegetables and more vegetables to look forward to for dinner.

I flick on the light as I step into my office and do a double take. My desk has been moved to one side of the room, flush up against the wall. A new, second desk, with that goddamn pink laptop and a new box of pink tissues, takes up the other half of the office space.

'Izzy!' I shout, moving out to the balcony. She's not tired any more; she's laughing hysterically, bent over her knees. 'You think this is funny?'

She holds up a hand as she tries to speak. 'I ca... I can't... I can't even...'

'It's not staying.'

Everyone in the gym has turned to look from me to Izzy; even those wearing headphones are taking them out.

'I need somewhere to work, Brooks.'

'Where did it come from?'

'I bought it online and had it delivered.'

'Well, have them collect it again because it is not staying.'

I storm into my office and pace the floor until she comes upstairs. 'What a stupid waste of money,' I snap.

She's not laughing any more. 'It's not a waste. I'll use it while I'm here. Plus, it's my money to do what I like with.'

'You know, I had you pegged from the moment I saw you. You think the world owes you some kind of favor because you're rich.'

'Excuse me. You know nothing about me. Don't lay into me over a bloody desk. What about you? Mr Miserable Obnoxious Adams. Who made you hate the world, huh?'

'You need to get out. I'm hungry. I have a raging headache. And you... you are just not my kind of person.'

'Bloody ditto, Brooks. But we're in this thing together so you need to just suck it up.' She opens the drawer of her new desk and pulls out a hardback book. 'Here. If you're hungry, you can pick one of the main courses from my book. Those are your options for tonight. And I will know if you cheat.'

I snatch the book from her hand. 'More rabbit food. Fantastic.'

She turns on her heel to leave. 'Grow up, Brooks.'

'Me grow up? Me? Enjoy your steak tonight, princess.'

'Oh, I will. Enjoy your tofu.'

'I definitely will!'

'Fine!'

'Fine!'

* * *

Just when I think my day can't get worse, I'm in my local store filling a basket with tofu and bok choy, and then my cell phone beeps.

Omg Dad. Saw the pics of you doing salsa. Wtf?

I put bean sprouts into my basket and reply as I head to the cashier.

Do not use WTF in messages to me. I may be old to you but I know what it stands for.

Another beep.

But seriously. You're a dancer now, Twinkle Adams?

She's just about the only person who could make me smile right now.

Enough of that. It's a PR thing for 2 weeks.

Beep.

I read about it. Not like you at all. Anyway, check this out...

Typing...

And my day can get worse. Infinitely so. The twelve-week scan of Alice's new baby stares up at me from the screen. FML.

I've been so concerned with Izzy and work that my mind hasn't been on Alice and the baby. Cady's text plunges me right back there.

I manage to reply that I'm happy for them all. I guess on some level, I am.

As I walk home, I try to imagine how life would have been. Alice, Cady, maybe another kid or two. We could have been happy. But her parents, their background, and their need to marry their daughter off to some rich kid ruined us.

Instead of cooking food I don't want, I pick up my guitar and slump on the sofa. When my cell phone tells me I have another message, I contemplate ignoring it, but I could never ignore Cady.

How's the tofu?

Izzy.

Still sitting in a plastic bag. I seem to have lost my appetite. How's the steak?

Beep.

About to go in the pan. It's filet. How long should I cook it for?

Ah, that's the last thing I want to hear.

Don't torture me. You get to eat steak and you're going to ruin it.

Typing...

How about we call a truce long enough for me to make your tofu edible and for you to cook me a steak?

As I ponder the options, my cell announces another text.

I have hot oil in the pan...

Screw it. Even Izzy's company beats the hell out of dwelling on what could have been.

On my way.

14

BROOKS

Day 2

I admit, the tofu wasn't so bad when Izzy cooked it with Thai spices. She's a good cook. I say that with surprise because I got the impression she has had a butler to do her cooking all her life. I'll also confess, it was nice having company. That's maybe the truth behind why I'm knocking on her apartment door right now, under the guise of making her eggs for breakfast.

'Hey, come in. Sorry I'm not dressed; you've got me up a heck of a lot earlier than I'm used to.'

I follow her tiny bed shorts and white T-shirt to the kitchen, not sorry at all.

'What culinary delight do I get today?' I ask.

'You get a blueberry smoothie. Don't look like that. It has banana in there; it will fill you up.'

'If only that were true.'

Sticking her tongue out, she puts the lid on the blender she has already filled and sets it whirring.

'You're going to wake the whole damn building up with that thing.'

'What?'

'You're waking my cock up wearing those tiny things.'

'I can't hear you!'

Chuckling to myself, I move around her and take eggs from her fridge. We shuffle past each other, finding glasses, pans, and cutlery as we each make the other breakfast. When she doesn't have an audience, she isn't so bad, I suppose.

'You're very messy in the kitchen, mister. Haven't the women in your life ever taught you how to clean as you go?'

'Careful, Coulthard, I could still spit in your eggs at this stage.'

She nudges my shoulder.

'No, to answer your question. The only woman I've ever lived with is my mother, and she was really more of the take-out type.'

Izzy stops clearing the counters and turns to me. 'You haven't lived with anyone? I assumed maybe... Never mind.'

'Go on.'

She shrugs. 'I just thought... I mean, you're thirty-five and, you know...' She gestures from my toes to my head.

I fight back a smirk. 'I don't know. Go ahead.'

'Shut up. You know you're not exactly unattractive.'

Now I have to laugh. 'High praise from Her Royal Highness, Izzy Coulthard.'

'If you're going to keep saying things like that, it would be much more entertaining if you used my Sunday name, Isabella.'

'No way.'

'What? Why are you laughing?'

'The shoe, or should I say the crown, fits, that's all. Isabella,

Claribella, Crystabella, Arabella, Marybella. The bellas are a posh group of names.'

She only half smiles. 'Yes, well, it's part of Mummy's show for the outside world. My sister is Annabella. What? Why are you looking at me like that?'

'You sound like someone I used to know very well.'

Someone I loved.

The mother of my child.

Her eyes narrow, as if she's waiting for more. Getting into deep and meaningful is not my thing. It is definitely not my thing with a woman whose goal in life seems to be driving me nuts publicly.

She nods, as if she's accepting my unwillingness to go on.

'So,' I say, 'let's get back to your saying I'm good looking.'

She shoves me in the shoulder and sets about pouring us each a glass of water. 'I said you're not unattractive. There's a difference. And I just figured you were maybe divorced or something.'

'No. No divorces. No relationships long enough to move a woman into my place. How about you?'

She takes a seat on a stool while I finish making her breakfast. 'Ha, no. Two longish, or medium-term, relationships. One with a pretentious arse my parents wanted me to marry. One with a guy I dated to antagonize my parents... shaved head, tattoos, working class.'

I keep my eyes on the pan in front of me but clench my hand around the wooden spoon. She really is just another Alice.

'Brooks, I'm sorry. I didn't mean any offense.'

'No, hey, none taken. You obviously didn't mean me because I don't have a shaved head.'

I force myself to smile. She offers a meek curl of her lips in return.

* * *

Studio A is becoming the bane of my existence. Today, our audience has grown to four reporters. The two new additions are, 'Important bloggers in the fitness circle,' to quote Madge.

Izzy has put one of her YouTube classes on the big screen and she's standing to one side, her arms folded across her chest, her back pressed to the mirrored wall, one foot casually resting against glass, distracting me because the glass was just cleaned this morning. I decide to choose my battles and this is a small one that wouldn't give satisfaction worth the effort.

Instead, I focus on Izzy on the screen; there's a smile on her face as she dances. She looks happy, an infectious kind of happy that makes me want to smile. Thing is, I can't because I'm too damn frustrated trying to get my feet to do what I know in my head they should be doing.

'Just keep moving,' Izzy tells me.

So, yeah, I end up doing some kind of Chandler Bing dance that isn't even in time to the music, all in a bid to work up a sweat.

Laughter bursts from Izzy first, followed by the reporters.

'That's it. I'm done. This is ridiculous!'

Izzy comes to the middle of the room where I am. 'I'm sorry, I'm sorry. I think it's your stiff hips.' She drops her hands to my waist and turns me to face her. 'You need to get more rotation here when you're doing Latin dances. It will help you keep your rhythm and it will stop you from looking like such a buffoon.'

I scowl down at her and see her amusement in her shining irises.

'Put your hands on my hips.' I do and she starts to salsa, her hip bones rotating under my palm. 'Can you feel that movement?'

Yeah, in my groin.

She shifts position so she's in front of me, her back pressed to my chest, her head against my shoulder. She takes my hands again and places them on her hips. I feel every movement through her yoga pants as if she's wearing nothing.

'Let's do it together. Ready? Forward on the right. One, two, three, pause. One, two, three, pause.'

I move with her, my hips pressed to her ass, her shoulders moving over my chest, her scent filling my nose, her hair tickling my neck.

'That's it. You've got it.'

Her hands come up to meet mine on her hips and she interlaces our fingers as we dance.

'Let's take it to the side on the next count. One, two... that's it.'

I'm lost in her. The roll of her hips. The feel of her soft skin; a contrast to my harsh, weight-lifting hands. We move easier, more freely. When she turns to face me, I keep my feet moving as she taught me and drown in her gaze, as if plunged into serene, warm waters, floating weightlessly through a new world.

When the track ends, we're brought back abruptly to reality. A camera flash makes her squint and I remember the reporters.

Clearing my throat, I tell her, 'I think I've got it.'

She wipes imaginary dust from her leggings. 'Right. Yep. I'll just be... you know... over there...' She waves a hand through the air in no particular direction, then sets off for the right side of the room and turns, before switching to the left side with a nervous giggle.

Well, who knew? Dancing can be hotter than screwing. I really am feeling hot and sweaty now.

* * *

Yesterday's argument seemingly did not have the desired effect because I'm sitting at my desk, trying not to stare at the delicate line of Izzy's neck as she sits in the desk she never moved from my office. My stomach grumbles like a JCB picking up gravel.

'Izzy, come on, I need something to eat. I can barely concentrate here.'

She checks her watch. 'You can have carrots as a snack.'

'I'll take anything.'

'I'll ask the bistro to cut some up for you.' She pauses. 'And for me... It's three in the afternoon – what am I supposed to be gorging on for my six millionth meal of the day?'

'I'll get Angie to fix you a strawberry protein shake.'

'Bulk in a cup. How tempting.'

If only she could be the quietly sexy Latin-style dancer all the time.

'Let me finish this e-mail and I'll go down.'

'It's fine,' she says, already standing. 'I could use a change of scenery. I'm not doing anything anyway.'

'Really? Not writing another blog about how I'm trying to cheat on your plan by ordering eggs on toast? Yeah, I saw that. I also saw the shitty pictures of my dancing yesterday. Thanks for making me look like a tool.'

'You know what, I've changed my mind. You can get your own bloody carrots.'

Before my retort comes, my cell phone rings and the image of teenage Drew, wearing a school tie around his head, lights up my screen. Never fails to entertain me.

'Drew, what's up, buddy?'

'Did you get that hockey game fixed up for tonight?'

'Yeah, I was going to send everyone a message. I've booked Sky Rink for an hour at eight. Can you bring a puck? I couldn't find mine this morning.'

'No worries. Catch you later.'

When I hang up, Izzy is standing by my desk with her pouty lip thing going on and her hands on her hips.

'Are you arranging to play hockey? You can't do that. You have to follow my plan.'

I push out from my desk and lean back in my chair. 'It's a game of ice hockey with my friends. You can't tell me not to go out with friends.'

'I'm not telling you not to *see* friends. I'm telling you to eat and drink what I say and exercise as I tell you.'

'Oh really, and what are you going to do: photograph me and cry about it on your little blog?'

She takes a breath that lifts her chest and flares her nostrils. 'You're a twonk.'

'A twonk?'

'Yes. A twat-wanker.'

'What the fu—'

'And I've changed my mind; you can't have carrots.'

As she slams my office door behind her, I ball up the first piece of paper I put my hand on and launch it at the door.

I put in a call to my friend who manages the ice rink at Chelsea Piers and call Drew back.

'Hey, it's me. Change of plan. The rink is booked for nine o' clock now. The fun police have intervened.'

'Should I ask?'

'No, man, just remember me how I was before my ruin.'

15

IZZY

Little blog. I'll show him.

I pull up the hood of my black zip-up, which I've teamed with black skinny jeans for the task at hand. I'm definitely more unobtrusive in the low light of dusk than if I were wearing my luminous yoga pants.

I had a cab drop me a couple of blocks from Sky Rink and I'm walking, with my head down, along the sidewalk to the building. It's seven forty-five. I figure if I can get into an inconspicuous position before Brooks and his friends arrive, I'll be able to take pictures of him entering the building. Hopefully, I'll follow them inside and catch him in action, playing hockey after I've expressly told him not to.

Then we'll see how he likes my blog.

I can visualize the post title now. *Brooks Adams, Cheat.* It's going to be fabulous.

In the parking lot, I start to use the stationary vehicles to shield my approach to the main entrance. I tiptoe, checking my blind spots as I move, until I come to the wall east of the entrance. I tuck in behind it and take a moment to channel my inner ninja, checking to make sure my camera, well, iPhone, is still in the back pocket of my jeans.

There's no sign of Brooks and his friends just yet.

At the sound of an incoming car, I pop my head around the wall and look. I wait for the driver to turn off the engine and step out, holding my breath.

It's not Brooks. Darn.

A tap on my shoulder startles me. I jump back against the wall and find myself looking at a tall man wearing a security uniform. Oops.

'Ma'am, can you explain what you're doing here?'

'Yes,' I whisper. 'I'm sorry, sir; I must seem suspicious but I promise I'm not causing trouble. I'm spying on someone, that's all.'

'Why are you whispering?'

I look left and right as if I'll find the answer and whisper, 'I don't know.'

'Then I'll ask you again. What are you doing sneaking around these premises? I'd appreciate it if you could speak up.'

Clearing my throat and straightening my back, I tell him. 'I'm spying on someone. He's going to play ice hockey and I need to get a picture of him.'

With a perplexed look, the security officer tucks his thumbs into his thick leather belt. 'I see. Ice hockey is code. Is this someone having an affair?'

'Huh? No. He... it's a long story. He's supposed to salsa dance and only salsa dance. He can't play hockey. It's against the rules.'

'The rules? Ma'am, are you feeling okay? Would you like me to take you somewhere to lie down?'

'What? No, you don't understand.'

'No, ma'am, I don't. Listen, I can't have you sneaking around here in an outfit like that. You must know that you look like you're up to no good.'

I look down over my hoodie, jeans, and black ankle boots. 'Erm, well, I can see why you would think that.' I check my watch and sigh. 'Damn it, it's past eight. I'm going inside, sir. I won't be troubling you any more.'

'Look, I have no idea what you are or aren't doing but you seem a harmless kind of insane. How about you take down your hood, head inside, and don't sneak around here in future?'

'Yes, sir. Sorry, sir.'

I slip down my hood and walk, like a normal person, to the main entrance. Inside, I put my hood back up and tiptoe to the ticket desk. The woman behind the counter looks up at me.

'How can I help?'

'I need access to the ice rink, please.'

'Do you have a session booked?'

'Ah, no. Actually, I just need to speak to someone who does.'

The lady taps on her computer keys. 'I'm sorry, the rink isn't booked right now.'

'It isn't? Are you sure? I heard my, ah, colleague, say he had a reservation for 8 p.m. tonight.'

'You can go through and take a look if you like, but that rink should be empty.'

'I will take a look, if that's okay?'

She shrugs. 'Be my guest.'

I follow signs for the ice rink, still hunched over, still tiptoeing, still hooded. When I get to the rink, the rental shed is empty, except for one worker playing on his phone behind the desk. The rink is dimly lit by an overhead light but it is 100 per cent, truly, really, empty.

I take out my phone and dial Kerry.

'He isn't here. I think he played me. I don't think he was ever coming.'

'Conniving, deceitful... Well, you're going to have to think of something else, Izzy. Posting about him ordering eggs just isn't going to draw enough interest.'

I hate this. I hate that my book isn't enough to sell itself. But I have something to prove. I must remember the bigger picture.

'I'll think of something.'

I walk to the edge of the rink and lean on the wood wall around the perimeter. The chill from the ice hits me and takes me back to memories of my childhood. Running my hand along the rim of the rink, I make my way to the gate and bend down, sliding my fingertips along the cold ice.

Gosh, I remember how it felt. I remember how the cold would seep through my clothes when I fell. How it would chill me to the bone at first, until I got moving.

I walk over to the guy behind the rental desk.

'Excuse me. Can I help you?'

'No, thank you. I thought a friend was supposed to be here right now but I must have been mistaken.'

'The rink is free if you want to skate?'

I put my hands in my pockets and look back at the ice, remembering that last fall. The fall that gave my mother leverage to tell me to quit figure skating. God, I loved it before that. One broken arm was all it took for my mother to make the seed of fear grow. Just another thing I loved that she stopped me from doing. All because she wanted me to focus on more 'highbrow' life options.

Could I do it? Could I still skate?

I look back at the guy and past him to the rows of equipment. 'Do you have any figure skates?'

'Sure do.'

I give him my size and the next thing I know, my feet are

strapped in and I'm standing on the threshold of the gate and the ice.

I used to be an amazing skater. I had so many friends in my classes. But when things got serious, when the competitions started to take up time that my mother thought should be spent doing spelling and maths, she started talking to me about how I could hurt myself. She planted the seed and it grew until the fear made it happen.

The overhead sound system breaks into my trance. 'Defying Gravity' from the musical *Wicked* begins.

I take a breath and step onto the ice. I let the gentle momentum nudge me forward, until I can no longer hang on to the side.

Eventually, I nudge myself forward with one foot and glide slowly with the other. Picking up pace, I'm soon halfway around the enormous rink, then back to where I started.

I grip the safety of the gate and start to laugh. I made it. I push off again and do another lap, then another, and another. Each time I get quicker.

On my fifth or sixth lap, I dare to turn and skate backward. I pick up speed and start flying around the rink. The wind of my motion blows against me. I hold out my arms and close my eyes, letting my feet guide me around the slick ice.

My skin feels flushed. My lungs are working hard. My pulse is racing, as I go and go and just keep bloody going. I feel light, weightless, free, and defiant all at once.

Maybe I used to be scared but now I feel the exhilaration that follows when fear is conquered. Fear can lead to freedom.

I have no idea how long I skate for before I start to do tricks. First, I skate on one leg, then I kick up into a flying camel, amazed I can still do it. On my final lap, I build my speed until I can't go any faster, like I've reached the peak of a mountain I've been climbing. I bring myself to the middle of the ice and start to spin on the spot, a basic one-foot move. In a split-second, crazy decision, I bring one leg behind me, bending it toward my head, and take hold of my skate. I'm stiffer than I used to be but I'm doing it. I'm doing the bloody haircutter spin! I turn and turn, elated and energized, until my momentum stops and I stop with it.

I lower my leg and bend over my knees to catch my breath, laughing with pure joy, the kind I don't often feel, the kind that should be cherished.

16

BROOKS

The first thought I have is, *So she did come here trying to catch me.*
The second thought is, *Wow.* Drew and Kit stop alongside me and
we watch Izzy skate. She flies around the rink, fearlessly, like a
fine sports car, smooth and wild all at once, magnificent.

We watch her move into the middle of the rink, and as the
music builds to a crescendo, so does she. She starts to spin, and
then her leg is up toward the back of her head, her back bowed.
All I can do is watch in awe.

'Tell me this is the woman who is driving you half-insane,' Kit
says.

I can't take my eyes off Izzy. I'm fixated, like a child seeing
something enchanting, magical, for the first time.

"Cause all I can think is, are you in-freaking-sane for not
wanting to tear this woman's clothes off?'

I wrench my eyes away from Izzy just long enough to glower at
Kit, then turn back to the scene in front of me. She stops twirling
and bends over her knees, giggling. She looks happy. Truly happy.
Exquisite.

Her laughter stops in an instant when all eleven of the guys

I'm with start to clap and whistle. I can only concentrate on stopping my heart from pounding right out of my chest.

Izzy starts to skate toward the exit of the rink, and the guys sit on benches to suit up. Drew is last to move. He drops a hand on my shoulder.

'You like her.'

'Nah, she's just another Alice. A rich girl messing with a poor kid's head.'

'Except you're not that kid any more. From where I'm standing, you're in big trouble, Adams. Big trouble.'

'I'm starting to worry about that.'

I hardly feel my legs as they move me, mindlessly, toward her.

She steps off the ice, the change in momentum bringing her closer to me than she probably intended.

'So, you changed the rink time to fool me.'

Up until this moment, I had completely forgotten about that.

'So, you tried to catch me cheating. I may not have a degree in English Literature from Cambridge, and I may not have come from much, but I'm not stupid. Look how your master plan backfired, Coulthard. Now I'm the one with you on camera not sticking to my rules.'

She swallows so hard I see it in her throat. 'I don't think you're stupid. And how do you even know I have a degree in English Literature?'

'I read the bio on your blog.'

'Whatever. What are you going to do with the pictures?'

Since I have no actual pictures because I was too busy gawking, I'm not going to do much. But she doesn't need to know that.

'I want to run,' I say.

'Excuse me?'

'I want to run, in place of two dance sessions a week, or in addition to them. And I want to do light weights.'

She plants her hands on her hips and stares at me. I can almost see her cogs whirring. 'Two runs, no longer than an hour, and toning, with your own body weight.'

'Fine.'

'And you'll call a truce on the skating?'

'You also have to let me play hockey.'

'Fine.'

'And I want protein. Something lean. Chicken will do.'

'No. I draw the line at running, toning, and hockey.'

It was worth a try. 'Fine. Agreed.'

'You'd better be true to your word, Brooks Adams.'

'If I'm anything, I'm a man of my word.'

She nods. 'Shake on it?'

I take her offered hand. Despite her pink cheeks, her finger-tips are cold.

'Off the record, you looked unbelievable out there.'

I see the flicker of a smile before she puts her pout back in place. 'There's no room for compliments in business, Adams.'

She struts off, as well as she can in figure skates, and my lips curl as I watch her walk away.

'Brooks! Let's play! Get your skates on,' Kit shouts.

'Coming.'

17

BROOKS

Day 3

'You're late,' Izzy says, moving the breakfast shake she has already made along her kitchen counter toward me. The easygoing, happy Izzy from the skating rink is gone.

She's wearing one of those T-shirts and tiny shorts again. The skin of my neck heats.

'Sorry, I had a few e-mails to deal with.'

I lie through my teeth. In reality, I woke before my 6 a.m. alarm but when I woke, my member was as hard as steel. I don't remember the specifics but Izzy showed me a damn good time during the night. That rich-girl attitude didn't make an appearance. I spent twenty minutes willing myself back to the dream version of the woman in front of me. It didn't work. Seemingly my conscious is smarter than my subconscious.

I rustle up an omelet for her and we sit next to each other on stools to eat. Or, in my case, drink breakfast. I seriously can't wait until I'm allowed to eat real food again. I can feel my body shedding muscle and pounds. It's killing me.

'How are you feeling?' I ask, wondering if she's struggling as much as I am.

'Fat. Incredibly fat. It's starting to make me feel... never mind.'

'Go on.'

She stares down at the omelet she's pushing around her plate. 'Ugly.'

'Ugly? Are you joking right now? Izzy, you couldn't look ugly.' The words seem to leave my mouth without my synapses firing messages. Yet, I don't try to qualify the statement. It's true. With the exception of the first day we met, she hardly ever wears makeup. She's in sports gear most of the time. And I've never met a more naturally stunning woman in my life.

She exhales heavily. 'I understand what you say, you know, about me putting on some muscle. I just find it hard.' She looks at me, as if she's wondering whether to continue. We don't exactly do heart-to-hearts. For some reason, she decides to talk. 'I went to an all-girls private school. You're probably thinking lesbian activity, right?'

'I swear I wasn't until you put that into my mind. Now, yes, I confess I have a few questions about the shower cubicles.'

She pushes my shoulder roughly, but her forlorn look changes to a smile. 'It wasn't like that. It was bitchy and pretentious. It was a constant competition to be the best at everything. Academics. Sports, of the right variety, like polo and dressage. The way you dressed and did your hair. Your weight.

'Half of it was the parents. If they had the smartest, prettiest, slimmest daughter, they somehow had elevated social status. Being skinny became something that I had to do, not for me, but to please my mother. It's hard for me to change that mindset. I mean, I love feeling clean but I wish I could eat out without feeling guilty. I want to drink alcohol sometimes. God, I've lost so many friends, or at least people I used to think were friends, because I'm just no fun any more.'

I don't know why but I feel compelled to touch her. I drop my hand to her thigh.

'We'll work on it together.' She looks down at my hand and I realize it is touching her bare skin. Energy powers into my finger-tips and courses through each vein and capillary in my body. I pull my hand away. That's dangerous ground. 'Your sense of humor failure, I mean.'

She hits me harder this time. 'Bugger off!'

* * *

I'm spotting for my PT client as he does bench presses. We've upped his weight today and he's feeling the increase as he grunts and barks his way through each lift. He's doing well. The problem is, I'm not. It's past lunch and I'm still surviving on this morning's shake. My hands are trembling, my arms are weak, and I'm wondering whether I'd be any use to this man if he were to get in trouble.

I'm damn annoyed!

This whole damn PR stunt is making me put my own health on the line, but worse than that, it's making me take risks with my clients. One of my other trainers, Leon, is doing his own workout on the multi-gym.

'Leon, can I borrow you, buddy?'

He comes over. 'Sure, man, what's up?'

'Can you spot for me? I'm not feeling great.'

'You got it.' I move aside and let Leon take my place. As I watch him assist in my session – the first time this has ever happened – the dull ache that's been building in my head for the last few hours starts to throb incessantly.

Once my session is finished, I trudge up the stairs to my office. I'm drained, I'm irritable, and I'm in real pain with this headache. I close the door behind me and sink into my desk chair. It feels like my brain is pounding against my skull. The room shifts around me and begins to move in and out of focus.

I'm going to faint.

Bending across my thighs, I drop my head between my legs. Beads of sweat form on my temples as I take deep inhalations.

'Brooks! What's wrong?'

I feel Izzy's hands on my shoulders. I want to slap them away. This is her damn fault.

'I need some goddamn food, Izzy.' My words are little more than a mumble toward the ground but she must hear them.

'Are you feeling lightheaded?' she asks.

'Understatement of the century.'

'Do you have a headache?'

'I've never had a damn headache like it before. I'm fairly certain this is a migraine.'

She presses her thumbs into my shoulder blades as she massages me. 'It's withdrawal, that's all. Your body is craving sugar and fat you're not getting. It's the detox working. You're fine.'

That's it. I dart up from my seat. 'Fine? Look at me. I'm a mess. You're feeding me like a petite woman. I can't even spot for—'

Whoa, shit.

I plant my hands on my desk as my body sways. My vision starts to tunnel. I do what I tell my clients to do when they overexercise; I lie on the floor and raise my legs. I'm vaguely aware of Izzy leaving the room. Probably finding this whole scene fucking hilarious.

When I start to come around, and stop sweating like a racehorse, I pull myself up to sit against my desk. The very last person I want to see returns.

'Izzy, not now, all right. No more of your shi—'

She bends down in front of me. 'Here. It's your afternoon shake. I had them add a spoonful of protein powder.' I take the glass from her and immediately sip through the straw, feeling like a patient to her nurse. 'You can have these too.'

She opens a packet of almonds and I dive right in, groaning as I chew.

'Real food.'

'You're such a wimp. Do you know that?'

'Don't be pissy with me because your plan doesn't work for anyone other than a one-hundred-pound child. This is exactly why I said your methods don't work. When it comes to your exercise, I'll admit I can feel muscles tightening around my waist and hips that I don't usually work out. But your nutrition advice is way off the mark. You need to tailor your plans to suit individuals, like I did for you.'

'I told you this morning that I feel fat. How is that tailored?'

'You only feel fat because you normally eat like a mouse. As your muscle builds, you'll be using that extra protein. Honestly, I've added about four hundred calories to your diet, and you needed them. No one can survive on the bird feed you recommend.'

She stands, and the version of Izzy I know best – pouting, hands on hips, childish attitude – is back. 'You're an arsehole.'

'Oh, real mature, Izzy. Walk away because you hate the truth.'

'Get your arse up. You're working out in half an hour. Kerry and Madge are here to speak with us before then.'

I tip my head back and fill my mouth with nuts, not caring that I'm starting to drool or that I have hamster cheeks. Hey, that's a thought. Maybe I should store some for later.

18

BROOKS

Recovered from my episode and feeling a hell of a lot better after some real protein, I head into Studio A. Kerry, Madge, and Izzy are sitting on the chairs that have been set out for the reporters who seem to want to watch me make a fool of myself every day.

I kiss Madge on the cheek, make a barely audible grunt in the direction of Kerry, and glower at the British sadist as I take a seat.

'Ah, glad the weakling could join us,' Izzy says, pretending to check out her nails, which are perfectly manicured and painted, in case you were wondering.

'If I could make someone mute with my mind, it would be you,' I snarl. I look from Izzy to Madge and find her smirking.

'So, you two are still playing nice,' she says.

'The reason we're here,' Kerry begins, 'is to let you know that this hate thing is working out well for book sales, and Madge tells me your gym isn't suffering, either.' She flicks a hand in my general direction. 'But what's really working, is this...'

She hands Izzy and me each a printout of a trashy online magazine. I read the headline:

From Haters to Lovers

There's a picture that takes up half the page, of my hands all over Izzy as we dance the rumba. Her hand is reaching behind her to grab my neck. Her mouth is parted, as if she's panting and wanting more. Hot. As. Hell. The look I'm wearing says I want to devour her.

Well, fuck me, I'm turned on looking at us together. My dream comes back to me. Or, at least, the thoughts I had and the things I was feeling immediately after I woke this morning. My throat feels dry and my skin hot. I hand the printout back to Kerry and focus on anything other than what is screaming at me from my boxers, begging to be satisfied.

I try to concentrate on something other than my raging cock. I find myself silently singing 'A Little Less Conversation.' In my mind, I sound just like Elvis Presley.

'We want you to keep playing with the press like this,' Kerry continues. 'They're lapping it up. Give them more of the same. Heat up the dancing and, I don't know, think of something.'

'No,' Izzy says emphatically. 'I can hardly stand to look at him, let alone hang around his neck.'

'That must be the first thing we've agreed on. I'm not whoring myself out for her quest for fame. No.'

'It's helping you both,' Kerry says, impatience obvious in her tone. 'Honestly, the way you're behaving, I wonder if you aren't secretly attracted to each other.'

Scowling, I open my mouth to retort. Madge leans toward me before I do. 'Brooks, you should consider it. It's no more than you have been doing. A few looks, a few smiles. In fact, Izzy should come along for drinks tomorrow night. Make sure you get seen heading out together. I could even arrange it.'

'Drinks with my friends on a Saturday night? No way is she coming. I'm not inflicting her on everyone else.'

Izzy glares at me. 'Inflicting me? Am I really that bad?'

'Yes.'

Ignoring me, she says, 'I'd love to come along, thanks, Madge. Do you have a phone?' Madge hands her cell to Izzy. 'There, you have my number; you can let me know the time and place.'

'So, there's just one other thing I wanted to mention,' Kerry says. 'AMTV USA has asked if you two would do a slot on the breakfast show on the last day of your contest. You would talk about the experience, give the results of the two weeks, and so on.'

'I'm not doing a TV show,' I growl. 'This whole thing has gotten out of control.'

'You might want to look at these ratings figures before you say no.' Madge hands me a piece of paper. 'And that figure on the bottom is what they want to pay you. Each.'

'There's surely a zero too many on that?' I ask.

'Nope.'

As I exhale, the thought of the things I could use this money for whirl around my mind. I could buy Cady a car. I could provide better accommodation for her while she's at college. I could keep the money for a down payment on her first pad.

'I'm in!' Izzy declares.

'Of course you're in. It's money and attention, your two favorite things.'

'You don't even know me, Brooks. How can you say that?'

'Because I know people like you.'

Like Alice.

She drops her shoulders from their offensive position and lowers her screechy tone. 'Come on, Brooks. It will be the last thing we have to do together. Then you never have to see me again.'

'Sold.'

'You're in?' She bounces excitedly on her seat. It's not surprising she's excited. More attention for Little Miss Fame and Fortune.

'I said so, didn't I? Are we starting this workout or what?'

'I'll let the reporters in,' Madge says.

As the back of the room fills with reporters, Izzy loads a YouTube video of her and a male partner talking about the basic steps of the tango.

From my lone spot in the middle of the studio, I hold up a hand and Izzy pauses the video.

'How am I supposed to tango alone when the video is you in a couple?'

'Erm, I guess I could dance with you.' Izzy walks over to me.

'Did you plan this?' I ask for her ears only.

She opens her eyes wide and looks up at me through her lashes. 'No, of course not.'

'So, this isn't some game concocted by you and Kerry?'

'No. I forgot this video shows a couple. Let's just get on with it, shall we?'

Feeling like I'm being played is doing nothing to soothe my anger.

'Fine,' I snap. 'Why are you smiling like that?'

'Because that nasty little frown of yours is perfect for the tango. It's a heated, passionate dance.' She leans in and whispers to me. 'Dance it like I get right under your skin.'

As I feel her breath, hot on my neck, I admit to myself she is under my skin, in more ways than one.

I refuse to do the pointed toe crap but otherwise pick up the steps relatively easily; at least I think I do. Izzy doesn't seem to be growling at me too much, so I take that as a good sign.

We watch the full dance through on the big screen twice and I try to follow the steps of the male dancer. All I can think is how fantastic on-screen Izzy looks, with her legs drawing shapes, her hips twisting, her sultry attitude. But something that irritates me even more than Izzy's damn diet plans is watching her with her hands on another man.

'I think you're ready,' Izzy says, grabbing my attention. 'Let's try it. Remember, if you mess up, just keep moving to get your workout.'

I miss half the steps, but we manage something like a dance. She's smug because she knows she is outclassing me in front of the reporters.

When I spin her into me, she raises her leg to my hip and I take hold of it behind the knee, pinning her to me. I lean into her ear and tell her, 'For the record, this dance is too slow to be a workout.'

I wonder if she feels the slip of my hand up her thigh, the way I pull her pelvis against mine.

She looks at me and her lips part. Her leg squeezes harder against my hip. 'And yet you're sweating, Mr Adams.'

Like I watched the man in the video do, I move backward, dragging her long straight leg along the studio floor. She wasn't expecting the move and the glint in her eye tells me so.

'As are you, Miss Coulthard.'

Her lips curl, slowly at first, then form a beaming grin. She throws her head back laughing and I fall into it with her. We end the track like that, both of us bent over our knees, neither one of us able to catch our breath. For a second, I forget that we despise each other. I almost forget what a dick I must have looked like dancing the tango.

It's getting late in the day and we have the reporters around so we move straight into the gym for Izzy's session. I set her off on cardio, then we move to weights, adding a small amount now that I know she can cope with it.

We finish on lunges. She holds two eight-pound weights as she sinks for three reps of fifteen on each leg. On the last lunge, she hisses as she pushes up. I immediately put down my clipboard and go to her, taking the weights. I notice a photograph being taken in my peripheral vision. I can imagine the headline now: *Brooks Rushes to Help His Lover.*

'Are you okay?'

'Yes, I'm fine. I just felt a twinge in my hamstring, that's all.'

'Okay, we're done for today, anyway. Let's make sure we stretch you out good.'

She follows me to the mats. We do a few standing stretches, then I tell her to lie on her back.

'Keep your base leg straight and lift the right for me.' I take hold of her leg and raise it straight up, flexing her toes toward her body. 'How does that feel?'

'Good but I can go much further than that.'

'All right, I'll push you but take it steady. Tell me if you feel anything.'

I start to lean on her leg, moving it toward her body. It comes so close to her face she's almost doing a split, and I'm hovering above her, looking down at her with my crotch pressed to her thigh. I'll be damned if I'm not completely turned on.

There's a sexy, knowing glint about her eyes. Jesus, I want her. I have to fuck this woman or lose my mind. I have to do this for the sake of mankind.

'Let's give them a show,' she whispers.

I waste no time moving my body closer to hers, bringing my mouth just inches from her inviting lips. 'There's nothing fake about this.'

Her face creeps toward mine. Then I remember where the hell

I am. I'm in my gym. I'm not some farcical performing puppet. I'm a businessman. I'm a father.

'Let's stretch out your core and arms.' I reach out my hand. She takes it and I help her to stand, but the look on her face is as bewildered as mine. What the hell kind of spell does this woman put me under?

My cell phone rings and I'm so freakin' thankful for the distraction, I answer without even looking at the screen.

'Brooks Adams.'

Izzy plants her hands on her hips and waits for me to get back to her cooldown.

'Dad, it's me.'

'Hey, baby. What's up?'

'I'm in the city and have half an hour to spare if you want to see me. But it has to be like right now.'

'I would love to but I'm busy.'

'Is it her? Are you with the dancer woman?'

I hear in her tone that what she's really asking is whether she's being pushed aside by her other parent too.

'Hey, it's just work. You know that. You have nothing to worry about. Any other time and I would have been there. This will be over soon and we'll be back to normal.'

'Sure. It's no big deal.'

'Speak soon.'

I hang up and drop the phone into my back pocket. 'Right, where were we? Arms?'

'Oh, you can see me now?'

Wow. Where did this new hormone burst come from?

'What? I took a call.'

She shakes her head. 'Whatever, let's just get on with it so you can get to your booty call.'

My booty call? I just turned down a chance to see my daughter.

'You know something, Izzy, you can go to hell. I'm done with you and this whole damn thing.'

'Because I got in the way of your sex life?'

'Are you serious? Are you on your period or something? Or is it that you're so used to getting everything your own way, a fifteen-second phone call makes you act like a spoiled kid?'

She steps toward me and gets in my face. 'Spoiled. There it is again. You and this obsession with money.'

'It's not an obsession with money, Izzy. It's the realization that you act like you think everything should just be given to you. Some people work their asses off to make their own luck. Even then, they don't get what they want.'

'At least I have a goal, Brooks. As far as I can see, you just plod through life, with your gym at max capacity but doing nothing to expand, with your apartment and its shitty view when you must be able to afford better. Maybe you should work out what you want, then you might have a shot at getting it.'

'What are you even arguing about? I took a call.' I drag a hand through my hair. 'Oh, I get it. You're jealous.'

'I am not jealous.'

I close the space between us. It isn't just me who gets hot under the collar. This gorgeous, infuriating, sexy-as-hell woman wants me too.

'You want me,' I whisper close to her lips.

She swallows and runs her tongue over her lip, confirming what I have already worked out. She pushes my chest and storms out of the gym, leaving the reporters gaping. I follow her to the women's changing rooms, where she knows I can't go. At the door, another woman comes out with her sports bag over her shoulder.

'Is there anyone else in there?' I ask.

'Someone just came in. Just one.'

I nod because I can't believe what I'm about to do. But I can't take this any more. I can't hate her and be pent up with frustration because I want her all the damn time.

I pause, knowing that if I go in there, this can only end one way. I push through the door and lock it behind me. I move through the changing area to the shower cubicles.

One shower is running. I lock the door out to the pool, kick off my cross trainers, pull my shirt over my head, and ditch it with my phone. Then I walk toward what has been stuck in my head for days.

'Izzy.'

She doesn't speak, but the cubicle lock is pulled back. I nudge open the door to see her naked, standing beneath the hot steam of the shower.

We stay in the moment, both breathing heavily, both staring at each other.

'Yes, I'm jealous,' she croaks. 'I hate myself for it but I am.'

Whether it's the admission, or the water running down the smooth curves of her body, I'm done for. I step into the shower and lift her legs around my waist, pressing her back to the wall. She takes hold of my face and crashes her mouth against mine.

Kissing her is like an inferno. The slip of her tongue. Her soft, plump lip between my teeth. It sets off a blaze that I feel in every part of my body. It travels my limbs and explodes like a firestorm in my chest.

I lose myself in her: in lust, desire, desperation. The energy I've been missing for days is here now, taking her weight as I rid myself of my sports shorts.

She groans into my mouth and pulls hard on my hair. It's a crazy mix of desire and pain. That's exactly how I feel. Conflicted. I've never wanted someone so much, while at the same time, alarm bells are screaming in my mind to stay away.

I take my mouth from her lips to her earlobe, nipping the soft flesh. Water runs between us and clouds my eyes as I move my mouth down her neck, along the thin skin of her collarbone.

'Brooks, just do it. I want this.'

I raise my head at her vulnerability, her breathless begging. Her sass is gone and she's just here, with me, stunning, wanting this as much as I do.

I hoist her higher, my eyes closing. And in my darkness, I come to my senses a little.

'Fuck, Izzy, I don't have anything.' I break the contact of our upper bodies and drop my head back in frustration. 'I can't.'

'What?'

I lower her legs to the floor and run a hand over my wet face, trying to think with my head and not my hard-on.

'You have no idea how much I want to, Izzy, but I can't.'

'I'm on birth control.'

I grimace, wanting her so much I could burst, but... 'It doesn't matter. I can't, Izzy. It's double or nothing for me when it comes to this stuff.'

She turns off the shower, but her eyes still fill with water. I've hurt her. Or embarrassed her. Either way, I'm so freaking sorry. But I tell her again, 'I just can't.'

She barges past me, leaving me standing alone in the cubicle. Shit.

When I leave the shower, I find my wet shorts and pull them on before unlocking the door to the pool. The energy I had moments ago is gone. I retrieve my T-shirt and pull it over my head as I move into the main changing area.

Izzy is already half-dressed. I stand at a distance behind her, afraid to move closer. 'Izzy...' I have no idea what to say to her.

She meets my eyes through the mirror, then turns her back on me. Outside the changing room, there's no sign of the reporters. I trudge up to my office and change into dry jeans and a clean T-shirt. I don't care what time it is; I'm done. What the hell was I thinking?

In reception, I tell Charlie, 'I'm going home.'

Her brows scrunch as she checks her watch. 'Is everything okay, boss?'

Her words fall on my back as I leave.

I walk home via the convenience store and pick up what I need for one of Izzy's salads.

It was the right thing to do, I tell myself. Since Cady, I've been careful with every woman. I've always had backup contraception. Her covered, me covered. The one time I didn't do that was eighteen years ago. That didn't work out so well.

But the look on Izzy's face. I'm not sure I'll ever forget it.

Hours after the shower incident, I'm eating my salad alone on my sofa with my guitar next to me. It dawns on me that I miss her. As crazy as it sounds, I even miss arguing with her. I wonder if there's any part of her that's missing me too.

19

BROOKS

Day 4

Rather than eating breakfast alone, I have Angie rustle up my green shake in the bistro. There is no sign of Izzy all morning. I keep checking between my PT sessions, and when I have half an hour to myself, I find myself sitting at my desk, staring at the empty chair next to me.

At lunchtime, Angie makes me a garden salad and I eat on a stool, talking to her both for company and for distraction. I miss Izzy. I don't know how or why but I do. You know the phrase *I've missed you like a hole in the head*? It's supposed to mean, you wouldn't miss a hole in your head, therefore you don't miss the person you're talking about, right? Well, suppose you did have a hole in your head. It's painful as hell most of the time but one day it closes up. The ache is gone and it feels like something that has become a part of you has disappeared. That's the only way I can describe the peculiar way I wish Izzy was here. I miss her like a hole in the head.

At two thirty, the agreed-upon time for our Saturday salsa session, I head up to Studio A. The number of reporters is fewer by half today, no doubt because it's the weekend. I have no idea whether Izzy will show, so I have no idea what to say to them. I just stand in the middle of the room, waiting. Feeling exposed and ridiculous.

After five minutes of standing around, my legs seem to lose their energy and I sit on the floor in the middle of the room.

'Where is she, Brooks?' Steve Sitwell asks.

'I really don't know, man. Sorry.'

After ten minutes, I lie back on the wood floor, my knees bent. Two reporters leave. I don't care. I just want to see her and say I'm sorry.

When fifteen minutes have elapsed, my sympathy for her, my guilt because I kick-started our almost sex and abandoned it midway, are gone. I stand up and turn to the remaining four reporters, or bloggers, or whoever they are.

'Sorry, folks, I guess she couldn't handle two weeks after all.'

'Oh, wow! Sorry I'm late.' Just then, Izzy walks in and dumps bag after bag of what look like shoe boxes and clothes in the corner of the room. 'There was an enormous sale in Prada.'

She finally meets my eyes and there is fire in her own. But not like the flames between us last night. No, these are satanic flames.

'My apologies, Mr Adams, I made a unilateral decision to change something we had already committed to.'

I feel my eyes narrow. 'That's how you want to deal with this?'

She clears her throat, her focus moving from pressing a remote control in the direction of the large projector screen back to me. 'I'm sorry, this?'

'Wow, you really do only know how to get your own way, don't you? Screw doing the right thing.'

She lets out one angry laugh. 'Screw. That's funny. You don't seem to screw much.' She dumps the remote and moves to the wall by her bags, leaning back with her arms folded across her chest. 'I've decided you can dance the Charleston today, Mr Adams.'

'You're joking, right?'

I'm no dancer but I do know this is that ridiculous, freakin', Gatsby-era dance.

She turns on the fakest smile I have ever seen. 'I most certainly am not.' Glancing at the reporters, she tells them, 'You might want to get your cameras ready for this.' Then she hits play.

I take a breath that fills my lungs to the max and bite down hard on my cheeks. She wants me to dance the Charleston? I'll give her a Charleston.

After five minutes of on-screen Izzy – a much-improved version than the reality – I've got the two basic moves. Step and tap, back and tap. Stay on the toes. Swivel, swivel, swivel.

It's not so bad. I look like a fool but it's just the feet that have to move. And it's actually working up my heart rate. Screw you, Izzy Coulthard.

On-screen Izzy steals my attention. 'Now, we're going to introduce the hands, like this, side to side.' I growl under my breath. I am starting to look like a bigger fool now with twinkle fingers. 'And the last thing we'll add is a subtle wag of the head, like this. Let's put it all together to music.'

'I'm not wagging my head,' I snarl at the real-life Izzy.

'Oh, but Mr Adams, it's all part of the deal. Unless, of course, you can't keep up with my plan?'

Fuck you. Fuck you so fucking hard.

'Fine.'

The music starts and I'm like a dancing goddamn bear on cocaine in the 1920s. I just need a striped suit, a twirling mustache, and a cigar.

Blanking out the snorts and laughter of the reporters behind me, I dance to the end of the music. Then I make a quick exit from the room, but not before coming to a stop, face-to-face with the Devil.

'You think that's funny, Izzy? Making a bigger dick of me than I already look?'

'From what I saw last night, you weren't a big dick at all.'

I curl my fingers into a claw, fighting the urge to wrap them around her neck, and ram the side of my fist into the studio door to open it.

Thirty minutes later, Izzy is wishing she never played hardball. I've increased her interval training in speed and length. I increase her weights and number of reps. To finish her off, I put her back on the treadmill and give her ten more minutes of sprint training.

By the time she's done, she hits stop and rolls back off the belt. Her legs wobble beneath her as she tries to walk to the mats.

'Stretch yourself,' I tell her, before retreating to my office, so incredibly pleased that I stopped what almost happened between us in that shower.

* * *

Sitting around two old whisky barrels in Rocky's Sports Bar, I'm wedged between Madge and Sarah, both of them relentlessly asking questions about Izzy and me.

'There's really nothing happening?' Madge asks.

'No. Like I said, the sooner this whole thing is done, the better.'

Kit and Drew make their way over with their hands full of drinks for the five of us – Marty is out of town on business, and Becky and Edmond will be joining us after service at the restaurant has finished. They nudge past a few small groups of people standing around the dingy bar. It's the type of place that fills with sports fans on Saturdays and Sundays. A place we can wear jeans and hear each other speak. Plus, there's a karaoke bar on the basement floor and when she's had enough wine, Sarah likes to get in on that action.

Kit sets down a club soda and a bottle of beer in front of me, then steps back, holding out his hands as if to ask, *What did I do?*

'Just in case the soda gets dull,' he says.

'Don't tempt me, man. This whole thing has got me wanting beer more than ever.'

'And by "whole thing", he means Izzy,' Sarah says, winking at me as she leans forward to take a handful of Bombay mix from a ramekin.

'Is this going to go on all night?' I ask, sipping my club soda and leaning into the high-back stool.

'We've all seen the pictures, Brooks,' Kit adds.

'Whose side are you on, man?'

'His wife's,' Madge says definitively, finishing with a swig of white wine for added effect.

'Sorry, Brooks, but she controls my balls.'

'Yeah, I can see that.'

'Hate to get in on this but those rumba photographs looked like pretty damning evidence to me,' Drew adds.

I shake my head because I can't fight all four of them.

'Ah, screw it.' I reach out for the bottle of beer. Before it reaches my lips, a familiar and unwelcome voice comes from over my shoulder.

'Put that down right now, Brooks Adams.'

I put the bottle down and drop my face into my hands, wondering whether I'm starting to hear her voice or whether the demon really is on my shoulder.

'Izzy, we're so glad you could make it,' Madge says.

'Are we?' I ask from behind my hands.

'Give Izzy your stool, Brooks. You can get another one.'

I raise my head to Sarah and she giggles when I give her a look that says, *Are you joking me?*

She's infiltrated my friends. My *friends*. I met this woman less than two weeks ago and she's turned my life upside down.

As the women start talking bags and shoes and giving out compliments like it's Christmas, I get up from my stool, not looking at Izzy. I won't spoil the get-together because she has turned up and her very presence ticks me off.

There isn't a spare stool in the bar so I head back to the barrel-cum-table empty handed. Since she's now in conversation with Drew, I see no harm in finally looking at Izzy. Her blonde hair is down, not in her usual ponytail. As she talks, she pulls it across one shoulder. The ends fall down her chest and between her breasts, exposed by the scoop neck of the expensive-looking, pearlescent tee she's wearing with her jeans. She crosses her legs, and I get a look at her new Prada heels. I quite like those shoes – for very different reasons from Madge and Sarah.

How could she ever have doubted whether she was slim enough or pretty enough at school?

I start talking sports with the guys, and a group of men next to us join in as we talk football, somehow transitioning to Formula One. When it's my round, I bring a tray of drinks back to the barrels. As I hand Izzy a club soda, I meet her eye for the first time. Her expression is cold. Heartless. The Izzy I met on the first day at the gym. She doesn't even say thank you.

I lean against the barrel and continue the sports chat, but my mind is not on the conversation and my gaze keeps flicking – without my say-so – to Izzy. More than once, I catch her looking back at me, wearing a scowl.

By the time Becky and Edmond come into the bar, the others are already merrily on their fourth or fifth alcoholic drinks. I wish I were too, because the way Izzy's ignoring me is starting to drive me crazy. Part of me wishes I could go back to that shower and finish the job.

As we move downstairs to the karaoke bar, something seems to light up in Izzy. I watch as she excitedly discusses with Sarah what Sarah should sing, walking behind her as she descends the steps, ready to catch her in case she trips in those fuck-me heels. With the aid of the stair rail, she makes it safely down to the concrete shell, where the karaoke is already in full swing.

The basement is dimly lit. The 'stage' area for the budding karaoke stars is lit by eighties-style multicolored bulbs. It's an awful place, but we've had some seriously good times in here. Two men in vests and shirts are onstage taking the parts of George Michael and Elton John as they slur-sing their way through 'Don't Let the Sun Go Down on Me.'

We gather around one tall table. Sarah already has the songbook and she's looking through it with Izzy.

'Another Brit to keep me company,' Becky says, leaning toward me but inclining her head to Izzy.

'Not you too. She's not a permanent feature.'

Becky smiles, that cute, dimpled smile she has. Drew drapes a lazy arm across her shoulder and kisses her cheek. 'You giving my friend grief, baby?'

'I'm just saying it's nice to have another British infiltrator around here. I approve of the choice. She was really sweet when I met her in Barnes & Noble the other day. And it was kind of you to set that up for her.'

I wiggle my head subtly. I don't want Izzy to know I sent them. But I don't know whether I cut Becky off soon enough, because when I glance at Izzy to check, she is as still as a statue, staring back at me.

'What will you sing, Iz?' Sarah asks, stealing her attention.

With his free arm, Drew drops his hand to my shoulder. 'Hate to tell you, buddy, but once Sarah has gotten involved, it's a done deal.'

'Can no one see that the woman is going to put me in a mental asylum?'

This time, Izzy definitely overhears. She glowers at me before turning back to Sarah. 'I've never done karaoke sober. It's your night tonight.'

'Or we could remedy that,' Kit says, returning from the bar and planting a glass of wine in front of her, then a beer in front of me.

Damn, I want that beer. My eyes are fixed on Izzy's. She wants it too. But she says, 'I'm okay, thanks. I don't really drink.'

'Yeah, that's why she has no friends,' I quip belligerently, knowing it will rile her.

'That was a low blow, tit-face.'

I pick up the bottle of beer and snort-laugh as I take a drink.

'Ha! I knew you couldn't stick it!' Izzy shouts so loud, other heads twist to look at us.

I remove the bottle from my lips and look at it as if it picked itself up and climbed into my mouth. 'Damn it!'

Izzy laughs and starts doing some goofy dance on the spot. 'I win!'

'What the hell is that?'

She stops dancing.

Sarah lifts up the wineglass in front of Izzy and wafts it under her nose. 'Why don't you two call a truce and just have some fun with friends for tonight?'

I see Izzy swallow hard. That reached her and I know why. She takes the glass and holds it up in my direction. 'One night and one night only.' She takes a large drink and so do I.

An hour later, she's draining the last of her second glass of wine as I come back from the toilets. I've seen this play out enough times to know that if she doesn't slow down, this night could end badly and her morning tomorrow will be even worse.

'Go steady, Izzy. You don't usually drink.'

She registers my hand on the small of her back before I do. I snatch it away from her. 'We called a truce, Brooks. You can't tell me what to do tonight.'

I lean into her ear, the soft fruit smell of her hair filling my nose. 'I'm not fighting with you. I'm trying to keep you from feeling like death tomorrow.'

She spins sharply to face me, the tip of her nose almost touching mine.

'You didn't care yesterday how bad I would feel this morning.'

She tries to storm away in the fashion I'm becoming accustomed to. I grab her hand and tug her back to me so fast, I have to lean back to stop our heads from clashing.

'You have no idea why I stopped things from going further. It's something I feel strongly about, all right?'

'I know exactly why you stopped, Brooks. You saw me naked and you touched me and kissed me, and...' Her eyes fill. The sight is like someone driving a roundhouse kick into my gut. 'Don't. Don't touch me. I get it. I wasn't what you expected or wanted.'

'Izzy, please.'

'Please, what? Huh?'

Before I can think of the right words. Before I can tell her she was more beautiful than ever when she was naked, that kissing her was like my entire world breaking from the safety of orbit and spinning into outer space, her name is called by the guy running the karaoke.

She tugs her hand out of mine and makes her way to the stage. I move into the group as Sarah, Becky, and Madge start whooping and whistling.

The music begins to play and I recognize the track right away. Cher's 'Just Like Jesse James.' Izzy stands on the slightly raised stage. She is looking down when she first starts singing. *Hot damn, this girl can sing.* When she dips into her lower register, her voice is husky, yet soft, with a British lilt. It drives straight to my groin without stopping to look for hazards.

When she glances up, there is no mistaking the intent in her eyes or who she's aiming her words at. Her voice grows sterner as she calls me out with the lyrics of the track.

The others start to talk about how good she is. Then I hear a few comments about Izzy and me. Someone asks if I'm certain there's nothing going on between us.

All I tune into is Izzy, as she sings, 'If you're so tough, come on and prove it.'

One night.

I push aside everything running through my head telling me this is a bad idea. *It can't be one night. There's tomorrow, in the gym. She's just another Alice. You're setting yourself up for a painful letdown.*

Tilting my head back, I drain the last from my bottle, and pull my wallet from my back pocket. I slap sixty dollars on the table for the next round and make my way across the bar, with only one thing on my mind.

She watches me make strides toward her. Her voice falters but she keeps singing to the final note before making her way off the stage, where I'm waiting.

Using the lyrics she directed to me, I ask, 'So, you want me to show you what my loaded gun is for, Izzy?'

As she looks up at me, her lips part, and I think she might have stopped breathing. I wait, praying that this is going to end the way I want it. My heart is thumping so loud, she must be able to hear it. My entire body is charged with desire. I want her. Hell yeah, I want her.

Eventually, she nods.

I lift my hand to her cheek. She watches me, unmoving, until I slide my fingers into her hair. She closes her eyes and I press my mouth to hers. Her lips are as soft as I've been remembering. Her taste, something that's delicious and distinctly her, is mixed with wine. It's a heady concoction.

'I'm taking you home.'

She opens her eyes and licks her lips. 'One more,' she says, before grabbing my T-shirt and pulling me to her. She kisses me in a way that makes me need to get her out of here.

I take her hand and lead her through the bar, noticing how her fingers seem to fit between mine, as if we have been holding hands for years.

The arguments are gone. Forgotten. Because in this moment, all I can see is her smiling and laughing, making me laugh.

20

IZZY

Day 5

With his bulky, unshaven, tattooed appearance, and his crabby, don't-mess-with-me personality, Brooks is not my type. Everyone else seems to love him. His clients and friends adore him. He's obviously Mr Charming with other people, but with me he's like a hungry baboon 24/7 – and that was before I actually made him hungry 24/7. In fact, he's exactly the kind of man I would date just to narc my mother.

So, yeah, I'm just as surprised that I sat at home last night brooding because I missed him. I missed Brooks Adams. There, I said it. I didn't just hate that we hadn't had sex in that shower and that he made me feel like the last woman on earth he would ever sleep with, but I had no one getting in my way when I made my dinner. There was no one bickering over everything I said. God knows why, but it made me feel so lonely, I eventually gave in and went to the bar to see him.

Now, lying tucked into his side, the sun's first light warming my bedroom, it somehow makes sense. I won't overthink this. I know I'm leaving in just over a week. I also know that Brooks and I are truly incompatible human beings. But here, in this moment, tucked under the heavy arms that I decided last night have a very good purpose, I've fallen and I'm happy to just let that be.

Brooks shifts beneath me and inhales as he drops his lips to my hair.

'Morning.' His voice is gruff, as if we were up all night. Oh wait...

I smile to myself as I roll onto my stomach and rest my chin on my hands, lying on his firm chest. 'Morning.'

He tucks my hair behind my ear and smiles, a full, dashing smile that reaches his eyes. It's a rare and alluring sight. The tame side of the beast. And the way he looks at me makes me feel like Belle.

'You're pretty when you're quiet,' he says, chuckling.

'Hey!' I grab a pillow from my side of the bed and bash him with it. Then I settle back on his chest.

'What are you thinking about, Izzy Coulthard?'

'That we may have finally found something you're good at, Brooks Adams.'

He laughs, filling my chest.

When he sobers, I tell him, 'Actually, I was thinking I want you to know that I didn't go to the bar last night for anyone but me. I didn't go to make sure my picture was taken. I won't be writing about it on my blog.'

He seems to take in what I'm saying, then this cheeky almost smirk that I'm getting used to comes. 'That's because you broke your own rules.'

'Ha. Maybe.' I turn onto my side and trace the lines of his tattoos with my finger.

He strokes my hair. His touch raises goose bumps on my skin. 'Why did you come?'

'A few reasons.'

'A few reasons you want to share?'

I contemplate not telling him, but he doesn't make me feel vulnerable now. 'I told you I lost friends and didn't really get invited places any more because of the whole exercise and not drinking thing and, to be honest, not being a Chelsea wife or a lawyer or doctor. Well, it felt nice to be invited somewhere. I know Madge invited me because of the PR thing but, I don't know, it was nice to be in a group, talking to people.'

'For what it's worth, the guys liked having you around. I think Sarah might move back to the UK with you.'

'She does seem to like the accent an awful lot.'

I find a rose inked on his hip and trace the outline of the petals.

'Thanks, Brooks.'

'There's no need to thank me for the truth.'

'Still, it's nice of you to say.' I also want to thank him for sending his friends to Barnes & Noble but last night, when I overheard Becky mention what happened, it was clear he didn't want to talk about it. So I keep that tucked away.

'I'm actually more interested in the other reasons you came. You said there were a few.'

'More like one, really. But I don't want to tell you.'

'Come oooooon…'

'I can't really make sense of it. I just, I was in here last night, having dinner. Alone. I guess I missed having an obnoxious, arrogant man around.'

His chest bounces as he laughs. 'I kind of missed fighting with you too, Iz.'

I don't let him see how that short statement warms me to the core. I continue drawing shapes on his chest. 'What is this?'

He glances down at the all-blue bird I'm tracing; its wings span both pecs. 'A phoenix. It's actually covering a tattoo that went wrong years ago.'

I move my fingertips along the rays of light bursting from a sun beneath the phoenix, then glide up his torso, through clouds, into trees. The tattoos are all so different but together, they paint a magnificent picture. In the trees are small birds with musical notes coming from their beaks. Against one trunk sits a man with a guitar.

'What is this?'

'Me, I guess.'

'You play the guitar?'

He nods.

'Me too! We do have something in common. I had you down as more of a wicky-wicky dance track kind of man.'

'What was that? That thing you just did with your hand on your ear?' I chuckle as I do it again.

'It's a turntable. I was being a DJ.'

'You're a real crazy kind of cute,' he says, pulling me to straddle his hips.

'Shut up. Not cute. Cool.'

'Whatever you say.' He runs his hands down my thighs, and my skin is sensitive under his gentle touch. 'And I do like dance music when I'm working out. I like country and rock too. I try out most stuff.'

'Can I hear you play sometime?'

'Maybe.'

'Maybe?'

'We'll see.'

Shaking my head, I get back to continuing my exploration of his tattoos, following another tree down his right arm. Next to it is a rabbit and a clock. An image I recognize. 'This is the ticktock clock, right?'

He nods again.

I notice the tensing of his muscles. 'From *Alice in Wonderland*?'

'Yeah.'

'Why would a tough guy like Brooks Adams have *Alice in Wonderland* tattooed on his arm?'

He stares at me for long seconds. In them, I see a story he doesn't want to tell. He shifts beneath me.

Though he kisses the tip of my nose as he moves me off him, I can sense his mood has changed dramatically. He moves to sit on the edge of the mattress, picking his boxers up from the floor and pulling them on.

'I'll start breakfast. I have to get to the gym,' he says without looking back at me.

'Have to, or want to?'

Now, he faces me. 'With you naked and that little sheet the only thing between me and you, I think it's safe to say I need to go.'

I watch his mighty fine buttocks flex as he strides out of the room. I guess I can't ask him to tell me everything overnight. It was only last night we were fighting. Does sex really change everything? Or was I already falling before then? Was I smitten from the first time I met him?

Rolling onto my back, I cover my face to hide my delighted giggle. Never before have I felt the way he made me feel last night. All four times.

As I make his breakfast shake, his eyes are piercing me through the white T-shirt I am now wearing, his T-shirt, which he wore to the bar last night. He still hasn't spoken since the *Alice in Wonderland* question but he doesn't seem to be brooding, either. Maybe there was nothing to it after all.

I switch off the juicer and pour its contents into a glass before placing it on the counter in front of Brooks, who is staring at me with hungry eyes – hunger that could be related to food, or the fact I intentionally forgot to wear any knickers.

Finally moving his eyes from my thighs to his glass, he says, 'My breakfast is purple.'

'I know, I made it. It's beetroot and there's a shot of protein in there, so drink up and stop complaining.'

'Grand,' he says sarcastically, wincing through his first mouthful. 'There I was thinking, if I slept with you and relieved some of that pent-up frustration, you might cheer up.'

He takes another mouthful of smoothie that empties half the contents of his glass. 'Do you have any idea how many calories the body burns having an orgasm?' he asks.

'No, how many?'

'A lot. Which means, not only are we both seriously calorie deficient right now, but if you want me to continue giving you four orgasms a night, you might need to give me some real food.'

'Well, that's certainly one way to bring up the awkward next day conversation. You presume there will be a next time, then?'

I can feel him fighting his own amusement as he moves around the kitchen counter and stands behind me, pressing his crotch to my bum, speaking against my neck. 'The thing is, Coulthard, I prefer when you're screaming my name in bed to you screaming at me for no good reason.'

He pulls away from me and takes eggs from the fridge. I rest back against the worktop and watch the muscles of his back as he moves, shirtless, around the kitchen and starts cracking eggs.

'Now, how would you like your eggs this morning? Over easy?' He flashes me a wink across his shoulder. In return, I launch the damp dish towel at him.

For once, I'm looking forward to my dose of protein. I don't feel fat today; I feel like I could climb Kilimanjaro.

21

BROOKS

Is there going to be a next time?

I'm sitting at my desk, tossing and catching a ball of elastic bands. I've been doing so for the last twenty minutes. Izzy has gone out for a walk because we've completed our sessions for today and she's bored of sitting around doing nothing. I'm waiting for my next PT client and though I may look like I'm doing nothing but tossing a ball, my mind is about as active as it has ever been.

There's no denying I liked waking up with Izzy in my arms this morning. I enjoyed finally falling into a sated sleep curled around her. I am definitely not complaining about the amazing sex. In fact, I'm not complaining or regretting anything, except maybe the point where I led her to believe it could happen again.

Can one amazing night change who she is, who we are? For years, I've dealt with the backlash of falling in love with a girl whose upbringing and parents tore us apart. I had a kid with her, for Christ's sake. Even that wasn't enough to outweigh prejudice. I'm okay in my life. Yeah, I get bored and occasionally I wouldn't mind company, but I have the gym. I'm here every day for most of the day. It keeps me occupied.

I stand up and continue throwing the ball as I wander around my office.

I've fallen for Izzy. I knew it before last night, and I knew it definitively when I looked in her eyes as I made love to her. Yes, we fucked, and it was incredible. But there were moments when it felt like more than that. I can't even describe it. It's something I haven't experienced before. More than a youthful desire to have sex or even sex with a first love. More than perfunctory sex with one end goal. It was like I had to be with her. I had to be touching her, inside her, connected to her.

I feel it now even, just thinking about her. And the question I would like my messed-up mind to answer is this: how in the hell did you fall for that pompous, fame-hungry Brit?

She's funny, my mind shouts back. She's vulnerable and seems lost sometimes. How can that same person be so obsessed with book sales, best-seller titles, Prada shoes?

She has a shitty attitude and she wants to damage my reputation for her own personal gain. Then again, she said she didn't come to the bar last night for media attention or more readers for her blog.

Ugh. I launch the ball at the office wall and catch it when it bounces right back at me. Its's like the back-and-forth of my chaotic brain.

The thing is, it doesn't matter what my mind tells me, because the erratic thumping in my chest when I think of her wins out. That's why I'm terrified. That's why I can't let myself be in this position, again.

She's another Alice. In any event, she's going back to London in just over a week. Why put myself through that? Yet, even as I think that, I'm craving more of her touch. More of her scent. More of her taste. She's gone for a walk and, unbelievably, I miss her relentless jibing. I'm a horrible person around her. The worst. But she's like an insatiable craving for something I know I shouldn't want. It's a hunger, a thirst, a need like oxygen. Fighting with her, laughing with her, even at her, is the most awake I've felt in eighteen years. I'm high on her.

The ringing of my cell is a welcome distraction. 'Hey, Sarah.'

'Hey yourself, charmer. I have to tell you, I loved your dramatic exit last night. Slamming down money, sweeping her off her feet. You were like Richard Gere, only without the limousine and billions of dollars. Tell me, how hot was the sex?'

'Did you call for a reason or can I hang up?'

'Look what she's done to you. You're normally so laid back you're horizontal, but Izzy Salsa Queen has got you all in a tiz.'

I sit back in my chair. 'I'm going now.'

'Wait, wait. I'm just teasing. I did call for a reason. I wanted to say, stop what you're doing.'

'Huh?'

'I know you, Brooks. That's how I know you'll be sitting on a weight bench or in your office chair right now, thinking of all the reasons you shouldn't be with Izzy. Think of me as your subconscious, but prettier. I'm here to tell you to stop thinking of all the reasons not to and concentrate on the reason you should.'

'Which would be, exactly?'

'She makes you breathe. Do you know how long we've all been waiting for you to breathe?'

'Sarah, she's—'

'I know. But she makes you smile and laugh, but she also makes you angry. People only fight when there's something worth fighting for, Brooks.'

I throw the elastic ball at the far wall, this time letting it bounce to a stop.

'Maybe you're right.'

'Of course, I'm right. I'm always right. Hey, she isn't with you, is she? I'd like to try out some new British words on her.'

'You're the one who has psychic powers. You tell me.'

'Um, let it be noted, I do not appreciate your tone. And if she isn't with you, go goddamn get her.'

* * *

With my hair still wet from showering, I knock on Izzy's door.

'One sec,' she calls. I smell meat cooking, sensitized to it like a wild beast, and decide she must be making her own dinner tonight. I don't have time to be disappointed before she is standing in front of me. Her hair is also wet, and she's wearing a white shirt. Only a white shirt.

She looks from me to the guitar in my hand. 'What's that?'

'You asked to hear me play and you said you were bored.' She reaches out to take the six-string acoustic from me but I stop her. 'Ah-ah. That's for me. First, I'm going to cure your boredom.'

I step inside and set the guitar against the wall, wasting no time before picking her up and wrapping her naked legs around me.

She kicks the door closed, kissing me back as frantically as I'm kissing her. The urgency, the overwhelming need I felt last night, comes back to me. I walk us into the living room.

'Wait, wait. I'm cooking.'

My mouth locked on hers, I carry her into the kitchen. She turns off the gas under the frying pan. I start walking us away.

'No, no, the oven is on too.'

I pull back from her and raise a brow; she just giggles. I like that I can do that to her. She fiddles with the oven knobs and, finally, I get her to the sofa.

I bring her down in my lap, her legs straddling mine, and as our mouths meet, as I feel her chest press against mine, I know Sarah was right. I just need to go with it.

As I run my thumbs down her neck, she rocks her head back, giving me access to her soft skin.

'You seemed distant today,' she says, breathlessly. 'I wasn't sure this was on the cards.'

'I was thinking, that's all.'

'Dangerous. What did you think about?'

'I decided we should think less and kiss more.'

She smiles and presses her lips to mine for a lingering, torturous kiss.

If I were a religious man, I would curse God right now. Why send this incredible feeling to me in the form of an antagonizing, self-righteous, amazing woman?

* * *

We are lying together on the sofa, our breaths beginning to slow, my racing heart starting to calm. Izzy runs her fingers over me, her soft touch blissful.

'You never did tell me about this tattoo,' she says.

I don't have to open my eyes to know she's talking about *Alice in Wonderland*.

It's the opportune moment to tell her, or at least give her something. Mention Alice, drop in Cady. But I don't because I haven't got this all straight in my own head yet and right now, I just want to be uncomplicated Brooks who can simply enjoy this woman touching him.

'A guy called Crazy Joe from Brooklyn gave it to me. It was my first tattoo. Before I really thought about how they would all look together. He was an old veteran who went mad. When he died, he left me some money – not a lot – and said in his will that I was to open my own gym.'

'Wow, and that's where it all started?'

'Yep. Why don't you tell me about the tiny love heart I've noticed on your hip bone?'

'It's pitiful really, isn't it?' She looks down at the solid inked heart, which can't be bigger than a thumbnail. 'I wanted to defy my parents but didn't really want a tattoo. I wanted to do just enough to tick them off but didn't dare go further.'

'Your parents seem to have quite a lot to answer for.'

She shrugs and pushing up on my chest until she's kneeling. 'Not my dad. He was never around enough to have anything to answer for. At least not when the business took off. I was still young then.'

I sit up so that we are facing each other and peck the tip of her nose. 'What business is your dad in?'

'Have you heard of Russell's Crackers and Rumble Tum biscuits?'

'Um, no.'

'Well, they're just two of the better-known brands owned by my dad's company. They're very big in Europe.'

I whistle through my teeth. 'You really are a rich girl.'

'No, my parents are. And, boy, does my mother like everyone to know it.'

Feeling her mood shift to something less than happy, I hold her face and kiss her.

'You must be ready for that steak now,' I say, guiding her off the sofa.

We retrieve our discarded clothes from the lounge floor. I pull on my jeans and Izzy re-dresses in the sexy white shirt she had on earlier. Between us, we make an outfit.

She puts a large bowl of green salad on the kitchen counter

with two plates, while I get us two glasses of iced green tea – actually not as awful as it sounds. After ten minutes of messing with the stovetop, she puts a sirloin on her plate, then turns to the oven and takes out a tray. I watch in astonishment as she uses a spatula to put a chicken breast on my plate.

'What's this?'

'A peace offering. You were right; maybe I do need to think more about tailoring plans to different needs.'

'I see. And by tailoring my plan, what you really mean is giving me sufficient food to power your orgasms.'

She plants a hand on her hip and points the spatula toward me the way she'd point a finger. 'Do you want the chicken or not?'

'Hell, yeah. I also want the orgasms.'

She snorts as she laughs.

'Real attractive, Iz.' My words only make her laugh harder.

After dinner, we sit on the sofa and I get the guitar.

'Here, it's yours, on loan, until...' I can't bring myself to finish that sentence.

She takes the guitar from me and rests it across her knee. 'Why?'

'Because you're bored and I decided today that I would rather have you rattling away at my guitar than walking outside where I can't see you.'

She looks up at me with wide eyes.

'What?'

'I think that might be the sweetest thing anyone has ever said to me.'

I fight my curling lips. 'Yeah, well, you need to get out more.'

As I settle into the opposite corner of the sofa, she starts to strum a song I don't recognize. She stops to tune the guitar and then sets off again. It's a delicate picked opening, using only the bottom three strings. Then she starts to strum, and a gentle, melodious voice follows.

She sings about a soldier leaving for war. About the people he leaves behind and the friends he's going to make. The song and her voice are enchanting. I'm drawn in by the smooth flow of her wrist, the gentle shuffle of her fingers, the movement in her neck as she forms the lyrics.

When she's finished, she hands the guitar to me. 'Your turn.'

I take it from her. 'You didn't tell me you could play the guitar like that, as well as sing. What was that song?'

'It's actually something I wrote. Did you like it?'

'Like it? Izzy, that was amazing.'

Her cheeks flush as she curls her legs beneath her and rests an elbow on the back of the sofa. 'It's what I used to want to do.'

'Sing?'

'All of the arts, really. Singing, dancing, songwriting, theatre.'

'Why didn't you stick with it?'

Suddenly her warmth fades. 'Because my mother stopped me at every opportunity. Because it wasn't taking steps toward being a doctor. Because it wasn't guaranteed to earn money. It was like the figure skating. As soon as I started competing, she stopped me. When I wanted to apply to the Royal Academy of Dramatic Arts, she refused to let me.'

'So now you sort of dance for a living but don't?'

'But don't. That's funny. Now I pretend I know what I'm talking about and make YouTube videos and I wrote one book but don't have enough material for another without completely going against my own advice. I never go out and I have no friends, so who won?'

'If you don't enjoy it, why do you do it?'

'There's a question.' She forces a smile that doesn't reach her eyes, then sighs and rests her head on her palm. 'I love dancing and being fit and healthy. If the book is a success, then… I don't know, I guess I feel like I have something to prove.'

'To your parents?'

'It sounds silly, doesn't it? You don't even have to answer that. I'm twenty-eight years old and I still give a shit about what my parents think.' I swallow hard, knowing this is another opportunity to mention Cady. I don't. 'You want to break free of your parents, defy them, and make them proud all at once. It doesn't sound silly so much as limiting.'

'How do you mean?'

I run my thumb gently down the strings of the guitar, thinking of the right thing to say. 'At some point, you need to start living your life for you and not other people.'

The irony of that statement is not lost on me. For so long, I've been living for what could have been. Under some illusion that maybe if I was good enough, I would get Alice back, that we would be a family with Cady. In reality, my daughter is about to go to college and her mother is never going to be mine.

Maybe Izzy's right. Maybe it is time I think about what I really want from life. Maybe I need a new plan.

I sit forward, set the guitar across my knee, and start to play the chords to Johnny Cash's 'Hey Porter.'

I set all other thoughts aside and in my best version of Johnny Cash's southern accent, I sing the opening lyrics to the song.

The sound of Izzy's laughter is reason alone to keep playing and forget everything else. I strum faster and sing harder. Izzy stands on the sofa and starts wiggling her hips and turning her arms to the beat. Soon, she's singing along. Both of us are happy and carefree.

Tonight, life is better than okay.

22

BROOKS

Days six and seven are a blur of sex, bickering, makeup sex, chicken, steak, kale, and laughter. We find it amusing to play up to the reporters but when we aren't giving them much of a new story, they seem to get bored.

We never mention Izzy's leaving in a week. We steer clear of the topic of family and difficult questions. Instead, we talk music, sports, movies, and mundane things, like which brands of running shoes we prefer. Izzy educates me on how to make a perfect cup of English tea and I tell her about JFK and the Kennedy family.

We are in a bubble that we decide to make unbreakable by not letting in any deep thoughts or outside influences. It is one of the best times of my life and I can say that without needing years to reflect.

* * *

The bubble just popped. I'm just getting out of the shower at my place before going to see Izzy for dinner. At the sound of my phone ringing, I wrap a towel around my waist and find my cell.

'Hey, Cady.'

'Hi, Mr Adams, it's not Cady. It's her friend Meghan.'

My mind immediately goes into red alert. 'Where's Cady?'

'I'm with her but she's really drunk.' I can hear now the alcohol in Meghan's words too.

'Where are you?'

'We're at her boyfriend's house. There's a party and she's been drinking a lot.'

I move to the bedroom and start to pull on clothes, still talking to Meghan as I grab my car keys and she relays the address.

'Are you with her?'

'Yes. We're in the bathroom. She's sick. She can't really walk and she only wants you.'

'Okay, Meghan. You two stay in the bathroom. I'm on my way.'

In my panic, I almost forget about Izzy.

I double back and knock loudly on her door. What the on earth am I supposed to tell her?

'Izzy, come on, I need to speak to you.'

When she pulls open the door, I'm struck by the smell of vanilla from the candles burning around the living room. I wasn't prepared for candles. I really wasn't expecting to see Izzy in stiletto heels and a short silk robe. And I definitely couldn't have anticipated her running her fingers down the silk and parting the robe to reveal a black lace bodice, stockings, and a garter belt.

Goddamn it.

'Izzy, I'm sorry, I have to be somewhere.'

'Somewhere as in not here?' She closes the robe around herself.

'Yes. I'm so sorry. Christ, I'm more sorry than you know but I have to go.'

'I… what? Is everything okay?'

'Yes. No. I can't explain right now. Ah man, you look so hot.' Growling, I drag my hands over my face. 'I'm sorry, Izzy, really fucking sorry.'

In my truck, I burst from the underground garage and concentrate on nothing except looking for police and getting to Cady as fast as I can. I ignore the part of my mind that knows I've just brought a shitstorm down on Izzy and me.

The address Meghan gave me leads me to a tired-looking block of apartments, seven or eight stories high. As soon as I step out of the truck, I can hear and see the party on the first floor. Multicolored lights flash behind curtains, and dance music bellows. There are students outside the main entrance, smoking and drinking from brown paper bags. There's a distinct stench of cigarettes and the sweet smell of marijuana in the air.

A few girls whistle as I pass by them and dip into the building. Two guys exit, staggering. The corridor, full of people making out and otherwise acting like dicks, leads me to the party.

Inside, music pounds in my ears. Teenage girls are wearing too few clothes and the air has a musty, stale-sweat smell. I peel the hands of a young girl off my chest and ignore the glares I receive from drunk young men, who really shouldn't mess with me right now, as I search for the bathroom.

A line of girls gives me a pretty good idea where I'm going.

'Is this the bathroom?' I yell above the music.

'Yeah, but someone has been in there forever.'

I knock on the door. 'Cady?' I rap harder. 'Cady! Open the door, it's me.'

When there's still no answer, I kick the door. Once is enough to tear the feeble lock from the wall.

'Jesus, Cady.'

She's alone in the bathroom, propped between the shower cubicle and the toilet, black streaks running down her face, her eyes barely able to open. Her phone is next to her on the floor but there's no sign of Meghan.

'Dad?'

I hunker down in front of her and take hold of her cheeks. 'Look at me. Cady, look at me. Is this just alcohol?'

She nods weakly.

'Promise?'

'Yes,' she murmurs.

I open her eyelids with my thumbs. I've seen people on drugs, and her white irises and normal-sized pupils let me know she's telling the truth. I stuff her phone into my back pocket.

'All right, baby, let's go. Arms around my neck. Good girl.'

I hoist her up in my arms. She clings tighter to me and rests her head on my shoulder as I carry her out of the party to the safety of my truck. I buckle her into the passenger seat and rummage in the back for a bag of sorts. I find an old gym towel that will have to do.

Bringing the towel to the front with me, I start the engine. Before I even pull away, she retches. I manage to get the towel under her and catch most of the vomit.

'It's just a little sick, baby. You're fine.'

'I'm sorry, Dad,' she cries.

Despite feeling irate with her, my heart aches at the sound of her tears.

'We've all been here, kiddo. Let's get you home.'

I toss the towel in a dumpster and drive us home, trying not to weave or turn too much. We make it back to the basement garage without any more vomiting.

I don't waste my energy asking if she can stand; instead, I

unbuckle her and pick her up. A guy I recognize from the building is making his way out of the garage. He helps me by closing and locking the truck. then opens the garage door and helps me to the elevator.

Cady seems to come to inside.

'I have vomit on me,' she says, crying again.

I don't tell her I'm fully aware of the stench of it. As I carry her along the hall toward my apartment, she starts to unbutton the shirt she's wearing.

'Cady, you can't take your clothes off here. We're almost there.'

'I want them off. Take them off me.'

I struggle to hold her and open the door. Inside, I carry her to her bedroom and lay her down on the bed. As I start to untie her boots, she begins heaving again.

'I'm going to be sick, Dad.'

I catch the first round in her wastebasket, then carry her to the bathroom and sit her next to the toilet, where I finish taking off her boots. She throws her guts up again, almost 90 per cent hitting the target. I hold her hair back and rub her shoulders as round four comes.

She seems more with it when she sits back against the white tiled wall. I slip down to the floor, one knee bent, my back against the bathtub, and hand her a box of tissues.

'Thanks. I'm sorry, Dad.'

'Don't tell me you're sorry, kiddo. Tell your head in the morning.'

'It's going to hurt, isn't it?'

'Like a bitch.'

She starts crying again.

'Do you want to tell me what all this is about?'

'I got dumped. Spectacularly. In front of an entire room full of people. And that was after I caught him with his hand up some other girl's skirt.'

'Do you really want to be with a guy who can do that when he's with a knockout like you?'

She part smiles. I'll take it. 'You're my dad – you have to say things like that. And no, I don't want to be with him but it can still hurt, right?'

'Yeah, it can still hurt, baby. Were you supposed to be going home tonight?'

She shakes her head. 'I was going to stay with Meghan.'

'Then I won't call your mom until tomorrow, but I'll text her and tell her you decided to stay here instead.'

'Thanks.'

'As for that Meghan character, she left you on a bathroom floor in a very vulnerable state. You might want to rethink your close friendships.'

She blows her nose like an old man.

'How are you feeling? Like you want to be sick again?'

'Not just yet.'

'Come on, then, let's get you to bed.' I stand and put paste on her toothbrush, then hold it out to her.

'Do I really have to brush my teeth?'

'Not if you would rather they fell out from all the acid you vomited over them.'

'Point taken.'

I help her stand and hold her steady as she gives her mouth a half-hearted clean. Then I walk her to bed.

'Do I need to help you get into pajamas?'

She gives me a drunken, tired laugh. 'You should see the horror on your face right now.'

'Get into bed; I'll bring you some water.'

When I return to her room, she's already tucked under the covers.

'Here, drink up. You'll thank me tomorrow.'

'I don't think I'll do much of anything tomorrow.'

'Nope, I have to agree with you on that one.' She drinks a few mouthfuls of water, and then I set the glass down on her bedside table. ''Night, baby.'

''Night, Dad.'

I settle into the pink chair in the corner of her room and watch her go straight out like a light. My mind goes to Izzy just two doors down. She's probably in bed now. Alone. Tomorrow, whether the timing is right or not, I'll have to let her in on my past, and my very present daughter.

At some point, I must have fallen asleep because I wake sweating under the sunlight, realizing I forgot to draw the curtains. Cady is snoring, her mouth wide open like she's catching flies. I check her bedside clock.

'Shit.'

It's after nine. Izzy is probably already at the gym. Regardless, I have to make double time to get to my first PT session at nine thirty. Deciding I'll have Angie make up a breakfast shake, I have a quick shower and pull on my gym clothes. When I go to check on Cady, her bed is empty.

'I'm in here.'

I follow her hoarse voice to the living room. Her hands tremble as she brings a cup of coffee to her lips.

'Feeling good, kiddo?'

'It feels like a man made of concrete sat on my head, then dragged razor blades along the lining of my stomach.'

'Graphic. Nice. Listen, Cady, I've been a teenager but last night, you were underage drinking in a place you shouldn't have been and you put yourself in real danger. Anyone could have put something in your drink or taken advantage of you.'

She looks down at the mug in her lap. 'I know.'

'My view is you've probably thrown up enough to learn your lesson but I'm willing to bet your mom won't take the same approach.'

Her head darts up. 'You're not going to tell her, are you?'

Moving to her, I ruffle her hair and kiss her temple. 'I don't need to because you're going to do that as soon as you've finished that coffee.'

I throw my sports bag over my shoulder and open the front door to leave. 'Also, wash your hair, it smells of vomit.'

Scowling, she follows me to the door. 'Thanks, Dad, for last night. I'm sorry I dragged you out to get me.'

'I'm not happy about the situation but I'm glad you called me. Stay here as long as you like. There's food in the fridge and money in the pot.'

'I love you.'

'Love you too, baby. Behave yourself!'

23

IZZY

Day 9

'There's food in the fridge and money in the pot... Love you too, baby.'

So, the woman I took a picture of in his arms last night stayed over and he's in love with her.

Devious. Sly. Lying bloody bastard.

I quietly close my apartment door as Brooks heads down the corridor. I back up, as if the door might reveal a lethal weapon and come after me. And I stop when I back into the kitchen counter. Other than anger, I don't know what I feel, but my eyes cloud with unfallen tears, and the pain that strikes my stomach is so fierce, it makes me fold forward.

I slide my back down and come to sit on the cold, tiled floor, wondering how I didn't see this coming. Of course he has someone else. We never go to his apartment. He doesn't talk about himself beyond the kind of movies and music he likes. He gave me a full lesson in the difference between American football and rugby but when I ask about his tattoos, he clams up.

He's thirty-five and looks impossibly good. I mean, come on, Izzy.

I feel ridiculous. Like, once again, I'm on the outside of a circle, only it's not skinny girls and ladies who lunch in the middle, it's a guy I have possibly fallen in love with.

How can I be in love with him? I don't even know him.

How could I have been so naïve as to think that a few days of sex and laughter are the basis of anything real?

My head is awash with tears and fury. I don't know what to do. I don't know because I've never felt about anyone the way I feel about Brooks. He makes me question who I really am and what I want. No one has ever made me question that; they've only directed me to be something different. Brooks likes me the way—

No, he doesn't like me for who I am. He doesn't give two hoots about my happiness. He wanted a shag.

Well, screw him. Screw this whole damn experience. He can get stuffed if he thinks I'm just going to swan into the gym today and act like he didn't leave me in stockings and suspenders in a candlelit living room while he bonked the person he's really in a relationship with two doors down.

Tears roll down my cheeks and I have no idea what I'm crying over. My own embarrassment, or that I lost something I never really had.

Angry, I swipe away the wetness from my cheeks.

As I stand, my mobile rings. My sister's name illuminates the screen. A familiar voice.

'Anna.'

'How's it going over there, author extraordinaire?'

The sound of someone who loves me brings back my tears.

'It's okay. I'm ready to come home.'

'Are you crying?'

I take a deep breath and pinch the bridge of my nose. 'No, I was cutting an onion.'

'Isn't it morning in NYC? Izzy, you never cry. What's wrong?'

'Oh, you know, fell for the guy I'm supposed to be in competition with. Slept with him and found out he has a... someone.'

'Bastard. He's married?'

'I don't know about married but there's someone else for sure.'

'Dirty bloody wanker. But he's not worth tears, surely? You've only been there a few days. I mean, you helped him cheat on someone. It's not the end of the world. Maybe Mummy is right about his type.'

'Excuse me?'

'You know, tattoos, no brain. He's hardly husband material, is he?'

'You're unbelievable, Anna. The last thing I would expect from you is an I told you so. I'm going.'

'Wait, Iz, I'm sorry. I'm just trying to make you feel better, that's all. You had a fling with a bad boy; don't let it get you down.'

'Too late.'

'What are you going to do about it?'

'There's not much I can do. Get through the next few days and never see him again.' That thought stabs like a blunt knife in my chest.

'Well, it may be the vindictive journalist in me, but don't you have a well-read blog? If it were me, I wouldn't let him get off so easily.'

'I couldn't blog about it. It's my life too.'

'I'm not Yoda – take or leave my suggestion. Bet it would make you feel better, though. Otherwise, go get yourself a tub of Ben & Jerry's and a bottle of wine and stew Bridget Jones-style. Anyway, I have to go to a meeting. I was just checking in. Mummy asked me to call because she's too proud to call herself when she doesn't agree with your, how does she put it...?'

'Life choices,' we say in unison.

'Thanks, Anna.'

'For telling you I told you so?'

'Erm, more the other stuff. It's just nice to hear from you. I'll see you soon.'

'Be safe, sweetie.'

'You too.'

* * *

After speaking with Anna, I wash my face and go out for a run. I had intended to clear my head but for the two hours I'm running, I just keep thinking, *Brooks will be standing in the studio waiting for me to dance now.* And, *Brooks will be sitting in the bistro, asking Angie to make him a breakfast shake.* Or, *I wonder if he makes love to the other woman as good as he did when we were together.*

Did it ever mean as much to him as it did to me? Didn't he feel like the earth stopped spinning? Like we were no longer part of a mundane routine but we were starting something different, new, and exciting; something remarkable?

I don't know how to answer my own questions or put an end to my chaotic thoughts. So I find myself here, in Walgreens, taking Anna's advice.

'That'll be nineteen thirty-five,' the cashier tells me as she bags up my bottle of New Zealand sauvignon blanc and a tub of Ben & Jerry's.

I pay her and walk back to my borrowed apartment. By the time I've showered, it's noon, a perfectly acceptable time of day to fill my body full of toxins and watch *P.S. I Love You* on my Mac.

While I've always preferred the book – it had me a blubbering mess from page forty – and I am one of those people more than a little angry that the movie was set in New York rather than Ireland, I'm dripping tears into my melting pot of ice cream within the first ten minutes. Subsequently drowning said tears with large gulps of sauvignon blanc, which are traveling straight to my head. Perfect!

When Brooks calls for the fourth time, I don't send him straight to voice mail; I turn off my phone altogether. You choose another woman; I choose Ben, Jerry, and Gerard Butler all at once.

As I watch Hilary Swank playing a young widow, dancing around her apartment in her dead husband's clothes, singing along to the TV through her hairbrush, with drips of ice cream decorating my white string vest, I ask myself what on earth I am doing. I didn't lose someone who loved me enough to marry me. No, sir, I dodged a bullet.

My resolve wanes when Hilary Swank receives the first love letter, written by her husband when he was dying. I blubber away, opting to drink directly from the wine bottle rather than topping up my glass.

Halfway down the bottle – now room temperature – I start to think my sister is right. Why should I be the one in tears? Why should I be crying over spilled milk? Brooks is like the worst kind of milk: full-fat dairy. He deserves to curdle and smell like cheese.

I take another mouthful of wine from the bottle wedged between my crossed legs, then place it on the coffee table. I minimize the *P.S. I Love You* screen and pull up my blog.

In the blog title box, I type:

Brooks Adams: Hound Dog

Ha, that's funny. I take a much-deserved drink of wine and start to type.

I've learned a lot about Brooks Adams over the last week or so. Like how he has two left feet and his hips move as if they're stuck between steel girders. How he has tantrums when he can't get his own way and needs anger management when he's hungry.

In the last couple of days, I've also learned how he can lure women in, put them under a spell. He can be the guy singing country tracks on his guitar and the man who likes black-and-white movies.

My biggest discovery came last night, when I realized Brooks Adams is a lying, no-good scumbag.

I take another large gulp of wine before writing the next part.

I fell for the act. Shame on me. But once Brooks had left his mark on me, he turned to another woman, or his other woman.

I interlace my fingers and push my hands out until my knuckles crack.

The worst part is, if Brooks is reading this, he's still trying to deceive me. He still thinks I don't know that he carried this woman to his bed last night and kissed her goodbye this morning.

Here, I copy and paste the photo I took of her outside his apartment.

If you're reading this, girl with the pink hair, and Brooks did the dirty on you, I'm so sorry. I had no idea you existed. I have never, nor would I ever, intentionally cheat. If you're reading this and you, Pinky, knowingly did the dirty on me, I consider you the filth that lines sewage drains, just like your lover.

Well, Brooks Adams, you ain't never caught this girl and you ain't no friend of mine.

Ha, that's witty. Very funny, Izzy. Very funny.

I'm too drunk to bother with spell-check, so I move my cursor to the submit button. There's a part of me that knows this is childish and petty. There's a part of me that doesn't want to humiliate the man I had come to respect. But I remember, he was lying to me the whole bloody time, and I click the button to publish the post.

I stare at the screen, waiting for the moment to come, the moment when I feel a thousand times better about this whole situation. It doesn't. In fact, I think I feel worse. Now the world knows I'm a fool, as well as someone who has to try all the worst tricks to get people to buy her book, someone who doesn't even follow her own advice.

I finish the wine and ice cream and watch the credits roll on *P.S. I Love You*. Then I hit play on *Bridget Jones's Diary*, because at least she will understand how I feel.

24

BROOKS

Kit stands outside the boxing ring, talking to Drew and me as I hold pads for Drew to hit.

'Just to recap. She was in the full Agent Provocateur–type getup. She'd lit candles all over the apartment. You're more into this woman than any other woman I've seen you with. If the way you two argue is anything to go by, she must be like fire between the sheets.'

'Too far,' I tell him, absorbing a hook from Drew.

'Sorry. But the point is, this was going to be a hot night, and you just left her there, with no explanation.'

'Cady was sick, Kit. She was wasted. Anything could have happened to her.'

He shakes his head. 'Man, your daughter has a lot to answer for.'

Drew stands down and we all move to the ropes. 'Come on, Kit, we've all been where Cady was. Brooks did what he had to do.'

'Would you have left Becky like that? God knows if Madge put stockings on for me these days, I'd feel like I won the jackpot.'

I help Drew unstrap his hands. 'Yeah, well, Cady got her karma,' I say. 'She was pretty sick. Again. And again. And again.'

'And Izzy just didn't show up today?' Drew asks.

'Not seen her. It gives me a good idea of how pissed she is. I've been stuck here but trying to call her all day. At first, I think she was sending me to voice mail, then she turned off her phone altogether.'

'How do you know if she sends you to voice mail?' Kit asks.

'It was a different number of rings each time before it transferred.'

'Huh. I'm going to look out for that. I'm sure Madge does that when I call from work.'

'To be fair, buddy, we all do that to your calls,' Drew says. 'Ah, I'd probably send me to voice mail too.'

For the first time today, I smile.

'What are you going to do?' Drew asks.

I shrug. 'I know I should have told her about Cady. I just wanted to be uncomplicated, you know? The man she was into.'

'I can speak from experience when I tell you, Becky once kept things from me for the same reason, and it didn't go well, buddy.'

I nod and bring my forearms to rest on the ropes. 'Yeah, well, I'm going to tell her everything tonight, as soon as I can get away.'

'Oh my God! Are you fucking kidding me?'

All three of us turn to face the door and see Cady storming toward me, red faced with eyes like thunder.

'I know you didn't just swear at me, kid,' I tell her.

'You deserve it! I can't believe this! How could you do this to me?'

'Whoa there, I don't know what you're talking about.'

'The goddamn blog!' She thrusts her phone toward my face, making me step back. When I take it from her, I see the heading:

Brooks Adams: Hound Dog

Then the picture of me carrying Cady into my apartment last night. The blog post makes it sound like Cady is my lover and I'm a cheating scoundrel.

Rage gushes over me like a tidal wave, bowling me over so I can see nothing else.

I knew I offended her, but this?

'Oh my God, my friends are going to see this and think I'm sleeping with my dad!'

'Cady, calm down. Your name isn't in there and your face is cov—'

'It's my goddamn pink hair! My boots. My skirt. Everyone will know it's me.'

I glance around the boxing room, thankful that there are only a couple of other people working out on bags, both wearing headphones. Although Cady is screaming loud enough to wake dead cats in Dumpsters.

'Kit, lend me your phone.' I dial Madge and ask her to have Kerry take down the blog. 'Tell her if she doesn't do this, I will bury Izzy and that fucking book in lawsuits.'

During the call, both Drew and Kit have a chance to read the blog.

'You really pissed her off,' Kit says.

'Yeah, no shit,' Drew adds.

'Cady, I'm sorry. The blog is coming down. Your friends won't have had a chance to see it. As for the pink hair, you'll change that in a week anyway.'

'This is not okay, Dad! If you want to dance for cameras and get laid, that's one thing, but—'

'Enough, Cady! Enough. I'm going to straighten this out, but don't you forget who you're talking to. Let's go. I'll take you home and you can go tell Alice what a shitty dad I am.'

God knows it's true.

As we walk back to my block, my anger doesn't wane; it heightens with every goddamn step. What a typical Izzy, dumbass thing to do. I should have known better. Being mad at me is one thing, but to go public with this crap...

When we're home, I send Cady straight to the basement garage and tell her to wait in the truck while I head upstairs, too irate to put off confronting Izzy.

I hammer on her door. 'Izzy, I know you're in there. Izzy, goddamn it, open the goddamn door!'

She eventually appears, with one eye closed and her hair falling out of the knot on top of her head, as if I've just woken her up.

'Brooks.' It seems to take her a second, then memories of her blog post must come back to her. Her eyes widen and she rubs the back of her head. 'What are you doing here? Shouldn't you be out with your girlfriend?'

'What am I doing here?' I push through the door and slam it shut behind me. Izzy takes a step back but she doesn't wilt like a flower; she straightens her back and folds her arms across her chest. 'Are you out of your mind? Even if I did have a girlfriend, which I don't, you just put our personal lives on your stupid blog!'

Her wince tells me she knows it was a senseless thing to do, but she doesn't admit it.

'Maybe you should think about the consequences of your actions before you get your dick out of your pants. And don't bullshit me about not having a girlfriend. I saw you carrying her into your apartment last night, as if you were newlyweds, and I heard you tell her you love her this morning. You played me for a fool, Brooks Adams. And do you know what hurts the most? I fell for it.

Call me naïve or stupid or whatever, but I actually thought you had feelings for me. But no, it turns out I was just sex.'

'God, you're incredible. You were never just a sex, but now, I wish I had kept my dick in my pants, because you are exactly what I was afraid you were. Just a spoiled rich girl who needs to have everything her own way and to hell with other people's feelings.'

'How dare you! You are the one who cheated on me! Or her, but definitely someone.'

'I didn't cheat on anyone, Izzy. She's my goddamn daughter.'

She leans away from me, her brow furrowed. 'Excuse me?'

'Cady. The girl with the pink hair. She's my eighteen-year-old daughter. She went to a party and got drunk. I had to pick her up. That's why I left.'

'You have a daughter?'

I scoff. 'If she'll still call me Dad after this. You just plastered her picture all over the internet and made out like I'm sleeping with her. How freakin' reckless can you be?'

'Reckless? How can it be reckless if I didn't know who she was? I mean, bloody hell, Brooks. You have an adult daughter and you didn't think to tell me? How could you not have told me that? Oh, I get it. Just play with me and ship me back off to London, right? There was no need to tell me anything about your family. Who is the mother? Are you... together?'

'Jesus. Back to me having an affair. I'm not even entertaining this. I should have told you about Cady but maybe, deep down, I knew the kind of person you are and decided not to bother.'

I watch as her eyes fill and she rolls her jaw. 'Great, yeah, put this on me being a shitty person. I'll take the blog down, and please tell Cady that I'm sorry. But you're still a liar, Brooks Adams, and I want nothing more to do with you.'

'That makes two of us.'

I turn and walk out of her apartment, leaving her there with tears in her eyes, my own throat locked tight with emotion.

Cady and I don't speak as I drive her home. She looks out of the window and I maneuver around the bright headlights of cars, my elbow on the window ledge, my fist propping up my temple. All I see is Izzy. Tears in her eyes. Smelling of wine.

I stop on the corner of Alice's cul-de-sac and Cady climbs out of the car without speaking, slamming the door behind her. I watch until she makes it inside the house and closes the door behind her, not once looking back.

Well, Brooks, you royally fucked this one up, buddy.

I stick the car into gear and just drive, to anywhere, nowhere.

25

BROOKS

Day 10

When I walk into Studio A, a small group of reporters – two I recognize and two new – are already gathered. Izzy doesn't meet my eye or speak to me as she loads a salsa video. Once the video is loaded, she leaves the room.

After my workout, I shower. As she said would happen, now that I know the moves, I can build up a sweat doing her routines. I head up to my office and stop in the corridor when I hear her soft, high voice singing to the gentle strum of my guitar. I lean back against the wall and listen. Each strum and each word peels back a layer of my anger and bares my feelings for her. I have to force myself to remember that she's childish and petty and this whole thing is just one big game to her. A game she is playing to win.

As she sings about feeling alone, I recognize the lyrics. Not because I've heard the song before; I haven't. I recognize the sentiment. That she can feel alone in a crowd of people.

Of course, if you write blog posts claiming the guys you are sleeping with are also sleeping with their daughters, it is a surefire way to make yourself lonely.

I don't have the energy for this. No more. I seek out Elliot – one of my best trainers – and ask him to cover Izzy's session for me.

In my office, Izzy is frantically scribbling on a piece of paper. Crossing out words, writing down guitar chords. She stops when she sees me and puts the guitar down, returning to her desk and her blank laptop screen.

'Elliot is going to take your session this afternoon,' I say. 'He's one of my best and he has your notes.'

She lifts her head but her expression is unreadable. She nods, then stands and walks out of the room.

* * *

I hold the punch bag that hangs from the ceiling of the boxing room as Drew pummels his fists, knees, and shins into it. Kit is slumped on the floor with his head between his legs, recovering from his session.

'Give me a left-right-left. Nice. Right-right-left. Good hit.'

As I talk Drew through his usual routine, throwing in a few different patterns to keep him sharp, Elliot comes into the room with Izzy following behind. He raises his chin in greeting. Izzy doesn't look our way at all.

'Give me five knees each side,' I tell Drew, who is now dripping with sweat and grunting through each move.

I watch Elliot strap Izzy's hands, my entire body tensing when he holds her wrist, his skin on hers. It's a small touch. I'm mad as hell at the woman. Yet it riles me. She takes Elliot's instruction without giving him any grief. I wish the music weren't playing so loud so I can hear what she's saying. It's a small comfort that she isn't laughing or smiling.

'Roundhouse, hook, jab. Five on each side,' I direct Drew.

Izzy starts punching at her bag but her technique is off. Her arms are too straight or too bent at the wrong times. She isn't punching through the bag. That's what I'd be telling her right now.

Elliot picks up on it but rather than telling her how to fix it, the bastard moves behind her, his chest to her back. He interlaces his fingers through her right hand and demonstrates technique by moving through the punch with her.

I don't realize I'm reacting until Drew stops his workout and follows my gaze to Izzy and Elliot. In the same situation, maybe I would be doing the same thing he is now. Would I? Would I hold my client's hand and move through the punches that way?

My fists ball at my sides. When Elliot is satisfied, he moves back to his position behind the bag. Before she starts up again, Izzy shoots me a glance, her eyes connecting with mine for a second that feels like an hour. Then she's punching through the bag, her back to me.

I wonder if she's imagining my face.

'I should have told her about Cady,' I mutter.

'You should have. But her reaction was out of order,' Drew says in my defense.

Oddly, I feel an irrational need to justify her insane actions. 'She was hurt.'

'She could have spoken to you in private.'

'I know. I think she knows that too. She's mad at me about Cady. And maybe she's right. I mean, she wouldn't have got wasted and posted anything if she had known I have a daughter.'

'How is Cady?' Drew asks.

'I'd love to answer that question, but she won't answer my

calls. Neither of them are speaking to me. How in God's name did I get here? You know what the really messed up thing is? I don't wish I hadn't met her.'

It strikes me as I say that, just how similar that reaction is to how I feel about Cady and Alice. My life went to crap because I got my girlfriend pregnant. I spend all my waking hours in this gym to avoid being home, alone with my thoughts. Yet I don't wish I had never met Alice. I don't wish we had never had Cady. And, even though she drives me crazy, there's not even a small part of me that wishes I'd never met Izzy.

I watch her drop her arms to her sides before Elliot hands her a bottle of water. Ah, I can still enjoy watching her suffer through her hangover, though.

'Hey, Iz!' I shout. 'Are you wishing you didn't drink a bottle of wine yesterday?'

She glowers at me across her shoulder. 'Don't you have somewhere to be? Someone to lie to?'

'Not right now. Hey, maybe you could take a picture of Drew, Kit, and me and put it on your little blog thing. Tell the world we had a threesome.'

She flips me the bird, then gets back to the bag, punching and kicking harder than she had been just moments ago.

'I take it back,' Drew says. '*She's* not childish. You *both* are.'

He's right. But those are the first words Izzy has spoken to me in twenty-four hours. I've had my fix. Now I can go back to being pissed at her.

I try calling Cady one more time before I leave the gym for the day. This time, I know she sends me to voice mail.

After making myself a quinoa salad – don't eat that stuff unless someone pays you to do so – I slump down on the sofa. I reach for my guitar. When my hand grips nothing but air, I remember Izzy has it.

No guitar. No Izzy. No Cady. No Alice. No plans with friends. Have I mentioned it's blasted Friday night?

Opening my fridge, I see at least I have beer to keep me company. I reach for a bottle but stop and take the can of club soda next to it. Not because Izzy would tell me not to have a Bud. Not because I would break another rule by having a beer. But because I don't want to turn to drink when I'm alone. I choose the can of club soda for me, no one else.

I pop the ring and take it to the window, where I stare out at the red bricks of the building opposite. I have lived with this view for six years, knowing I could afford something better but not wanting to waste money. Not wanting to spend money I could put into Cady's college fund. Not wanting to admit that I came from nothing but now I do have money. That I have made my own wealth. But I've saved for Cady's college fund now. So what am I trying to prove by staying here? That I'm not like Alice?

Through the window of an apartment in the building opposite mine, I see a woman answer a door and welcome friends into her place. I think of my friends. I think of Drew and Sarah. How they try to push me to be better. How Drew wants me to franchise the gym. He's offering to help me and I haven't even looked into it seriously.

Is it because I'm done trying to make something better of myself to prove that I deserve Alice? What about what I want?

I'm thirty-five years old. I can't work myself to the bone training forever. At some point, I need to let younger guys come in. At some point, I should take my own advice and decide what the hell I want to do, for me.

My cell chimes and I rush to it. I wonder whether it will be Izzy, alone and wanting to call a truce. Do I want to call a truce?

The reason I don't want to is the very face that is flashing on the screen.

'Cady.'

'I'm still pissed at you. But I've been talking with Mom and, since I'm on house arrest otherwise, do you want to have breakfast tomorrow?'

I chuckle. 'Yes, baby. I would love to take you to breakfast tomorrow.'

26

BROOKS

Day 11

Cady chose the quirky café we're sitting in. It's Japan meets New York. The wall of windows looks out toward the Hudson River. One wall is brick – city-style. Another is painted with two geishas holding fans and standing outside a Japanese teahouse. The third wall is lined with shelves that are decorated in an array of teapots: fine, floral-patterned china, Asian-style pots with iron handles and matching miniature cups, English teapots with images of the royals and Big Ben.

Apparently, this week's thing is tea. Cady has become a tea connoisseur, as well as a brunette. I decide not to comment on her change of hair color, knowing exactly why she has lost the pink look. The tea focus could be the result of an article in a magazine, or the fact Alice has placed her under 'house arrest' for throwing her guts up earlier in the week.

She orders blueberry pancakes with syrup and a tasting tray

of different teas. I contemplate bacon and eggs but opt for a mango smoothie made with coconut milk, boosted with a shot of protein, and finished with blackberries. It was the berries that clinched the deal.

'Okay, who are you and where did my dad go?' Cady asks when our server leaves us.

'Some of these shakes aren't so bad. They make you feel sort of... clean. Just don't ever tell Izzy I said that.'

I wince once the words are out of my mouth, knowing I went straight to the most taboo topic I could have chosen.

'It's okay, Dad. I'm cool about it now. I mean, I'm still pissed at you both, but Mom and I had a chat about it...'

She shrugs.

'You and your mom talked about Izzy and me?'

Something inside me flutters. But what's new is, the reason isn't the mention of Alice, or that Alice has been talking about me. It's that simple phrase: *Izzy and me.*

'Do you think I don't know why you never drop me at home?' she goes on.

I shuffle in my chair, out of my comfort zone.

'Don't worry, Mom says she thinks it's because you don't like knowing I live with someone in a father-figure role who isn't you. But I know you don't really have girlfriends. I know if it weren't for Uncle Drew and Aunty Sarah, you would spend all your time between the four walls of your apartment and the gym.'

'What does that have to do with anything?'

'Stop being childish, Dad.'

'What the—'

'Shh, just listen. I know by the way you talk about Mom that you never got over her. Thing is, you always talk about the two of you when you were teenagers. Younger than I am now, even. So, I don't agree with Mom. I think you don't pick me up because you're stuck with an idea of what could have been.'

I lean back into my seat and roll my jaw. I'm about to argue, tell her she's wrong, but she has nailed me right on. It's just as impressive as it is annoying.

'When did you get so grown up?'

'I have my moments.' A server sets down Cady's selection of teas. 'Thanks. Anyway, Mom and I both agree on one thing.'

'Enlighten me, Dalai Lama.'

She sips from her first miniature cup of tea and rolls her eyes at me as she does. 'Izzy pulls you out of your comfort zone. She makes you do things you would never do. Like dancing and having public arguments. I'm not saying that's a good thing. My point is, Izzy seems to have an effect on you that no one else has ever had.'

'You and your mom spoke about this?'

'Yes. And we're both happy for you. Even if Izzy isn't "the one".' She uses her index fingers for air quotes. 'Maybe she's waking you up. I love you, Dad, but you should have more in your life than that gym.'

I stare at my daughter, wondering when she got so smart. Maybe she's right. Maybe I like to think of the old Alice, but she isn't the same person any more. Maybe I'm not the same boy I was back then, either.

'She told me to apologize to you, by the way. Izzy, I mean. She obviously never meant to hurt your feelings.'

'I know. I read her latest blog post.'

My stomach sinks. 'Christ, what has she posted now?'

'You haven't seen it?'

'If I had, I wouldn't be asking.'

She grunts, as if she's the adult fed up with my attitude. 'You should read it. You should also go see her after breakfast.'

'That's difficult, since she won't speak to me.'

'Because you never told her about me. It's okay. I get why you might not have wanted to. Sometimes we want to pretend we're something else, right?'

'I would never want to pretend I don't have the most amazing daughter in the world, Cady. I adore you, you know that. I guess it just didn't come up, and it was easier to show Izzy a simplified version of myself – a single guy who would argue with her for two weeks, then wave her off to London.'

'Well, the London part I can't really solve for you. But if you read her blog post, I don't think you will be so afraid to see her.'

I feel my eyes narrow. 'What does this post say?'

'You'll see.'

27

IZZY

Brooks hasn't turned up at the gym and it's almost eleven. I know he has a client booked for a session in half an hour.

Will he show? It's Brooks; of course he'll show.

That thought doesn't make me feel less nervous; it makes me feel worse.

Will he have seen the blog post?

Sitting at my laptop in the bistro, I read what I wrote for what must be the fiftieth time.

Public Apology

Two days ago, I wrote a nasty post about Brooks Adams. The post has since been removed and I won't repeat what it said. Suffice it to say, I hurt Brooks and someone very close to him.

To both of you, I am truly sorry for how I behaved.

I wrote that post in a hurt and catastrophically jealous fury. It was childish and I am deeply regretful.

The truth is, Brooks Adams is a good man. The best, even. I think I have brought out the worst in Brooks since we met and

I know he brings out the worst in me. But here's the thing: I believe we bring out the best in each other, too.

The last two weeks have been the greatest of my life and I'll be sad to see our competition end. More than that, I'll be sad to no longer have a reason to have Brooks in my life every day.

From the bottom of my heart, Brooks, I'm sorry. Please find it in that enormous heart of yours to forgive me.

To the other person I hurt: I hope to get the chance one day to tell you in person how truly remorseful I am.

Izzy.

Why did I write that? Conscience. Guilt.

Sarah.

The last person I expected to see when I answered my apartment door at nine thirty on a Friday night was Sarah. My first moment of realization was staring her in the face and wishing it had been Brooks knocking on my door, because I would rather fight with Brooks than be in anyone else's company.

My second moment of realization came over a cup of Earl Grey tea on my sofa. Sarah told me how she lost her husband to a motorbike accident five years ago. I found it so hard to believe that someone as confident and outwardly happy as Sarah could be hiding something so painful inside. It occurred to me that I couldn't stand the thought of something so tragic happening to Brooks.

The biggest moment was when Sarah told me that she introduces herself to new people she meets as a single woman.

'Sometimes it's easier to keep up the front if I'm just Sarah, not Sarah the widow. Sometimes it's nice to just be uncomplicated, someone who isn't deep down scarred by the past.'

'Are you telling me Brooks was putting up a front?' I asked her. She put her hand in mine then. 'I'm saying maybe he just wanted to be Brooks with you. Not Brooks with baggage. Not Brooks with a broken heart. He adores Cady and she's a great girl. But honestly, Izzy, how would you have reacted if he had told you he has a daughter who is about to start college?'

I stared at her then, blankly, as I replayed that question in my head, thinking two things. The first: I probably wouldn't have fallen for him – the guy with tattoos and big muscles and a kid. The second: he would be an amazing father.

When Sarah left, I wrote the apology. In part because I wanted everyone to know that Brooks is a good man. The other reason was that I didn't know how to tell him to his face that I've fallen for him and I wish things were different. I wish we had met without this stupid competition between us. I wish I had my shit figured out and I wasn't such a 'brat,' as he so politely puts it.

As I close the lid on my laptop, Brooks comes into the gym. He walks right by the bistro and toward the staircase. I want to follow him, but my heart is hammering in my chest and I need just a minute.

I close my eyes and lean my head back with my hands across my face, trying to remind my lungs to breathe.

'Why isn't your desk in my office any more?'

I sit upright but keep my eyes closed, not able to tell from his tone whether he's still pissed at me.

'I don't want to upset you any more. I know you didn't want it there so I had it taken out.'

I feel him sit at the table across from me before I open my eyes to his.

'I didn't want your desk, but you put it there anyway and I like having you in my room. I like hearing that sweet voice singing to my guitar. Damn it, I even like arguing with you incessantly.'

'What about my shitty attitude?'

His lips rise at one side in the kind of half smile that liquefies women, this woman.

'Fuck it, I miss that too.'

'What about kale smoothies?' I giggle, less at what I'm saying and more at the giddy relief I'm feeling, which is making my body tingle.

'Too far, Coulthard. I draw the line at kale smoothies.'

'Well, for what it's worth, I've missed your steak and eggs.'

He winks at me and the power of that move, together with his half smile, has me melting like an iceberg in the desert.

'I'm sorry I didn't tell you about Cady. I should have.'

'I guess I understand why you might not have told me. I'm sorry I reacted the way I did. Even if you had been having a sexual encounter with an eighteen-year-old with pink hair, I shouldn't have gone public with it.'

'We both seem to have a few things to work on, huh?'

I nod. 'It would seem that way.'

'How about we get through the next few hours here and you let me take you home?'

'I'd like that a lot.'

'You know it sucks that I can't take you to dinner.'

'Maybe when our fourteen days are up.'

As I say those words, I feel the mood shift between us. It's day eleven. On day fourteen, we end this charade. On day fifteen, I fly back to London. We both know that a dinner date can't happen any time soon.

As if he hears my thoughts, Brooks leans across the table and presses his palm to my cheek. 'We don't have to think about that now.'

I lean into his palm and close my eyes, wanting to see and feel nothing but his touch.

* * *

I'm standing by a table in the bistro, my sports bag on a chair, waiting for Brooks to finish up.

My iPhone tells me I have six missed calls and two voice messages from my mother. I hit play.

'Isabella, we need to talk. This has got out of ha—'

I happily cut her off when Brooks appears through the double doors into reception. Charlie walks by his side. Otherwise, the gym is empty.

Brooks' lips break into a beam when he sees me. The kind that feels like he has folded me into his big, warm arms.

'Are you ready?' he asks.

'Yep.' Picking up my bag, I almost skip toward him.

'I'll lock up, Charlie,' he says. 'You have a good night.'

''Night, boss. 'Night, Izzy.'

'Good night, Charlie.'

I like her so much more now she's stopped scowling at me all the time.

On the sidewalk, Brooks locks the doors and tucks me under his arm. We walk like this all the way back to our block. When we reach the twelfth floor, he stops outside his apartment and takes my hand. 'Let's stay here tonight.'

I feel one eyebrow rise. 'The secret fortress?'

'Otherwise known as home.'

I run my hands down his back and bite his shoulder through his T-shirt as he opens the door, all the while I'm feeling like we've crossed an invisible barrier.

He flicks on the lights and takes the bag from my shoulder as we both slip out of our training shoes. I pad, barefoot, into the whitewashed space. It's similar to the apartment I'm staying in but this one feels bigger and cleaner. Homier too, although it does have a single-man feel about it.

I clock three guitar stands in the lounge. One holds an electric guitar, another a bass guitar, and one is empty. Brooks draws the sheer curtains across the floor-to-ceiling windows, hiding us from the apartments in the building opposite. He has a large flat-screen TV opposite an L-shaped sofa. The bright abstract artwork on the walls steals my attention. He has three canvases. One is splatters of bright paint on a white background. Another looks like a pathway to heaven – a long, gray path leading to the sky. Around the path are what look like random items – a guitar, an American football, a hockey stick, boxing gloves – but the more I look, the more I see Brooks.

'Did you commission this?' I ask, turning to where Brooks is standing watching me with his arms folded across his chest.

He shakes his head. 'Actually, Cady painted it.'

Right, his daughter. 'It's very impressive.'

I move to the opposite wall, lured by the third piece of artwork: a giant canvas of an eye that looks like a photograph blown up to size. The eye is beautiful. A bright-blue iris with flecks of gray and silver. The pupil is big, making me wonder whether the camera didn't flash when the photograph was taken. There are no lines around the eye, only soft, pale skin.

'This is stunning.'

I feel Brooks as he comes to my side, his arm gently grazing mine. 'That's Cady's eye.'

'She's a really big part of your life, isn't she?' I keep my focus on the image, knowing my words seem peculiar and not under-standing why I'm asking the question, except that I'm both jealous and awed. Such a strange mix of emotions.

'She's my daughter, Iz.'

Just like that. It's so simple to him. It should be to me too. If she's such a huge part of Brooks, I should want to know her.

'Do you think maybe I could meet her?' I ask, a small part of me hoping he says no.

'I'll see if she's free tomorrow.' He turns me to face him and takes the tie from my hair, letting the loose tendrils fall onto my shoulders. As he strokes his fingers through my locks and presses his lips to my neck, I roll my head to the side and close my eyes, indulging in his touch.

'I missed you,' he whispers against my ear, taking the lobe between his teeth.

I slide my hands beneath his shirt, craving the feel of his firm torso and the press of his warm skin against my fingertips. 'I missed you too.'

'I'd like to take you to my bed.'

I answer him by pressing my lips to his. There's something about this kiss that's different from before. Less frantic, sweeter, deeper somehow. Or perhaps it's the way it is making me feel, as if there's no room for anything more in my chest before it has got to explode.

He breaks our contact, taking my hand in his and leading me down the corridor to his bedroom. It's much bigger than mine and has a large en suite. He lights up the room, then dims the lights. He moves to the bed and sits, tugging me so I'm standing in front of him, between his open legs.

I reach down to his face and stroke the coarse hair around his jaw, the soft crinkles at the sides of his eyes, the straight line of his nose.

His eyes are fixed on mine as he hooks his fingers inside my yoga pants and knickers—fresh on after showering in the gym, just in case. He draws them down an inch and makes me hiss my next breath as his teeth and lips connect with the sensitive flesh over my hipbone. He tugs them another inch, then another.

Afterwards, he collapses onto my chest and I hold him tightly to me, feeling his heat, listening to his every breath in my ear, my heart beating with his.

We were in it together, like I was an extension of him. Everything about his touch was tender, gentle, loving. He made me feel adored, cherished.

I want to be an extension of him. I want to always be with him.

28

BROOKS

Day 12

'Why have you stopped here?'

Izzy looks through the windows of the truck at our surroundings, on the edge of the cul-de-sac where I usually pick up Cady.

'She lives just down there. This is where I pick her up.'

'But it's raining, Brooks.'

Her words irritate me. This is the routine. This is what we do.

'She'll have an umbrella, Izzy. It's only water. Here she is.'

Cady runs with an umbrella over her head, her brown bob bouncing. Her usual skater dress has been replaced by skinny jeans, but the staple black leather jacket has made the cut. She makes for the front passenger door, then remembers we have company today and jumps into the backseat, dumping her overnight bag next to her and the umbrella in the footwell.

'Already relegated to the backseat. Fast mover, Dad. Next you'll be shipping me off to college.'

'Or telling you to drive yourself into the city,' I say, turning to look at her.

'I'm working on that. Too many things happening at the same time. You know I've never been coordinated. So, you must be Izzy.'

Izzy peers between the seats. I can tell from her tentative smile and the way she's fiddling with her fingers in her lap that she's nervous.

'Hi, Cady, it's really nice to meet you. And, erm, before we go anywhere, I just want to say, I'm really sorry about the blog post.'

Cady shrugs. 'It was a shitty thing to do, but he shouldn't have pretended I don't exist. So, now that's over, where are we going for lunch? Are you two going to be all lettuce leaves and shakes? Because I would love a burger.'

Izzy and I look at each other, then back to Cady and we all smile, the tension in the car fading in an instant.

'Izzy is definitely allowed a burger.'

Izzy sucks in a breath and pouts, as if she's struggling with a conundrum. 'You can have a chicken burger. No bun, no skin. And sweet potato fries.'

'So, basically chicken breast and sweet potato?'

'Right.' She chuckles as I shake my head.

'Burgers it is.'

I dump the truck at home and we walk to a secret burger joint down a side alley in the city. It's not actually secret at all because it's always packed. But I figure it is a cool place to take Izzy, and Cady and I love the burgers.

After shouting our order above the music and chatter, we take a seat in a wooden booth, Izzy and Cady on one side, me on the other. The inside of the place looks like a huge garden shed: wood walls, roof beams, and furniture. Izzy checks out the art decorating the walls: old music and movie posters, handwritten graffiti.

She leans her head to the side as she reads two notes by my shoulder.

> *Mel was here '13.*
> *Sarah & Mitchel 4ever.*

'You see that Rolling Stones poster up there?' I ask, pointing. 'Check out the writing to the left of it, in purple felt pen.'

She finds the words and reads aloud: 'Cady and Dad 2008.'

'I drew the stick men,' Cady says, smiling across the booth at me. Izzy's lips curve up, but there's something else about her expression that I can't read. Something behind her outward smile.

'That's pretty awesome,' she eventually says. 'So, Cady, are you looking forward to college?'

Cady nods as she slurps her Diet Pepsi through a straw. 'Sure am. I'm going to NYU but I'm going to be living on campus. I get the best of both worlds. Dad and his wallet when I need him, Mom's washing and cooking, a place where neither one of them can see me behaving badly.'

Izzy's giggle turns to a laugh when she spots the scowl I'm throwing Cady.

'You need to learn a few life lessons, kiddo. Dad's wallet is paying your fees. You can get a job for the rest.'

She rolls her eyes and waves a hand through the air. She is saved from my addressing that damn attitude by our number being called at the counter.

'To be continued,' I say, pointing to her as I leave the booth.

When I come back with our food, Izzy and Cady are talking about Broadway shows: their favorites and which they've seen recently. I dish out two mouthwatering cheeseburgers to them, while I try not to outwardly grumble over the plain chicken breast in front of me.

'I adore *Wicked*,' Izzy says, as they unwrap their burgers in unison.

'Oh, me too. That song. You know, the big one where the witch floats up from the stage?'

'Defying Gravity!' they shout together.

As I work my way through my bland meal – which ought to be outlawed in a burger joint this good – I watch my girls.

They both lift the lids of their buns and remove the pickle and tomato slices from the top of their meat, placing them on the side of their burger wrappers. They don't stop talking as I reach out and take all four pieces of veggie for myself. Other than paying the check, I'm basically superfluous to this lunch.

By the time we leave the restaurant, the rain has started up again. Given we're so close to my apartment, we decide to make a run for it. We stop to pick up chocolate and ice cream, which I'll have to watch Cady and Izzy eat later, and somewhere along the way, a decision is made to play Monopoly, then watch a movie.

As much as I hate Monopoly because it usually drags on forever, I enjoy sitting around the living room, the three of us playfully jibing at each other. My enjoyment is helped by the fact I won. Another reason I don't usually like Monopoly... I always win, which is boring. Today, though, it was a close call.

It's after seven by the time we decide to wash up and put on lounge clothes for the movie. Unsurprisingly, I have no say in what we watch. Izzy connects her Mac to my flat-screen and Kate Hudson appears on it in some chick flick.

Cady curls her feet beneath her in the lounge-chair. I rest back into the L of the sofa and pull Izzy to sit between my legs. She's reluctant, I can tell from her rigid body, but she eventually gives in.

Cady offers chocolate to Izzy, which she takes and eats, delighting in my growl against her ear. It pleases me to see how she has become more comfortable with food. Cady pops the lid on a tub of Ben & Jerry's and dives in.

'I can't believe you're making me watch a chick flick,' I grumble.

'Shh,' both of them say, putting me firmly back in my box.

Around a half hour into the movie, I decide it isn't so bad. Perhaps it isn't the movie so much as the company. I rest my chin on Izzy's hair, breathing in her familiar shampoo, and tighten my arms around her. I watch Cady, focused on the TV, so much so her ice cream drips from her spoon back into the container.

It dawns on me that this is the life I always wanted. I've always wanted this closeness with Cady and Alice. It's broken my heart for eighteen years that I couldn't have it. I'm not sure I could cope if it was snatched away from me again. Just as quickly as the thought came, I swallow the tightness that takes hold of my throat. My chest constricts as my heart rate speeds up. I try to breathe calmly, without drawing Izzy's attention. But I'm panicking. I'm panicking like mad.

I love her. I'm in love with Izzy. I'm terrified.

As the credits roll, Cady stands and stretches her arms above her head with a loud yawn. 'Well, I'm pooped. Do me a favor and don't be loud when you're doing sexy time? I don't need to hear that.'

I feel Izzy's intake of breath as she sits bolt upright. 'We wouldn't, don't, I...'

'Cady, enough,' I say, raising my brows in a way that tells her she's crossing the line. 'See you in the morning.'

'Such a pooper! 'Night, Dad. 'Night, Izzy.'

When she's out of earshot, Izzy buries her face in my chest. 'Oh my God.'

Now, I laugh as I kiss her hair and stroke her back. 'I thought you handled that well.'

She sits back and slaps a hand across my chest. 'Shut up. I didn't know what to say.'

'I. A-ah. Erm.'

She picks up a sofa cushion and throws it at me. I grab her wrists and pull her on top of me. 'Seriously, Iz, thank you for today. I know it must have been... odd.'

She swallows so hard I see it in her throat and wonder what she isn't saying.

'She's a great girl, Brooks. She clearly loves you.'

I wait for more, for the 'but' that her expression seems to hold. It doesn't come.

'Shall we go to bed?' I ask.

'Yes, but I can't, you know...'

Chuckling, I kiss the tip of her nose. 'How would you feel about lying in my arms all night?'

She nods. 'I can't think of anything I'd like to do more.'

That night, Izzy's breaths are slow and deep as she sleeps across my chest. I lie perfectly still, scared I'll disturb her and that she might roll over, away from me. I need to hold her. As I lie here in the darkness of my bedroom, she's the only thing stopping me from losing my mind.

She's going back to London. Back to a life full of designer labels, where her wealthy parents pay for her apartment. A life like Alice's.

29

BROOKS

Day 13

Izzy comes with me to drop Cady home, both of them grumbling at how early it is but both knowing I have to get to the gym.

I stop the truck in my usual spot at the edge of the cul-de-sac. I can feel Izzy's eyes on me. It must seem strange to her that I don't drive Cady to the house. I get it. But how can I tell her this is what eighteen years of wishing looks like? How do I tell her it's just too much for me to see Alice's life without me in it?

'Well, back to Alice's house arrest,' Cady says, getting her things together in the backseat.

'Alice?' Izzy says, staring at me.

'That's Mom's name,' Cady says, not registering the shift in mood in the front of the truck. 'It was really nice to meet you, Izzy. Hopefully it won't be too long before you come back from the UK.'

Wow, way to add to the awkward-as-hell moment, Cady.

'Bye, Dad.' She leans through the seats and plants a kiss on my cheek.

'Bye, baby.'

Izzy is still looking at me as I knock the truck into gear and head back to the city. I force myself to look straight ahead. But as we pull into line behind traffic, she asks, 'Alice, as in *Alice in Wonderland*?'

I glance quickly at her and back to the road. 'Yes.'

'Your tattoo.'

I nod. 'It was the first tattoo I got, a long time ago.'

'Do you still… I mean, are you over her?'

'Am I over Alice?' I don't know why I feel the need to repeat the question. 'Izzy, Alice and I haven't been together since Cady was born. We were seventeen.'

'Why don't you drop Cady at home?'

I feel the muscles of my jaw tense and my nostrils flare as I breathe out. 'Cady has two homes, and I just don't, okay? Can we drop this now?'

'Yes. I'm sorry. Cady obviously has two homes. This is just all new to me.'

Guilt churns my stomach. I know it's new to her. And I wish I could give her answers to her questions about Alice. The thing is, I don't have them.

Am I over Alice? Will I ever be?

I know I feel different about Izzy from the way I've felt about Alice, or anyone.

Can I be in love with Izzy and not be over Alice?

Can I be in love with Izzy knowing that there is every chance she is going to break my heart?

30

IZZY

He has a child. Well, a young adult. Okay. I can handle the idea. We had a great day, yesterday. Cady is nice; she's funny. She reminds me of Brooks in too many ways to count.

But she's an adult, going to college, and I don't even know what I want to do with my life yet.

Brooks tells her to get a job and be responsible but even I don't have a real job. My parents still pay for my apartment.

Does it really matter? Am I beating myself up over nothing because I would never be number one if I were to be part of Brooks' life? I'm not just talking about Cady but Alice. Alice in bloody Wonderland. He couldn't tell me he is over her.

Oh, Izzy, grow up. Of course, he isn't over her; she is the mother of his child. She will always be there.

See, this is my point exactly. I need to grow up myself.

'Izzy? Does that all sound okay?'

I move my attention from my fingers to Kerry, as she and I sit with Madge and Brooks around a table in the gym bistro.

'Erm, yes. The studio will send a car. Brooks and I will drive to AMTV together. They'll ask about the results of the two weeks.'

Brooks puts his hand on my thigh and questions me with his gaze. I force myself to smile back at him.

'Great,' Kerry says, shuffling pieces of paper on the table in front of her. 'Next, we need to go over a few details of your London promo events when you get back. Brooks, Madge, you guys are free to go if you like. You're welcome to stay too.'

'We'll leave you to it,' Brooks says.

After saying their goodbyes to Kerry – Brooks seemingly increasingly less offended by her – Brooks and Madge move into reception. But as Kerry starts talking me through three book signing dates in the UK, I can't take my eyes off Brooks. He drags a hand back through his hair and across his chin. Madge reaches a hand to his shoulder, as if she's comforting him. Then she folds him into her arms and they linger there.

Sickness builds in my stomach. I can tell he's nervous about the TV appearance tomorrow but I think it's more than that. Has he realized I'm not right for him? Or, like me, is he dreading tomorrow because it is day fourteen, our last day together?

'You've fallen for him, haven't you?'

I look at Kerry through clouded eyes. I don't answer her question. There's no need. I know the answer will be written all over my face. I'm in love with him.

'You can always come back, babe. You don't have to stay in London forever.'

Right on cue, my mobile rings and 'Mummy' lights up the screen. I silence her – again. I know she will be freaking out after seeing my blog. She's my mother; she'll know there's something going on between Brooks and me. And she'll hate it. Since I already know that, what's the point in hearing it from her?

A text message follows the call and I delete it after reading the words:

Isabella Coulthard, you are ignoring me and I will not stand for it.

Kerry and I part ways and I go in search of Brooks.

'Are you ready to get some results?' he asks when I reach his office. A distraction.

'Yes, sure. Are we doing it here?'

He flashes me a sly look. 'Doing the tests here!' He chuckles. The sound thaws the ice that is starting to build around my heart to protect me from what is coming. 'We can take a few measurements here. We'll use the scales downstairs. I don't think we need much, just something to talk about tomorrow. Do you agree?'

'I do. Now, take that shirt off,' I say with a wink that has him laughing again.

I kick his office door shut and he draws the blinds before pulling his T-shirt off over his head. Taking the measuring tape from him, I close the space between us, knowing the one thing that will make me feel better about tomorrow is having his arms around me now, being with him completely.

Standing in front of him, I bring the measuring tape around his back and across his chest, my fingertips gently trailing his skin. I write down the size of his chest, then move to his side, wrapping the tape around his bicep, pressing my lips to his shoulder as I work. Bending to my knees, I pull down his shorts until his thighs are exposed. I nip the skin in my teeth while working out the girth of his solid quads.

'Izzy, if you don't stop, this is only going to end one way.'

I look up at him through my lashes and see the lust on his face, as if it is a mirror of my own. With my eyes on him, I run my hands up his legs and press my lips to his navel, his abs, his sternum. I need this.

Wrapping my ponytail around his hand, he pulls me up to him and crashes his mouth against mine with a growl.

'You're so fucking beautiful, Izzy.'

'Be with me,' I whisper. 'I need you. I can't stand the thought that tomorrow—'

He takes my mouth again, even more ferociously. All I can think of is him. Not tomorrow. Not the what ifs. Just him. Us.

He lifts me onto the edge of his desk. Just as we are about to really get into this, a knock on the office door startles us both to stillness, both of us looking at the unopened door. I'm sure we're both thinking we should have locked it.

'Brooks? There's someone calling on the main line asking for you.'

Brooks shakes his head quickly, as if trying to clear it. 'Charlie, Izzy and I are just doing some measurements. We won't be much longer. Can you take a message?'

I slap my hands across my mouth to stop my laughter from escaping.

'You got it.'

Brooks takes my hands from my mouth, pulling me up to sit as my amusement finally escapes and is matched by his. He pulls my top over my head, then holds me to him, his skin on mine. His amusement fades from his dark, hooded eyes and he kisses me slowly, deeply.

I feel like everything is charged around us, like I'm on fire, melting into this man who I am, without a shadow of doubt, 100 per cent in love with.

He tightens his hold on me and presses kisses to my hair. 'I wish we were in my bed so I wouldn't have to let you go.'

'Me too.'

* * *

We move downstairs to the weighing scales, passing through reception on the way. Charlie is back behind the front desk.

'Sorry about that, Charlie. Did you take a message?'

I can feel my cheeks turning scarlet.

'Yeah, but it was really odd. She wanted to know where you live and where Izzy lives. She seemed to know you are living next to each other.'

'Press?' Brooks asks.

'I don't know. It didn't really seem like a professional approach. Anyway, here is her number. She said her name is Mrs Periwinkle. She didn't give a first name.'

I dart forward, taking the notepaper from Brooks' hand. 'Let me see that.'

'Do you know who she is?'

I close my eyes and bite down on my lip. 'Yes. It's my mother.'

'Periwinkle?' he questions.

'It's a code name she uses when she doesn't want people to know who she's talking about. Like when she's gossiping about someone at lunch. She'll call the person Mrs Periwinkle so she doesn't get caught out or overheard.'

'What? Why would your mother call here asking for me and why would she leave her number with a fake name?'

I sigh, knowing my mother too well. 'Because she hoped you wouldn't tell me that Mrs Coulthard called. She wants to speak with you.'

'Why would she want to speak with... Because of us?'

I nod. 'And she asked where we are staying, which means... Oh God.'

'She's here?'

'Or coming.' And I know exactly what she's coming to stop.

31

BROOKS

I lean against the kitchen counter watching Izzy scurry around her apartment, frantically tidying.

'I thought you said you didn't care what they think.'

'And I thought you said I secretly do,' she snaps. She stops fluffing the sofa cushions. 'I don't care. It's just she's flown halfway around the globe.'

'Six hours.'

She launches the sofa cushion at me. 'Now is not the time to be a smartarse, Brooks.'

The truth is, it's all I can think to do because I'm afraid. I'm afraid her mother is coming here to tell her what a mistake Izzy will be making if she decides to stay with me. I've been here before. I know how this ends up. Me, alone, heartbroken.

I tuck the cushion under my arms for something to hold. A comfort. I'm already hurting, and I don't know if I should stick around for the main event.

'You know why she's coming, Izzy, and it isn't to tell you that your two-week rental is untidy.'

Izzy stops and faces me. After long seconds of us staring at each other, she says, 'I don't know why she's coming, Brooks.' Her words hold no conviction. Her shoulders sag and I am struck by a need to hold her.

I cross the living room, ditching the cushion and taking her in my arms. I hold her tight against my chest and stroke her shower-wet hair. 'She's your mom, Iz. What are you so afraid of?'

'Everything. Letting her down, letting you down, letting myself down. You don't know her, Brooks.'

And I really don't think I ever want to. I pull back and hold her cheeks in my palms.

'Look, she doesn't get here until after midnight. Let's go to my place and go to bed for a while.'

'No. I can't.'

'Izzy, tomorrow is our last day together. I don't want to be apart from you tonight.'

'But my mother is coming. I have to be here.'

'Fine, then let's go to bed here. Just let me be with you.'

The expression she offers could be apologetic or full of pity. Whichever it is, it cuts me deep.

'You can't be here when she gets in, Brooks.'

Those words finish me. I take a step back from her and nod, slowly. It's happening again.

'We have to be up early for AMTV, anyway,' she says, her words coming fast. 'It will take me ages to get ready in the morning. You'll have a better night's sleep on your own.'

'Yeah, sure. Thanks for thinking of me.'

I leave her apartment, slamming the door behind me. Instead of going to my place, I head outside and start walking aimlessly.

There's a cool wind that chills me through my T-shirt. I tuck my hands into the pockets of my jeans and keep moving west until I'm standing on the edge of the Hudson. The city's lights catch the ebb and flow of the water and take me back almost eighteen years.

On that day, I could hear Cady crying before I even got to Alice's parents' house. For a small thing, she had a big set of lungs. I didn't care that she was crying, again; I was just excited to see them both. It had been a long day at the garage. A few emergencies came in, on top of the cars we already had booked. And I had been to Crazy Joe's gym early that morning. I was exhausted.

But my feet started moving faster when I heard raised voices. I realized then that it wasn't Cady's normal crying; she sounded distressed. And Alice was shouting above her screaming and, between the two of them, no one heard me enter the large, suburban house.

I knew Alice's mother would kill me if I didn't take my work boots off before stepping on the new rug, so I fought with them, wrestling them off.

'But I love him,' Alice shouted.

I could tell from the noise that she was downstairs with her parents and Cady was upstairs.

'Alice, you're seventeen years old. You don't know what real love is,' her mom said.

'Real love,' her dad began, 'is providing for your family properly. Not being a mechanic at someone else's garage. Now, Brooks is a nice boy, but that's where it stops.'

'Look at his background, for goodness' sake,' her mom said. 'He comes from nothing and will come to nothing, Alice. We let you have Cady—'

'*Let me have* Cady? Is that a joke? She's my daughter. *Our* daughter. Mine and Brooks'. And he's a good dad.'

Her father's voice grew sterner. 'He comes over every night for two hours, Alice. How can he be a good father?'

'I only see you for two or three hours a night. Are you saying you aren't a good father?' Alice yelled.

'Now you watch that mouth, young lady. I put this roof over your head. I have given you a good education and, once this mess is straightened out, you'll go back to having good prospects.'

'Did you just call Cady and Brooks a mess?'

'Open your eyes,' her mom shouted. 'It is a mess, Alice. If you listen to your father, you might be able to salvage something of a life for yourself. You'll be lucky now to find yourself a good, wealthy man who'll take you on with baggage.'

I was rooted to the spot.

'I don't want a wealthy man. I want Brooks. I want my family.'

Her mom cackled, and I felt my face twist with hatred as I imagined her perfectly made-up face and salon-styled hair thrown back.

'We are your family, Alice. The people who put a roof over your head.'

I had heard enough and my baby was screaming. I walked upstairs and found Cady in her basket. I picked her up and held her to my chest. It surprised me every time I held her how tiny her head, her toes, her fingers were. How delicate she was. She was everything. And I would be everything for her.

I kissed her cheeks and swayed with her in my arms until her body relaxed and her tears disappeared.

'Brooks.'

I turned to see Alice, tears streaking her face, her eyes red and swollen. She still looked beautiful.

'I love you,' I told her because I had nothing else to say. Her parents were right. I was a mechanic and didn't even earn minimum wage.

She sniffed. 'I love you too.'

'I'll show them, you know. I will. I'll make something better for us, Alice. I promise.'

She crossed the room and put one hand on my head, the other on Cady's back. 'I know, Brooks. I know.' She dropped her cheek to my shoulder and we stood like that for what seemed like hours. Perfect. My family.

The next day, Alice broke up with me.

The wind rises from the Hudson in gusts. It hits my eyes over and over again, until they start to water. I can't do it again.

32

BROOKS

Day 14

I hate wearing suits. Men like Drew and Marty look good in suits. They own the look. I, on the other hand, look like the Michelin Man being squeezed into fine fabrics. I own two suits. One I wore to my grandfather's funeral when I was twenty-four, with skinny shoulders and about forty pounds lighter than I am now. The other is the one I'm wearing now: a suit Drew convinced me to splurge on for a networking event we went to last year. He told me it was an investment, which was why I eventually caved. This is appearance number two for the dark-blue two-piece.

I fight with my tie in the mirror, with one eye on YouTube and a video that's instructing me how to tie a Windsor knot. Once I'm finally suited and I've run product through my hair – enough to look like I've made an effort, not enough to make me look like Leonardo DiCaprio's Jay Gatsby – I shine my shoes and get set to leave.

When I receive a message telling me the car sent by AMTV is downstairs, I close my apartment door, really wishing I could spend the morning at the gym rather than a television studio.

The door to Izzy's apartment is ajar, as if someone exited and intentionally left it open so they could reenter.

'You don't know anything about him,' I hear Izzy say.

The voice that replies is stuffy, with overpronounced vowels and drawn-out consonants.

'I know that our friends and family have seen your blog. You've made your point, Isabella. You've flaunted a relationship with a man I could never approve of. Imagine what the ladies at the Savoy will think. The man is covered in tattoos. He's a weightlifter, for crying out loud.'

'He's a fitness instructor and he owns his own gym,' Izzy fires back, her words sharp, almost a shout.

'A fitness instructor, then. It's hardly a life I want for my daughter.'

'How can you say that? *I'm* a fitness instructor.'

'Oh, please, we all know what this is, Isabella. You wanted to show your father and me that you can do something on your own. You've done it now. The silliness ends here.'

'Silliness? This is my career.'

'No, darling, it's a flirt with dancing and a few recipes. Do you intend to write another book about breakfast shakes and salads? How long do you expect to salsa yourself to a size whatever? You never stick to anything. It's time for you to grow up and do something constructive with your life. Having some kind of public fling with that man is not a step in the right direction.'

'That man has a name.'

'I don't care to learn it. You can do your show. Then you will fly home with your father and me and we will get your life back on track. You have a very good degree in English Literature. We are well connected. If you want to write books, write something worthy of being read.'

'When will you realize that this is my life? I want to work in fitness. I want to date Brooks.'

'He has a grown-up child, Isabella! Do you really believe he is the man for you?'

Izzy's voice seems to lose its conviction. 'That's my decision.'

'We both know you are incapable of making good life choices. Now, let me tell you how this goes. You will come back to London and fix your life. You will stop turning your back on the people you need to socialize with to thrive in life. And you will walk away from that man.'

'But—'

'You will do it, or your credit cards will be cut off and we will stop paying your rent. Then you could really see how far your life choices have got you on your own.'

I'm startled by the sound of a throat clearing behind me. I knock into Izzy's door as I turn. A man stands before me, holding three coffees. He has Izzy's eyes and nose. He's tall and slim, with thin, gray hair and an immaculate suited appearance.

I swallow deeply. 'Sir. I'm going to take a guess that you're Izzy's dad.'

'That's correct. You must be Brooks Adams?'

'Yes, sir.'

He takes a deep breath and seems to stand even taller than before. 'I'm sorry you had to hear that.'

He gestures to the apartment door, sending my mind right back to the conversation I just overheard. I care less about her mother's opinion of the inked, muscled man with no prospects, and more about what Izzy didn't say. She didn't really defend me. She didn't stand up to her mother. She didn't say I was the man for her.

I nod to Izzy's father because I am struggling to form words. I'm seventeen again. My heart is breaking, again. It hurts every bit as much as it did then, maybe more.

'Could you tell Izzy the car is downstairs?' I manage.

'Yes, of course. We'll be down soon.'

'Thanks.'

Outside, I lean back against the apartment building wall, needing a few minutes of air before I get into the ridiculous stretch limousine that must have been sent so that Izzy's parents can ride with us. Great.

I can feel heat rising on my skin. Sitting in front of a camera, inches from the woman I love, knowing my eighteen-year walls have cracked... I don't know if I can do it. I yank my tie loose and unfasten the top button of my shirt, needing to cool down, needing to breathe. I ball the overpriced fucking tie in my fist and lean my head back against the wall, trying to get a grip on myself.

I was a fool to think it's possible to fall in love with someone after two weeks, that she would love me back, and that any of it would be enough to erase eighteen years of pain. I was an idiot to think Izzy isn't just another rich girl.

'We'll meet you in there,' Izzy says. 'I just need to speak with Brooks.'

I open my eyes to see her folks walking to the limo. Her mother has on a cream-colored suit. Her blonde hair is perfectly styled into a roll at the back. Pearls decorate her neck and ears. Even her goddamn shiny shoes look expensive.

'Brooks.' Izzy's hair falls in waves across her shoulders. I love seeing her with her hair down. She has on a peach-pink dress that sits off her shoulders, hugs her slender waist, and finishes below the knee. Her high heels make her entire body taller and straighter. What looks like a diamond bracelet sparkles on her delicate wrist. Her nails are painted to match the dress. She looks incredible and out of reach, all at once.

'You look beautiful.'

Her smile is soft and doesn't shape the rest of her face. 'You look good in a suit.'

Men in suits. That's what she's used to. It's not me. I'm just the mechanic who got lucky when Crazy Joe left a little pot of cash to me. The kid with no direction and no money is still inside me. The kid who got his girlfriend knocked up at sixteen is right here. The man who has an adult daughter and zero clue how to move on with his life is hiding behind the suit she likes.

'Brooks, what my mother said...'

I shake my head. 'It's fine, Izzy. I get it.'

'You mean so much to me, Brooks.'

'Just not as much as credit cards and a nice apartment.'

'That is unfair!'

'Is it? You and I are very different people, Isabella.'

'You're being a dick.'

I push off the wall so we're standing face-to-face. 'No, I'm being a realist. You come from money and you like money and wealthy circles. I'm just a small-town guy lifting weights in the city.'

'You know I don't think that.'

'Well, you sure as hell didn't tell your mother any different, did you?'

She exhales tightly and heavily, shaking her head. 'Well, you didn't manage to tell me that you aren't still in love with your ex. I guess we both have a lot to figure out before we hurt each other.'

It's way too late for that.

We stare at each other for seconds that feel like an eternity. I wish I could take her in my arms. I wish we could go back to the gym and bicker about the Charleston. I wish we could stay in bed, just the two of us, where we make sense. But that isn't real life. Real life grinds you down and tears you apart.

'We should go. We'll be late,' I tell her.

She looks to the ground, not meeting my eye again as she walks to the limousine.

* * *

When we arrive at the studio, Izzy and I are met in the lobby of the high-rise by Kerry. In her usual stylish way, she's in heels, a pencil skirt, and blouse. Her shoes make a clicking sound against the marble floor as she comes toward us.

'Wow, did someone die? You two are going to have to cheer up, at least for an hour. Brooks, I thought we agreed you would wear a tie?'

'I'm in a suit, aren't I?'

I hear Izzy's mother tut behind my back and feel Izzy tense at the sound. Her mother hardly spoke two words to me on the ride over. Her father asked a few questions and made small talk about the city. I can tell neither of them have an interest in getting to know me and I'm certain my life wouldn't be incomplete if they weren't in it. But I was polite, for Izzy's sake.

'True. It beats sneakers and running shorts. Follow me. We'll go up to AMTV's floor. Makeup might want to see you, and then there's a breakfast buffet.' As we reach the elevators, one of six opens and Kerry leads us inside. 'I'm sure you can fight over what you can and can't eat.'

Kerry leads Izzy's parents to some place in the studio, where viewers are permitted to stand behind the cameras. Izzy and I are brushed and fussed over by the makeup team – not something I take kindly to – then a studio runner leads us to the breakfast room.

Two guests of the show are already inside, sitting on a red sofa and talking about their upcoming political segment. We have short introductions, then they get back to discussing the latest Senate scandal. Two flat-screens on the walls show AMTV in real time. The clock in the corner of the screen tells me it is eight fifty. Izzy and I are on at nine fifteen.

I watch the show for a few minutes, then move to Izzy's side as she scours the breakfast buffet. Pastries. Muffins. Cream cheese bagels. 'I'm guessing I can't have any of this?'

She looks up at me quickly, I think surprised that I've broken our silence. 'You can have fruit,' she says, gesturing to the far end of the spread.

'Why don't you go for half a cream cheese bagel and add some of that smoked salmon,' I tell her. I hate that we are speaking to each other like robots. But I don't think there's anything meaningful left to say. That thought alone has me rubbing a fist against the lingering ache in my chest. My worry is, like the DOMS – delayed onset muscle soreness – this pain is only going to get worse tomorrow.

We plate our breakfast and each take a bottle of sparkling water from the minifridge. We stand to eat. Izzy picks at her bagel, her gaze focused on her plate the entire time.

'Are you nervous?' I ask.

She finally looks at me. 'We are still going to say what we agreed, aren't we?'

I should have known she would be less bothered about what is happening between us and more concerned about her public appearance. 'Yes, Izzy.'

'Please don't be like that.'

The runner is back. 'Ms Coulthard, Mr Adams. Can you follow me, please?'

We do, relieved – at least for my part – to be spared another discussion about how we just aren't compatible. The guy leads us to the edge of the studio, where we are wired up with microphones. Two presenters are sitting on a cream-colored sofa.

'All right, guys, you're up. Take a seat on the sofa here opposite Marcha and Aaron.'

We briefly shake hands with the presenters and take a seat opposite them. We both shuffle, crossing and uncrossing our legs, sitting taller, then more relaxed. Izzy settles for crossed legs and I settle for parted knees.

I glance around at the cameras and lights on us. I read the autocue, set up for Marcha's first line after the weather segment that is currently airing. I'm nervous as hell and way out of my comfort zone.

Izzy's hand comes down on my thigh, stealing my attention. 'You'll be great,' she says.

I lock my fingers in hers and squeeze her hand, grateful to have her next to me, letting her know I'm here with her too.

The moment is gone and we part our hands when Marcha welcomes back viewers.

'Next up, we have Brooks Adams and Izzy Coulthard on the sofa. Brooks, you are the owner of the gym Brooks Adams and a renowned trainer here in the city. Izzy, you are visiting from the UK to promote your book, *Be Green. Be Clean.* Now, to help any viewers who haven't followed the story, you two have slightly different approaches to health and fitness. That's fair to say, I think. Brooks, why don't you start by telling us about your methods?'

My nerves are back with a vengeance. Remembering Madge's advice, I try to imagine this is just four people chatting on two sofas in a private living room.

'My method really revolves around the idea that no one size fits all.' I feel my voice strengthen as my heartbeat calms. 'I believe a plan for exercise and nutrition advice should be tailored to each client. As a starting point, I would include cardiovascular and muscular training. I would include healthy carbohydrates and proteins. But the rest depends on what the client wants to achieve. They could be training to run a marathon, for example, or they might want to increase muscle mass.'

'Interesting. So, for you, Izzy's method of dancing and structured detox recipes would be incorrect?'

Izzy fidgets uncomfortably beside me. 'No. That's not what I'm saying. Incorrect is not the term I would use. For some people, dancing as exercise and going green, detoxing, would be a fine way to achieve their goals.'

'But it wouldn't work for everyone?'

I glance at Izzy, conscious that I don't want to say or do the wrong thing. She doesn't deserve that.

'In my opinion, it wouldn't work for everyone, no. But I will say, I feel good after following her plan for two weeks. There are some things I will take away and some that I'll continue to do.'

'Such as?'

'Well, I feel cleaner and leaner. I'll continue to include detox shakes and superfoods along with my regular diet.'

'Will you still do the Charleston as exercise?'

I don't feel like it, but I recognize that I should laugh with Marcha, Izzy, and Aaron, so I do. 'I don't think the Charleston will be one of the things that stays.'

Laughter seems to have suited Izzy. She appears to relax a little.

'So, Izzy,' Marcha begins. 'How did you feel following Brooks' plan?' She glances at me and smiles. I don't know if it's genuine.

'Honestly, I hated it initially. I felt like I was eating a lot more than usual. I missed dancing and disliked the regimented approach to exercise. But now, I feel great. I've actually gained weight but not body fat, which means it is all strength and toning. I feel better for it, physically and mentally. So, I do recognize that advice should be tailored. I stand by *Salsa Yourself Slim* and clean eating. I also appreciate that if you want to build muscle, or really enhance your cardiovascular fitness, introducing weights and interval training could be beneficial.'

Marcha leans forward across her knees and presses her hands together. 'This is interesting. For viewers who don't know, Izzy and Brooks' relationship has been dubbed 'love, hate, salsa, and weights' by some reporters. Which I love, by the way. Very catchy. But what I'm seeing here is definitely more reconciliatory. So, tell us, are the rumors true? Has this competition led to a blossoming romance?'

Izzy and I look at each other. What the hell kind of question is that? I glance at the cameras and see Izzy's parents looking on, worry lacing her mother's expression.

'We've certainly come to respect each other,' I say, the words catching in my throat. 'I'm sure we'll stay friends after this and continue to give each other grief about weight training and salsa dancing.'

Marcha laughs and pats Aaron on the arm. I keep my gaze on the coffee table between the sofas.

'What about a collaboration? Are we likely to see a salsa and weights book being released next?'

I open my mouth to speak but Izzy beats me to it. 'We both have things to work on as individuals. A collaboration is highly unlikely. Plus, I'm not sure I could stand more than two weeks of Brooks Adams. I like designer handbags and kale. Brooks hates extravagance and enjoys burgers.'

I look at her now. Though a fake smile is planted on her face, I don't misunderstand one word she said. She's acting like the Izzy she was two weeks ago, not the Izzy she wants to be. The fact is, she is going back to the Izzy of two weeks ago, and she isn't putting up any fight.

Whatever we were or might have been, we're done.

'Well, we think you both look great, and that you would look great together, don't we, Aaron?'

'We sure do, Marcha.' He turns to the camera. 'You can find the results of Brooks and Izzy's competition on our web page. Next, we have Nigel Anderson discussing his new sitcom, *Anything Goes*.'

After de-wiring, I chase Izzy along the corridor to the elevators. Her parents are already waiting on the landing.

'Izzy, can we talk?'

She spins on her heels to look at me. 'There's no need, Brooks. I got the message, loud and clear. You're right. We are two very different people. I have no clue what I'm going to do with my life. You have a business, Cady, and *Alice in Wonderland*. I'm supposed to move in circles with skinny, wealthy people and you like grungy karaoke bars. I want to be number one to someone. You already have a number one in your life. I'm not even mature enough to be able to accept that. We have nothing in common. This would never have worked. I'm a fool for thinking it could have.'

The elevator doors open and she steps inside. I don't follow.

* * *

I decide to walk from the studio, knowing it's miles from home. I don't care. I take off my suit jacket and hold it over my shoulder, my other hand in my pants pocket, as the sun beats down on me. After a while, I reach my street but I keep walking. I don't want to go back there. I don't need to see Izzy packing, getting ready to leave. I don't need to know she's only two doors away from me but will be gone by tomorrow.

My goddamn shoes start blistering my feet but I keep walking, all the while remembering why I prefer to wear sneakers. Without realizing, I find myself in Central Park. I sit on a bench, alone, watching families and tourists smile and laugh, feeling the rush of air as rollerbladers and runners zip by me.

She's right. We are two very different people. But I don't believe what she said about social circles and handbags. She hates those people. She's so much better than those people. They put her down, made her feel self-conscious and lacking. And we do have things in common, so much. Music, movies, sports, exercise. She challenges me. I thought I hated that at first, then I realized she makes me feel alive.

But she does deserve to be someone's number one and right now, I can't figure out how to make room for her. She isn't just talking about Cady; she's talking about all the other mess inside me. I'm lost. I've been lost for eighteen years because I've been so focused on Alice. Every move I've made, every thought I've had, Alice has been in there somewhere. Alice. Alice, who broke my heart.

Sitting here, I see the difference between Alice and Izzy. I feel it. Izzy has caused a different kind of hurt. Not deeper or more painful, just different.

But it ended the same. She'll go back to the life she hates, with her parents telling her who she can and can't date.

This time, I won't just accept it. Things are going to change.

33

IZZY

Day 15

'Are you ready?' Dad asks from the doorway of the bedroom, where I'm zipping up my suitcase.

'Yeah. Would you do me a favor and meet me downstairs?'

I need some time alone and though I know he feels the same way as my mother – that I'm better off without Brooks in my life – he can at least see that I'm hurting.

'We'll see you down there.'

When I hear the door of the apartment close, I drag my luggage into the living room and sit on the sofa one last time. I rub the cushion next to me, remembering where we made love. I look at the TV, remembering how we talked for hours about movies. I turn to face the kitchen and picture us making eggs and smoothies together. I smile at the thought of the first time he came over because he was worried I would cremate a good steak.

God, I'll miss him.

Summoning strength I don't feel, I pull my suitcases out to the hallway, closing the door behind me for the last time. Who would have thought I'd come to New York to promote a book and end up finding the only man I have ever loved? Who could have guessed that man would be Brooks Adams?

I drag my suitcases past his door, pausing, remembering how he wouldn't let me go in the first time we came here, wondering if he's in there or if he is already at the gym. Wondering whether he went right back to having eggs for breakfast. Wanting so much to go and make his breakfast for him.

I move on, as I know I have to do, making my way down the hall. Suddenly, my cases become lighter and leave my hands. My stomach sinks.

'Brooks.'

'I'll help you down.'

I don't know what I expected him to say. There are so many things unsaid between us, yet nothing to be said. We know how this ends.

'Thank you.'

He carries my luggage to the elevator and we ride in silence. Outside, my parents are waiting in a black Cadillac.

Brooks hands the cases to the driver. Now, there is nothing between us except heavy, silent air. He reaches out for my cheek, the way he does, and I lean into his palm, closing my eyes, wishing I could bottle his touch and always have it with me.

He steps closer to me, his hand on the small of my back. I give in to the temptation to touch him and wrap my arms around his waist.

He drops his forehead to mine. Finally, I open my eyes and find his gaze.

'What would you have said if I had asked you to stay?' he asks, a tremor in his voice.

'I have promotional stuff to do in London. I have to go.'

He presses his nose to mine and I smell fresh mint on his breath. 'What if I had asked you to come back, so I could take you to dinner? Or if I'd asked to come to England?'

I take a breath, hating what I'm about to say, but knowing the truth. 'I would have said, I wish that were the right thing to do. But we both know it isn't.'

His lips gently graze the tip of my nose and my body dissolves into his.

'The only part I wish we could change is the ending,' he says. God, he has no idea how much I want that to be possible. 'And maybe the Charleston.'

I laugh as much as my heart will let me and feel his chest shudder as he pulls me tight against him, my cheek pressed to his chest, his hand in my hair.

'Izzy, darling, we have to go,' my father says, leaning out of the car door, then moving back inside.

I pull away from Brooks' hold and run my fingers through his hair. 'Thank you, Brooks Adams. For the first time in my life, you have made me want to work on me, for me. I can't really explain that, except to say, thank you. You've done more for me in two weeks than most people have done in my life. You've made me want to figure out who I am.'

'I love you, Izzy.'

Tears build quickly and fall from my eyes. 'I love you too.'

He kisses me, long and slow. I grip his shirt, never wanting to let him go. Knowing I need to. When we separate, we're both crying silent tears.

I run my thumb under his eye, wanting to be here every time he breaks, every time he needs someone to hold him and kiss him.

He takes my hand and kisses my knuckles. 'Go. You don't want to miss your flight.'

I watch him walk back to the building, until the door closes and he disappears.

Sitting in the Cadillac, my mother says the last words I want to hear. 'It's for the best, Isabella.'

I cry all the way to JFK, endless tears that refuse to turn off.

34

IZZY

Day 2 Without Him

There's a gentle tap on my bedroom door.

'It's me,' Anna says, coming into my room uninvited.

I roll over in bed. 'Have a good day at work.'

I roll back to face the window.

She moves around the bed, picking up used tissues from the floor and putting them in my wastebasket. 'I'm not at work today. I worked last weekend. Let's do something. I could call Zara and Beatrice and we could go to afternoon tea? One of those healthy ones you like?'

'No, thank you. I'm happy here.'

'You've been in bed for a day and a half. You smell. This room smells. You've hardly eaten and you need to stop crying.'

'I was watching a sad movie.'

'Of course you were. Didn't you say you had some event tonight?'

'What day is it?'

'Friday.'

'I have a signing at Waterstones at 6 p.m.'

'Right. Let's pick something to wear then. Up you get.'

I pull myself up. Not because I want to but because she has just reminded me I have a signing and, unfortunately, I do have to go.

Anna moves to my wardrobe and picks out dresses on hangers.

'This? What about this Gucci? I adore this Tom Ford.'

God, it's no wonder I can't afford to rent my own place. My wardrobe could be a down payment on a mansion.

Dressed in a day-to-evening Dolce & Gabbana dress, which Anna has teamed with my latest Mulberry bag and Prada shoes, I agree to a late lunch with Anna, Zara, and Beatrice. Only because I have to eat something before going to Waterstones.

We sit around a marble-top table in one of London's finest hotels and order green salads and water. I hear Brooks as I eat. *If you eat like a rabbit, of course you'll be skinny.*

I laugh through a mouthful of water. The daggers I receive from Zara, Beatrice, and Anna tell me it must have been an inappropriate time to laugh. I cough until my amusement subsides.

'Sorry, it went down the wrong way.'

After tutting, Beatrice resumes whatever she was saying. 'He said he couldn't be with her any more if she was going to be friends with Tillie, because of course Tillie had been seeing – and by *seeing* I mean having sex with – Alfie. Then Tillie said she was pregnant, which was a lie, and she admitted it minutes later, apparently. So, he said, even if she hadn't been with Alfie...'

I zone out again, until I hear my name. 'Well done with the book thing, Izzy,' Zara says. I'm about to thank her when she continues. 'I mean, at least you showed willing to do something. Now you can relax for a while.'

'Sorry, how do you mean?'

'You know, stop pretending you want to make your own way. You can get back to shopping. Plus, you can start coming out with us again if you would like.'

'Wow, incredible.'

'Oh, nonsense. You're a friend. You know you are welcome. We only didn't invite you those other times because you were taking the exercise thing so seriously, and what with not drinking, you were a waste of a good invitation.'

'Actually,' Beatrice jumps in, 'about that book. I told Audrey about it and she was quite excited that we have an author friend. She was going to buy it but I said you would obviously give me copies, so if you could drop some in to me, that would be grand. Maybe five or ten would be okay. I don't know many people who will want it, but a few spares are always handy. It's nice to give people something to take away when they visit.'

I glance at Anna, expecting her to be as incensed by the conversation as I am. She sips her water and crunches through raw carrot, not concerned in the least.

'Sure, Beatrice. I'll sort that for you. You'll have to excuse me. I'm not feeling too well. I think I could use a walk before the signing.' I take my purse from my bag, find fifty pounds for my overpriced salad and water, and leave it on the table beside Anna.

'Izzy, I have Daddy's card.'

'Mm, I know. I want to pay my way.'

I walk toward the river Thames and saunter along the shoreline. Even when my toes begin to hurt in my high heels and I wish I had my running shoes on, I keep walking, feeling the cool wind in my hair.

I won't be like them. I'm not like them.

On the way to Waterstones, I resolve to start making my own way in life, for real.

Despite my book apparently selling ten thousand copies already, I only sign five books at Waterstones, which were sold to three people. As I sit alone, drumming my fingers on the tabletop, at a store just minutes from home and my 'friends' and family, I know no one else will come. Not one other person I know would have phoned friends to get them to come and buy my book just to make me feel less worthless. Only Brooks.

35

BROOKS

Day 5 Without Her

The gym is boring without her. Life is quiet when she isn't around. I train. I train others. I do gym admin. I strum my guitar, wishing it was her fingers playing and her voice I was hearing, instead of my own.

I want more. I need more. It's time to do something new and challenge myself.

I set my tuna steak and edamame beans aside – it's lean protein and greens, I can't be expected to be a kale convert after two weeks. Come on!

Opening the lid of my laptop, I sit at the kitchen counter and find Drew's e-mails about franchising.

After an hour, I think I understand the basics: someone else owns the land, someone manages the gym, but it's my style, my training regimes, and my brand they use. I make a note of things I need to ask. How do I make sure the quality of the training is maintained? Who pays for equipment and the fit-out of the gym? Do I get to dictate which suppliers are used and how many members the gym has?

I go to the fridge for a beer but when I reach inside, I decide to take a club soda instead. By the time I'm finished reading everything Drew sent me, it is after midnight and I am pooped.

36

BROOKS

Week 2 Without Her

Stepping out of the elevator, the first thing I see is the new gold sign saying:

Welcome to Statham Harrington

I'm so damn proud of my buddy for getting his name on the wall.

'Hey, handsome. Admiring the art?'

'Hey yourself,' I say, hugging Sarah.

'I'll take you through to the meeting room. Drew is just finishing up a call. Do you want coffee?'

Following her impressively fast strut in sky-high heels, which ought to be considered an extreme sport, I tell her, 'Actually, I'm not drinking so much caffeine.'

She stops, dramatically – in true Sarah fashion – and spins to face me. Holding her hand to one side of her mouth, she whispers, 'Don't let the attorneys hear you slander their best friend. Men have been killed for lesser things.'

I'm still smiling at Sarah as I stand in the meeting room and take in the view of Manhattan's skyline under the early morning sun.

'Brooks, my man.' Marty comes into the room and shakes my hand. 'I can't stay. I've got a mock deposition in two minutes, I just wanted to say hi. Are you coming to poker at Drew's on Saturday?'

'I'll be there.'

'Great stuff, great stuff. All right, got to go. When I make him wait, my client is like you when you're hungry.'

'Shit, you better get going.'

'I know, right?'

As Marty leaves, Drew comes in. 'Hey, buddy.' He shakes my hand and we take a seat at the glass table. 'Do you want a bagel or pastry or something?'

'No, I'm good.'

'You're turning down food? Sarah says you don't want coffee, either. What the actual?'

'Since you made me buy this suit and it's like two inches too small, I can't afford to eat pastries.'

'The suit is the perfect cut, Brooks. You're just used to elastic waistbands. Right, let's get down to it.'

'I'm ready. I'm in. Let's franchise.'

Drew smiles as he sips his take-out coffee. We talk through everything I think I understand. Drew fills in some blanks and answers my questions.

'What happens next?' I ask.

'We look for a property. I can get someone from Real Estate to help with that. They know good commercial realtors. Unless you have an idea already?'

'Not on the property front. I do have an idea for a manager, though. Do you remember Mickey and Brad, the brothers who bought my first gym in Brooklyn? Well, they did a good job of it. I'd like to float the idea by them.'

'Are you sure? I mean, are they commercial enough?'

'No.' I chuckle. 'But they managed to keep that gym afloat. They've never expanded it, but I know the membership is at capacity. They are capable of doing it and, more to the point, I trust them. Let's give them a chance.'

He nods slowly, as if contemplating. 'They're good guys?'

'Yeah, they're solid.'

'Your call, then. Speak to them.'

We end the meeting with a plan of action in place. It feels good to be taking an extra step, pushing myself. More than anything, it feels phenomenal to know that I'm doing it for me.

Drew shakes my hand and I pull him into a man hug. 'Thanks, Drew, for pushing this. I had to work through some stuff, but I wouldn't have done this if you hadn't been nagging me like an old wife.'

He thumps my back harder than necessary but laughs. 'I'm glad you're getting your head straight, Brooks.'

* * *

After thirty minutes of interval training on the treadmill, I hit stop and roll back with the belt until I'm standing on the gym floor. I smile at the thought of Izzy's jelly legs the day I added it on to her training because she'd pissed me off again. As I rub sweat from my face with a towel, I wonder where she is, who she's with, what she's doing. I contemplate sending her a message. Maybe telling her about the plans for the new gym.

The walk to the showers gives me time to think better of the idea.

When I'm back in my office, I have a missed call from Cady. I call her back.

'Hi, Dad.'

'Hey, baby. Did you call?'

'Yeah. I, ah, I'm sorry but we need to talk about me moving into NYU. I don't know who wants to drop me off, you or Mom. I mean, I would like it to be you and, you know, you could lift stuff better than Mom and Richard. But Mom wants to be there too. She'll probably cry or something, I don't know. Anyway, I don't know what you want me to tell her?'

I suck in a breath and exhale heavily down the line. 'You don't need to be in the middle of this, Cady. I'll speak to Alice.'

'Are you sure?'

'Yes, of course. What are you doing this weekend? Will you both be home on Sunday morning?'

'Ah, yeah, I'll check but I think so. Will you... are you saying you'll come *here*?'

I scratch my head, not sure at all, but there is no time like the present for conquering things I'm afraid to conquer. 'I'm sure. Let me know what time.'

A text message comes through to my cell a few minutes after we hang up.

Mom says 10am and she will make breakfast. K?

Breakfast with Alice. Well, fuck.

Sounds good.

37

IZZY

'Your technique is flawless, Izzy. I don't think it will take long for you to feel confident about auditioning for theatre, especially if you keep dancing every day.'

I can't hide my happiness as my dance teacher speaks. 'Thanks, Francesca. I'm really enjoying getting back into it. It feels like forever since I had to concentrate on the mechanics of it all. I'm having so much fun.'

'I can spread the word, if you like, see if anyone is auditioning? It wouldn't necessarily be in London but if you don't mind travel, I think we can find a theatre company.'

'I would love that, thanks so much.'

We leave the dance studio in London's West End and head off in different directions. I walk west, back toward my apartment, excited about the stop I am making on the way.

I reach Sam's music store just before he closes. It's a small place in Notting Hill. Old green wood is marked quite simply with 'SAM'S' above the entrance. The window is lined with sheet music, everything from the Beatles to Faith Hill.

A bell rings as I enter.

'Sam?' He's nowhere to be seen, which I have come to realize means he is probably drinking tea with three sugars out back.

He totters in, hunched from age in his old cricket jumper.

'Izzy. She's ready for you.'

I clap excitedly and do a little jig on the spot. Sam lifts my new six-string acoustic from its leather travel case. 'I've been calling her Betty, after my late wife,' Sam says. 'I think it suits her. Especially with that floral shoulder strap you had me put on.'

I take hold of the guitar, pull the strap over my shoulder, and strum.

'She sounds perfect. Betty, huh? I like it.'

I carry Betty in her case back to my apartment and up to my bedroom. I take another look inside my wardrobe and a thrill runs through me. At a guess, I would say 70 per cent of my designer labels are currently being sold online.

I sit down on the bed with Betty and a notepad and pencil. I write a song about a lost love. I call it 'Betty.'

> *No one will ever replace you, my love.*
> *I found in you something that will stay with me for a*
> *lifetime.*

But I don't see Sam's late wife in my mind. I see one man. *The* man. I see Brooks.

As I'm playing 'Betty' for the tenth time, or maybe more, Anna comes into my room. She looks at the almost empty wardrobe then at me.

'I still can't believe you're selling your clothes. What is even scarier is that you've cut up your credit cards. And what is scarier still is that you seem *happy* about all this.'

I laugh and shrug. 'I'm twenty-eight, Anna. It's about time I started standing on my own two feet.'

'This isn't like the time you went vegan, is it? Because if you change your mind in three weeks, you can't just get the clothes back.'

'No, Anna, it's not like that. Oh, hey, hold Betty.' I hand over the guitar as I move around to the other side of my bed.

'Betty?'

I ignore Anna's question.

'There is one thing I decided not to sell.' I take out my latest Mulberry, the one Anna desperately wanted when I bought it, the last one in the store, and hand it to her. 'It's yours. For putting up with my tears.'

Her eyes fill and I hold her to me, smiling. I cried over losing the love of my life. She cries over being given a Mulberry. I see how ridiculous I must have seemed to Brooks when we first met.

'All right, all right.' She pulls back and wipes the mascara shadows from under her eyes. 'What are you wearing to Marybella and Edward's engagement party tonight?'

'Urgh.'

'Izzy, stop. You said you would come. They are big family friends and you're shocking Mummy enough at the moment without refusing to go.'

'Fine. I don't know. I kept a few dresses. Can I wear black in honor of the inevitable divorce?'

'What a thing to say! Why would they get divorced?'

'Because she craves attention and money and he craves other women and money.'

'Ergo, they have a lot in common.'

I can't help but laugh. 'True.'

* * *

Mr and Mrs Rochester welcome you to celebrate the engagement of

Marybella Elizabeth Charlotte Rochester

and

Edward Harold George Wellington-Purrell

I stare at the gold-embossed sign at the entrance to the Rochesters' ten-bedroom home in Mortlake, one of the wealthiest suburbs of London. Anna and I went to school with Marybella. Mrs Rochester, or Victoria, is one of the leading LOLs – ladies of leisure – in my mother's clan.

I can imagine Brooks reading the sign and saying something like, *Who needs all those names? You only use one.* I curl my fingers against my clutch: gold, like my shoes, because Anna said I had to add some color to the black dress. I feel my mobile through the material of my bag and wonder whether I should call Brooks, or just text him. See how he's doing. See what he's doing.

'Isabella, come on, darling.'

My mother calls from the top of the steps that lead to the Rochesters' home, her arm linked through my father's. She's in a silver and blue sequined dress, he in black tie. Anna has already found a friend and gone inside. I'm quite pleased; her fuchsia dress was beginning to hurt my eyes.

The house has been turned into a gala hall, with waiters serving canapes and champagne as a concert harpist plays in one corner.

'Ah, Isabella, how wonderful to see you.' Claudia Huckleberry almost swings me by the shoulders to face her. I perform the obligatory air kisses. 'It has been too long. Your mother told me about your new book. She's very proud. Said it's a best-seller. *New York Times*, is it? A thriller? Oh, excuse me, I must say hello to Helena Delaney. Her daughter just got the results for her pre-university testing. It hasn't gone well. Everyone knows about it. Helena will be distraught. We'll speak soon.'

And I was just about to say hello, Claudia. Shame.

As a waiter passes, I take a glass of champagne. From the next, I take a caviar canape.

'Darling, do be careful,' my mother says. 'We are having a three-course dinner. You don't want to overeat. I didn't think you drank alcohol these days.'

'Mm, yeah, it's a new me,' I say, purposely leaving caviar in my mouth as I speak. I know I'm turning over a new leaf and doing things for me rather than to piss off my parents but, well, I couldn't help myself.

'Isabella, do not embarrass us this evening.'

'I would never, Mummy.'

A marquee has been erected in the grounds at the back of the house. It is lavish inside. Crystal chandeliers, red carpets, white-clothed tables with tall, floral centerpieces. They're going to have to really up their game for the wedding. As I think that, I snort-laugh at my own wit. People already seated at my designated table scrutinize me, then get back to their conversations. I take my seat, recognizing some of the faces from Chelsea's social scene. Boy-girl seating has been enforced, with a rule that we all rotate two seats to the left at the end of every course.

'Hi, I'm Marcus Hendrickson.'

I take the hand offered to me by the guy to my left. He's kind of puny but his suit has been cut to fit his thin shoulders and skinny arms. He has a big forehead that I think is shiny from face cream. His hair is slicked back with so much product, he looks like Leonardo DiCaprio's version of Jay Gatsby.

Brooks wears a suit far better than this guy, or any of the five men at this table, for that matter.

'Nice to meet you, Marcus. I'm Izzy.'

'Izzy...?'

Trying not to roll my eyes, I tell him, 'Coulthard. Izzy Coulthard.'

Now he can mentally assess whether I'm worth talking to. Whether I might be able to do anything for his social standing.

'Oh, you're Izzy Coulthard. I heard about your book deal. The stunt with the roughneck. Brilliant idea. I bet that sold a few extra copies.' He sort of laughs and sort of chokes on his red wine as he speaks. Whatever he does, it's disgusting. 'You know, I've been thinking about doing something similar, trying to get close to reality TV stars, to put my name on the map, so to speak.'

If Brooks were here, I think there's a good chance he would punch this Marcus guy in his upturned nose. Since he isn't...

'For your information, Marcus, it wasn't a stunt.' I rise, my chair scraping the floor as I stand. 'Brooks Adams is a million times the man you could ever hope to be.'

I drain the wine from my glass and bang the empty down on the table. Then I leave the trivial, stuck-up party and the farce of everything that is my life in London.

* * *

'Look, I told you I didn't want to be there. The guy was a dick.'

Anna stands in front of me with her hands on her hips, looking a little green. Maybe she should have slept off more of her hangover.

'You know what, Izzy, why don't you just go back to New York if you prefer it so much?'

I put my headphones into my ears. 'Be careful what you wish for. I'm going for a run.'

I set my wristwatch and start a half marathon. I run through Chelsea, Kensington, around Hyde Park, checking my watch at each mile. By the time I reach thirteen miles, I have shaved eight minutes off my best-ever time.

I bend forward and drag air into my lungs, then start to walk off the run. My smile is so wide, my cheeks ache. At the next store I pass, for the first time in as long as I can remember, I buy a chocolate bar. I take it to a bench in St. James' Park and I watch people walking by as I enjoy my treat, square by square. Brooks was right. If you work hard, a reward is fine. I don't feel guilty at all.

Working on cardio with Brooks was what got me to my best time today too. I take my phone from the bottom pouch of my yoga pants and snap a selfie.

I type the words:

You shaved eight minutes off my half marathon with your brutal cardio. You know the saying, nothing tastes as good as skinny feels? Well, it's bullshit. This chocolate bar tastes bloody amazing.

I hesitate before finally hitting send and then enjoy the last of my sweet treat.

38

BROOKS

'What do you think?' Drew asks.

I lean back against the window ledge and take another look around the second floor of the old building, just off Wall Street. It's the perfect location for the new gym. And the space is enormous. But the renovations were abandoned by the previous tenant, and it's hard visualizing a gym around polystyrene drapes and scaffolding.

A lady called Gloria is showing Drew and me around. She's a realtor his firm regularly works with.

'You need to think outside the box,' Drew says. 'The space always looks smaller when it's empty. Try to imagine yourself working out in here.'

I pace around the room but I'm not sure I can imagine myself here.

'I think the ceilings are tall enough to have office space on a mezzanine level, like you do in your current place,' he adds, walking around in jeans, boots, and a hard hat that's a match for mine, only his is red and mine is blue.

As I try to 'think outside the box,' I receive a text message. The name on the screen is the last one I expected to see and the only one I've been hoping for.

I smile at a picture of Izzy in her sports gear, who's sitting on a bench, eating chocolate, and admitting that my interval training has got her fitness up.

God, it's only one text message but I feel like I can breathe again.

I reply:

It's not just my cardio training. The squats and lunges have given you more power in your quads too.

She replies in an instant and I actually laugh out loud.

Smart arse!

With more energy than moments ago, I walk into the middle of the floor and turn on the spot. I see Izzy running on a treadmill, looking out on the view of the Hudson. I see her pummeling a punch bag, her music playing in her ears, or in the stretch-out area maybe humming her own songs as she winds down.

'I'm in,' I say.

Drew throws an arm around my shoulder. 'Let's make this happen, buddy.'

Out on the sidewalk, after exchanging details and agreeing on a time to talk through next steps, I have a thought. 'Gloria, do you also deal with residential apartments? I'm in the market for a new two bedroom. My only stipulation is a view.'

* * *

Stopping the car in the usual spot I would pick up Cady – on the edge of the cul-de-sac – I give myself a pep talk. *This is Alice. Just Alice. Sweet, beautiful Alice. She can't hurt you any more. You have to do this for Cady.*

Putting the car in gear, I drive down the road, following Cady's instructions. In front of a large, detached house, I see the black Range Rover she told me would be in the driveway.

Come on, dude, keep your cool.

Cady is already out of the house when I shut the door of the truck behind me. As she walks into my arms, I see Alice over her shoulder, standing in the doorway. She's older. She doesn't look exactly like my Alice. Her hair is a darker shade of blonde. There are a few different colors, not one light shade, not like *Alice in Wonderland*. And her hair is short, just below her chin. But her big, blue eyes are just the same. And she's glowing, like she did when she was pregnant with Cady.

'She won't bite,' Cady whispers into my ear.

For the first time, as I meet the stare of my Alice, I know she won't bite. I also know she is no longer mine. The strange thing is, it doesn't upset me, or bring me to anger. The relief I feel carries me to the door.

Cady steps inside ahead of me and disappears down a long corridor, leaving just the two of us. Up close, Alice's eyes are different. There are fine lines at the corners. Her once pale, clear skin has makeup partially covering freckles.

Her lips curve into a smile. That I recognize. The way her skin folds at the corners of her mouth. She's the same Alice and yet so different.

'Hi, Brooks.'

'Hi, Alice.'

It's hard to say which of us makes the first move. We end up locked in an embrace, squeezing each other hard. Holding the past and letting it go at the same time.

'Can we eat? I'm starving!' Cady shouts from somewhere, presumably the kitchen.

Alice and I pull apart, still smiling at each other. 'You always did look beautiful pregnant.'

'You always said that and I always felt dreadful.'

'I guess I missed that.'

'It's good to see you, Brooks.'

'It's good to see you too, Alice.'

I follow her along to the kitchen, walking over the high-polished wood flooring, passing white walls filled with pictures of countryside and beaches. Cady is already perched at the farm-house-style table.

'Richard, this is Brooks. Brooks, Richard,' Alice says.

Richard is around five ten in height and thinning around the crown. He turns from where he's putting bacon onto four plates, wiping his hands down an apron as he does. He holds out his hand and I shake it. Firm, but not aggressive.

It turns out Richard isn't the alpha douche I expected, ordering Alice around while he sits with his feet up in checked slippers, smoking a pipe all day. Go figure.

We eat bacon, eggs, and French toast. All cooked by Richard. It's not the nightmare I have thought about for years. It's... nice. Alice and I share a few glances and tell Cady and Richard a few stories of when we were kids. It's surreal but fine.

Eventually, we get on to Cady's drop-off day at college. We agree to all go with her. College fees are never mentioned. It was agreed a long time ago that I wanted to, and would be, paying those. But Richard does ask my permission to buy a few niceties to make Cady feel more at home in the dorm. I respect the guy for asking and I have no problem with it.

It's hard to describe the weightlessness I feel as I drive back into the city. It's like Alice, or the thought of her, has been a concrete block crushing my chest for so long, and now, everything feels easier, lighter somehow.

As I roll to a stop at a red light, my hand braced on the top of the steering wheel, I also realize for sure that what I felt, feel, for Izzy is nothing like what I have been feeling for Alice all these years. Alice was a sense of loss. Any happiness was nostalgia.

If Alice is water, Izzy is fire. What I feel for Izzy is not calm, passive, past. It's exciting, scary, hot, and so very present. It's real, tangible, and something I want back.

Alice is happy without me. I see that. She was young when her parents told her she couldn't be in love with me.

Maybe... what if Izzy isn't happy without me? What if she does want something different from what her parents want for her, and I was too afraid to wait and find out?

As the light changes, I look down at my bicep and the image of Alice in Wonderland I had inked on me a lifetime ago. I decide to make one more stop before I head home.

39

IZZY

Week 3 Without Brooks

I wake from a dream I can't remember but one that left me happy and sad and thinking of Brooks. I haven't heard from him since I sent that text message after my run.

He told me he loved me once. I haven't stopped loving him and craving him since I last saw him. Could he have stopped wanting me already?

I put on my dance clothes and head down to the studio. Francesca is working with two ballet students when I enter.

'Izzy, come in. We're almost finished and I have something I need to discuss with you.'

I nod and sit on the floor to start stretching. I haven't yet looked at my phone this morning but I take it out now and see I have a message from Brooks. My heart flutters and I press my hand to my stomach.

There are two messages. Both images.

The first is a picture taken through a window looking out toward New York's skyline. I recognize the Empire State Building immediately. The caption reads:

You were right. I did need a change of scenery. This is the view from my new pad.

'It's stunning,' I whisper for my own benefit.

I click the second image and it takes me a moment to realize that what I am looking at is Brooks' bicep. I recognize the inked forest that spreads from the beams of sunlight on his chest, the familiar birds and musical notes.

I gasp, dropping my phone. and then retrieve it to double-check what I think I see. *Alice in Wonderland* is gone. She has been covered by the face of a girl or woman. The image resembles Cady.

I decided it wasn't Alice I was clinging to. It was Cady.

I don't know why but I reply.

What happened?

I'm not sure if he'll understand from my reply that I'm asking what happened to make him change his perspective on Alice. But he does because, despite whatever unearthly hour it must be in New York, he replies:

I went to their place. Spoke to Alice. Met her husband. She's wonderful. But she's not the woman I'm in love with.

My heart starts hammering beneath my ribs, so fiercely I

wonder whether it is possible to break your ribs from the inside out. Does he mean he's over Alice or is he telling me he's still in love with me?

'Izzy, I have great news,' comes a voice, pulling me out of my reverie. I shake my head, trying to clear my erratic thoughts. 'I was tempted to call you last night, but it was late.'

I look from my phone to Francesca. 'I'm sorry?'

'I've got you an audition. If you want it. It's a new musical. It isn't big yet. And the audition is for a standby role only, but I think you're good enough.'

I jump to my feet. 'Oh my God, that's insane! Thank you, thank you, thank you.'

I throw my arms around her neck, which encourages her to say, 'But there is a catch...'

'Oh.' I step back. 'What is it?'

'The audition, and the production if you get through, they're in New York.'

Have you ever felt the earth move? Had a moment when you realize that everything in the universe is working toward one, glaringly obvious conclusion? That's what I'm feeling now.

'When is the audition?'

'Next week.'

I process that for a second. 'Can you get me ready, Francesca? Can you get me ready for New York?'

'We can work our hardest to try.'

I bite down on my lip as my eyes fill with happy tears.

'Well, all right, then.'

40

BROOKS

Week 4 Without Izzy

Kit lays punches into the pads I'm holding in the boxing ring. He's getting stronger. I might try sparring with him properly soon. Drew waits for his turn, his arms resting on the corner post of the ring as he watches us.

'When do you move into the new pad?' he asks.

'Two weeks,' I say, and then turn to Kit. 'Keep going. He's talking to me.'

'Fucker,' Kit says breathlessly, landing another punch.

'I'm looking forward to it,' I admit. 'Things are changing and I... I guess I feel good about it. I only wish I'd had my shit together when Izzy was here.'

'Have you spoken to her lately?'

'One-two, one-two, Kit. Keep up the pace. I sent her a couple of messages last week. Showed her the view of the apartment and, ah, the new tattoo.' Kit stops punching and bends forward over his knees, raising a hand in surrender. 'Good effort, buddy,' I tell him, patting his back with my pad-covered hand.

'She knows about *Alice in Wonderland*, huh?'

'Didn't take much working out.' Kit and I move to the corner of the ring while Drew steps in. 'Let's aim to spar properly next week,' I tell Kit. He nods as he drinks from his sports cap bottle.

Drew and I bounce in the middle of the ring, smirking, staring, generally winding each other up to spar. He moves first, as I expect. I block his punch and I get in a jab.

'So, what did they say, these messages?' Kit asks.

'I guess I was trying to show her that I'm changing.' I block another shot from Drew. 'When she left, we both knew we had shit to figure out. I thought... I don't know, man. She just didn't reply. Maybe I've been working on me and she got back to London and realized she liked being a spoiled rich girl.'

As I say that, I hope to God I'm wrong.

The distraction allows Drew to land a blow to my temple. Hard enough that I feel it, but not so hard it's going to hurt me – that's kind of the point.

'Did you outright say, "I love you, I was an idiot to let you go and I want you back now I've stopped acting like a pussy"?'

Drew and I stop sparring and I glare at Kit. 'I know you didn't just call me a pussy, man.'

'I did. And the reason you're not already over here putting your glove in my face is because you know it's true. Look at Drew. When he realized he might lose Becky, he got on a plane and flew to London, like a hero, to get her back. So, did your messages tell her you want her back or not?'

'Well, no.'

'Then you can't be sure she got the message.'

'We're not like Drew and Becky, Kit. When Izzy left, she said we both had stuff to work on. Just because I've been doing that doesn't mean she has, or that she still wants to, or even if she does, that she'll want me at the end of it.'

'God, I'm pleased I hooked Madge in college. This old-man love is complicated shit.'

'Kit, you're older than us both,' Drew points out. 'Can we spar?'

We get back to it, working up a sweat, laughing as we land and dodge punches, until Charlie comes into the room.

'Brooks, I'm sorry to interrupt.'

'What's up, Charlie?' I ask, still going at it with Drew.

'There's a bit of a situation. Some woman is making a scene downstairs. She isn't a member and wants to use a studio.'

I land a punch in Drew's side and block his next. 'Tell her no.'

'I have but she's very persistent.'

When I notice the smile on Charlie's face, I take my attention from Drew and look at the woman who has made her way to Charlie's side. The breath leaves my lungs and I drop my hands to my sides. As I do, Drew lands a punch I should have blocked, right into my jaw. The shock rocks my already shaky legs, and one knee gives.

'Fuck, Drew.'

'Shit, sorry, buddy. You should have had your hands up.' He stops talking when he follows my gaze to Izzy. 'I'm still claiming that as a KO,' he says, as I stand and walk to the edge of the ring.

Izzy swallows hard as she stares at me, looking immaculate in yoga pants and a sweat top that drapes off one shoulder. Her blonde hair is pulled back into her signature ponytail and she has the smallest amount of makeup around her eyes. My body is suddenly heavy with emotion and the urge to take her in my arms.

'Is this the one who's causing you trouble, Charlie?' I ask.

'Yes, boss.'

I don't take my eyes off Izzy, and I see my growing smile reflected on her soft pink lips. Of all the things I have wanted to say to her, the only one that comes to me now is, 'Hi.'

She steps up to the ring. Kit lifts the ropes for her to climb through. She comes up to me with her hand held out for me to shake.

'Hi, I'm Izzy. Hot mess but working on myself.'

I pull off a glove and take her hand, glancing down to make sure it is real, that I'm not imagining she is here.

'I'm new to New York. I don't really have a job. I sold a book once for a small advance and my sales are on a steady decline, but they're enough for me to afford a tiny studio apartment in the city. It has a terrible view of another block of apartments. But it's mine and I pay for it myself. I'm a singer-songwriter and I intend to do open-mic nights but I don't actually make any money from it. I'm currently living off money I got from selling my designer clothes online. Tomorrow, I have a dance audition for a small musical. Even if I get it – and there's a good chance I won't – it's for a standby role.' She smiles fully now. The kind I love. The kind that lights up her irises. 'But it's what I really want to do, for me.'

I absorb everything she said, still holding her hand in mine. I tell her, 'I'm Brooks. I'm a gym owner. My body is covered in tattoos. I'm the father of a young adult, who sometimes acts older than I do. I get along with her mother but I don't wish we had never split. I like meat, especially meat coated in sauce—the more sugar and fat, the better. I like beer, football, and playing the guitar. I have a swanky new apartment with a killer view. Maybe I could show you sometime when you get fed up with living in a box.'

She laughs, looking down at her feet as if she's nervous. I take a step closer to her and finally let go of her hand so I can lift her chin and look at her beautiful face.

'Why are you here?'

Her expression changes from happy to serious. 'Because I spent four weeks in London and realized I need, and *want*, a life overhaul. It's not complete yet. I don't have all the answers. But the one thing I am absolutely certain of is that arguing, laughing, and making love with you is the happiest I've ever been in my life. I love you, Brooks. I love everything about you. From the fact you hate wearing suits and eat too much meat to the fact you send shivers through me when you sing and play the guitar. You're the only person in the world who would call your friends to have them buy my books, even though you didn't really like me, just so I wouldn't feel bad. I love that—'

I crash my lips against hers and scoop her up, wrapping her legs around my waist. 'You talk too much, Izzy Coulthard. But I fucking love you. I love every annoying-as-hell bone in your body.'

She laughs as she kisses me again.

When cheers and wolf whistles start up around us, she buries her head in my neck and wraps her arms around me.

'I'm never letting you go, Izzy. You're mine.'

She kisses my neck. 'I only want to be yours, Brooks. Forever.'

ABOUT THE AUTHOR

Laura Carter is the bestselling author of several rom-coms including the series *Brits in Manhattan* which she is relaunching and expanding with Boldwood. She lives in Jersey.

Sign up to Laura Carter's mailing list for news, competitions and updates on future books.

Visit Laura's website: www.lauracarterauthor.com

Follow Laura on social media:

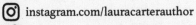
instagram.com/lauracarterauthor
twitter.com/LCarterAuthor
facebook.com/LauraCarterAuthor

ALSO BY LAURA CARTER

The Law of Attraction

Two to Tango

Friends With Benefits

Boldwood

Boldwood Books is an award-winning
fiction publishing company seeking
out the best stories from
around the world.

Find out more at
www.boldwoodbooks.com

Join our reader community
for brilliant books,
competitions and offers!

Follow us
#BoldBookClub

Milton Keynes UK
Ingram Content Group UK Ltd.
UKHW041307041024
2014UKWH00054B/716